Readers love
A Growl, a Roar, and a Purr
by K.C. WELLS

"As always, K.C. Wells does a great job at character development and she definitely knows how to sex things up, without making the sex the most important part of the book."

—Love Bytes

"In this paranormal romance, Wells explores the shifter and fated mates tropes in this fun action-adventure romp that includes an epic heist and a sweet romantic through-line."

—J.L. Gribble's Book Reviews

"The romance was definitely the key to this story. It leaped off the pages and heated up the sheets."

—The TBR Pile

By K.C. Wells

Published by DREAMSPINNER PRESS
www.dreamspinnerpress.com

A SNARL, A SPLASH, AND A SHOCK

K.C. WELLS

Published by
DREAMSPINNER PRESS

5032 Capital Circle SW, Suite 2, PMB# 279, Tallahassee, FL 32305-7886 USA
www.dreamspinnerpress.com

A Snarl, a Splash, and a Shock
© 2022 K.C. Wells

Cover Art
© 2022 L.C. Chase
http://www.lcchase.com
Cover content is for illustrative purposes only and any person depicted on the cover is a model.

Trade Paperback ISBN: 978-1-64108-374-4
Digital ISBN: 978-1-64108-373-7
Trade Paperback published May 2022
v. 1.0

Printed in the United States of America
(∞)
This paper meets the requirements of
ANSI/NISO Z39.48-1992 (Permanence of Paper).

For Parker Williams. You ROCK.

ACKNOWLEDGMENTS

THANK YOU to my wonderful beta team.

CHAPTER ONE

March

"HONEY, I'M home." Vic Ryder smiled at his habitual joke. Saul always got a kick out of it.

"In the kitchen."

Vic dropped his bags on the floor in the hallway, shrugged off his jacket, and hung it on a hook. Saul was a stickler for keeping the place neat. Vic stuck his head around the kitchen door and gaped. "You are *not* cleaning guns on our table." The surface was covered in rags, cleaning patches, brushes, solvent, degreaser, and various handguns and rifles.

Saul glanced up. "Why the hell not? I covered it first. Besides, I wasn't going to do this in the garage. Too freaking cold out there." He grinned. "At least this way I get to wear as little as possible."

Vic was trying not to stare at Saul's pointy little nips. The urge to lick and tease them was overpowering. Then he bent over to peer under the table. Saul's half-hard dick decided to attempt a greeting, and Vic straightened in an instant. "You're naked."

"See, remarks like *that* show why you're in Intelligence." Saul's grin had a lascivious air about it.

"But *why* are you naked? Did you run out of clothes? Because you certainly couldn't fit into mine." There were times—like *always*—when Vic hated clothes shopping with a passion, especially because he had to look in the teenage section.

Having a build like mine sucks.

Saul gaped at him. "You were coming home. I wanted to be ready." He grabbed a bottle from the table and held it aloft. "See? Even got my gun oil."

Vic coughed. "You'd better not put that anywhere *near* my ass."

Saul frowned and glanced at the label. "Oopsie." He gave a sheepish smile. "Hey, they're both lube. This one is for your gun," he said as he grabbed the second bottle. "And this one is for mine." He glanced down into his lap with a wide grin. Then he set the bottle aside. "So, how was Idaho?"

1

"Cold. Snowy. And interesting." Except that last word had to be the understatement of the year.

Saul cocked his head to one side. "You look tired." He wiped his hands on a rag.

Tired? He wasn't tired; he was shaken to the core.

"Vic?" Saul's brow furrowed. "What's wrong?"

He wasn't sure he could put the roiling mass of conflicting emotions inside him into words. "As an oral historian, I'd be the first to confess there's so much we don't know about shifters. That history goes back almost a thousand years, but when you look at what we've got, it amounts to *fragments*. And when I learn something new, it only adds to the big picture and brings me a little closer to better understanding where we came from."

Saul got up from the table and walked around it to where Vic stood. "I may not be a shifter, but I know when you're troubled. Whatever it is you've discovered, is it something you can share with me?"

Vic laughed softly. "Is there anything I *don't* share with you?" The sight of Saul's cock was a definite distraction.

Saul moved closer and put his hands on Vic's waist. "Okay, let me put it another way. Is it something we need to talk about, or do you want me to make it all go away?" Then Saul's lips were on his neck, and Vic shivered. Saul chuckled against his skin. "Oh, you like that idea." He moved his hands to Vic's ass, molding him against Saul's body, the heat and hardness of him sending waves of desire through Vic.

He locked his arms around Saul's neck, their mouths fused in a lingering kiss. "Missed you," he whispered when they parted.

"I think talking can wait." Saul cupped Vic's ass and hoisted him into the air. Vic wrapped his legs around Saul's waist and held on as Saul left the kitchen, carrying him as if he was no heavier than a bag of groceries.

"You forgot the gun oil," he called out as they reached the bedroom door.

Saul's throaty chuckle was such a turn-on. "Are you kidding me? We have lube in every room in the house." Then he kicked the door shut behind them, locking out the world.

THE BED was warm, the sheets rumpled, and Vic had aches in all the right places. Being away from Saul was always tough, but this time he couldn't wait to get back into his arms—into their bed. And judging by the way Saul had nailed his ass, the break had been hard on him too.

Does he need me as much as I need him?

It was a habitual thought. Vic still marveled at what Saul saw in him. Saul could have any guy, and yet he chose Vic, a world away from him in terms of physique.

That wise inner voice piped up. *Maybe he thinks there's more to you than that.*

He stared at the ceiling. Usually sex wiped him out, but something in his head wouldn't shut down. Then he realized what was niggling him. Whenever he and Saul made love, it left him feeling complete.

But not this time.

He couldn't imagine why. Saul fucked like a god, and then after, he was gentle and caring, cradling Vic to his chest, assuring him everything would be okay.

So why isn't it?

Vic rolled onto his side and found Saul in the same position, staring at him. Vic smiled. "See something you like?"

Saul's eyes gleamed in the lamplight. "Saw it, enjoyed it. Might enjoy it some more before the night is over."

Vic ran his fingers lightly over Saul's muscular shoulders. "Have I mentioned how much I like this?"

Saul grinned. "The way you kiss my guns when I flex might be a bit of a giveaway."

"It's not only your muscles, though. It's the hair too." Saul's chest was covered in it, and then there was the trail leading down to his pubes. The beard that hugged Saul's jaw was all kinds of sexy too.

"Got a thing for hairy guys, huh?"

Vic smiled. "Just this hairy guy."

Saul propped his head in his hand. "Now suppose you tell me what had you so shook up." He narrowed his gaze. "You're *still* shook up, so it must be bad."

Vic should have known he couldn't hide a bean from this guy. "That obvious, huh?" There was no way he'd tell Saul about the… incompleteness that had him so confused.

Saul leaned in and kissed his forehead. "Only to me." Then he went back to his original position. "I'm listening."

3

Vic took a deep breath. "I saw something I've never seen before."

"In Idaho? I doubt that."

Vic gave him a playful swat. "I need you to be serious right now. I mean it. This is… huge."

Saul's face lost all trace of humor. "Okay."

Vic swallowed. "You know I went there because Doc Tranter called?"

"That ex-military doc? Sure."

"Well, he told me there was a group of shifters I needed to meet. So I went there. There were six guys in a log cabin, plus the doc. Three of them were shifters."

Saul's eyes widened. "The others knew about them?"

Vic snorted. "God yes. All I did was ask if it was safe to talk in front of them, and one of them almost bit my head off. Mouthy bastard." That had been the one they called Crank. Stupid name. No one in Vic's unit would ever have such a dumb nickname. *Not someone I could easily forget.*

Saul frowned. "But I thought…."

Vic nodded. "Generally we don't share what we are with humans." He cupped Saul's cheek. "We do make exceptions now and again."

That was all it took for Saul to roll him gently onto his back and cover Vic with his body, his large hands gripping Vic's wrists and pinning them above Vic's head on the pillows. He rolled his hips, and Vic pushed out a soft moan as Saul's shaft slid over his own thickening cock.

"Talking here, remember?" He couldn't even *think* when Saul did that.

Saul leaned in to kiss his neck. "Just so you know? I'm not done yet."

"Yeah, I got the memo." Vic grabbed him by the chin and held him steady, his face inches from Vic's. "Neither am I." Maybe if Saul took him again, he would feel better this time.

Saul gazed into his eyes. "Good to know." His voice was husky. Then he rolled back onto his side.

Vic took a second to push down hard on his raging libido. "What makes these shifters so special? They're mates."

"I don't understand."

"Mates. These guys have somehow been… fated to be together. It's like they're soul mates or something."

"That's a thing? How come you've never told me about this?"

"Because I didn't know! This is what I'm trying to get across to you. I've never seen this before. I mean, I know shifters talk about it, but I figured it was merely that—talk. We possess the most complete archive of shifter knowledge in the world, and there's only a brief mention in there, so I thought it was, you know, like fantasy stuff." The light-headedness he'd experienced at the cabin was back, as was the tingling all over his body.

Vic didn't *do* agitation.

"So what is so special about mates?"

Vic shivered. "Oh, not much. Only that they can communicate via telepathy." When Saul stilled, his eyes wide, Vic nodded. "No lie. They have this… connection."

"You're sure they weren't putting you on?"

Vic was rock-solid sure. "It's genuine."

"Wow. Do you think you'll get to see them again?"

"I hope so." There were so many questions he wanted to ask them. "The guys who were with them? Ex-military. In the same line of business as me. One of the shifters, Horvan… I've come across his name before. He's got a good, tight team there." Even Crank had to have his uses.

Why the hell do I keep thinking about him? The guy was loud, brash, opinionated….

"You never know. Maybe you'll work together at some point." Saul traced a line from Vic's collarbones to his pubes.

"What are you doing?"

Saul smiled. "Letting my fingers do the talking."

Vic was more than ready for another conversation. Anything to stop the thoughts colliding in his head.

VIC KNEW he was dreaming, but *God*, it felt so fucking real.

"You gonna bend over for me?" The voice was gruff. Fingers dug into Vic's shoulder, and his unknown lover smacked what felt like a very meaty dick against his ass.

"Only if you ask nicely," Vic fired back.

"Not gonna ask, sweetheart, because we both know you want this inside you. I just wanna know how you want it." Then he slid his hot, slick, bare cock between Vic's asscheeks, and Vic's hole tightened. "Like this?"

Vic swallowed. "I want to see you." He wanted to look into the guy's eyes.

Then he was spun around, and cool blue-gray eyes met his. Vic's legs were hoisted onto broad, muscled shoulders, and he gasped as that thick head penetrated him.

"What's my name?" The words were almost a growl.

Vic stared up at him, panting as a solid shaft filled him to the hilt.

"What's my name?" Louder, harsher now.

Vic locked gazes with him, biting back a moan as the guy retreated, leaving him feeling so fucking empty.

"Answer me, Vic!" Then he drove his cock all the way home.

"Crank! Your name is Crank!"

VIC SAT up in bed, sweat covering his chest. *What the fuck?* Warmth coated his belly, and he touched it with tentative fingers. *Oh my God, I came.*

"Babe?" Saul was awake. "You okay?"

He shivered. "Not really, no." With a *click*, warm light spilled into the room.

Saul touched his chest. "Christ, you're wringing wet. What were you doing, running a marathon in your sleep?" Then he glanced down and grinned. "Ah, okay. I guess I *know* what you were doing."

Vic couldn't shake off the feeling that something momentous had occurred. "I've never had a dream like it." *And why about* Crank, *of all people?*

Saul snickered. "Pretty sure that's a lie."

Vic reached for the towel Saul kept by the bed and wiped away the stickiness, his head in a spin.

"Was it about me?"

Fuck. There was no way Vic was going to break the habit of several years and lie to Saul. They'd both sworn never to do that. "No."

Saul stiffened. "I see. So you shot your load dreaming about some other dude?"

Despite the tremors that rippled through him, Vic smiled. "You can't get pissed about a dream." *I'm not going to make a big deal out of this. It was nothing, okay?*

"Oh, can't I? Watch me." Then Saul's face softened. "Okay, then who was it about?"

Vic leaned over and kissed him. "No one you know, but I think you're safe. He's straight."

Saul smirked. "Lusting after straight guys now?"

"Not lusting after *anyone*. Why would I? Look what I've got right here." He kissed Saul again, then nuzzled his neck. "You have nothing to worry about," he murmured. "You're more than enough for me."

"Oh yeah?" Saul trailed his fingers over Vic's damp chest, moving lower, lower, until at last he slid them into Vic's still-slick hole.

Vic caught his breath. "Three times in one night?"

Saul let out a wry chuckle. "I'm on catch-up. You were gone a few days, remember? And my hand is no substitute for this tight little hole."

"Not so tight now. It's already taken you twice tonight."

Saul grinned. "Three always was my lucky number." Then he flipped Vic onto his belly and spread him wide with his legs, pushing at Vic's knees. Vic gave a low cry as Saul slowly filled him, and he tilted his ass to give him access.

"My turn to shoot a load," Saul whispered. "And I'm in no hurry."

Vic turned his head to receive the kiss he knew awaited him. "Neither am I. Take your time."

He wanted to lose himself in Saul's kisses, the warmth of Saul's body, the comforting smell of him that enveloped Vic in a warm, safe cocoon.

Most of all, he didn't want to think about Crank.

CHAPTER TWO

Still March, but almost April

"CHRIST!" CRANK sat bolt upright in bed, his chest damp to the touch. Then he realized what coated his fingers was not merely sweat but something a lot stickier.

Again?

He threw back the sheets, swung his legs out, and headed, naked, for the bathroom, shaken by the dream that lingered in his mind. He could still feel the water all around him. The tang of the salt on his lips. The glare of the sun on his head. That mouth….

Jesus fucking Christ.

He filled the sink with water, then grabbed a washcloth to clean away every trace. Crank stared into the mirror, noting his enlarged pupils, the flush in his cheeks, neck, and chest. *Is that how I look when I come?* He'd never been one for watching himself fuck in a mirror. That seemed kinda weird. He splashed water on his face, then dried himself with a towel.

This is getting to be beyond a joke.

Crank couldn't remember the last time he'd had wet dreams, but he guessed it had to be more than a decade. Lately, however…. And it wasn't so much the whole "waking up with a cum shot" that bothered him—it was the dream that preceded it, because it had been the *same fucking dream* every night for the last week.

There's some weird shit going on inside my head.

He switched off the lamp and went back to bed. After half an hour of lying in the dark, unable to switch off his brain as easily as he'd extinguished the light, he gave up. Crank pulled on his shorts and headed for the door.

The house wasn't entirely silent. When the first muffled cry reached his ears, he tensed, until he realized exactly what he was hearing. *Fuck, they give bunnies a bad name.* Dellan's bedroom, which he shared with Horvan and Rael, was at the top of the house, but *damn*, the sound carried. Crank hurried downstairs. He didn't begrudge the guys their extremely active sex life—the problem was it threw his own libido into stark relief.

Can't remember the last time I made someone moan like that.

Then he reconsidered. *Wait—have I ever made someone moan like that? Is it a shifter thing, or just a guy-on-guy thing?* He pushed that last thought from his head. *It's not as if I'm ever gonna get the answer to that question, right?*

God knew there had been times when he'd been curious. Not curious enough to do anything about it, though.

As he reached the kitchen, he noticed the light showing beneath the door. Crank froze. After the appearance of that leopard shifter last week, he was taking no chances. Then he relaxed. *No one could have gotten past Brick.* The polar bear shifter worked the night shift, patrolling the grounds.

Crank pushed open the door to find Horvan sitting on a stool, his phone in his hand and a mug of something steaming on the countertop in front of him. Horvan jerked his head up. His wide shoulders tensed, then relaxed. "Can't sleep?"

"You neither, by the look of it." Crank stilled. "Hey, what are you doing down here? Sounds like they're hot 'n' heavy upstairs."

Horvan chuckled. "I'll go on up when they're done."

"But… I thought you guys could only fuck when it's all three of you."

Horvan lifted his eyebrows. "Not that our sex life is any of your business, but you're referring to the first time we got together. Things have moved on since then." His eyes gleamed. "Take tonight as a for instance. The first two times, it was all three of us. Then I got off a third watching them. I'm sure they'll still be at it when I go back, and whether I watch or join in, there'll be at least a fourth orgasm in there somewhere." He grinned. "Besides, sleep after sex is incredible. You're far too wrung out to wake for anything."

"And yet here you are, awake and drinking hot chocolate," Crank noted.

Horvan grinned. "That's 'cause I'm not done yet." He shook his head. "You know me. You know how much I've always liked to fuck, right? But with these two…." He shivered. "It's never been like this. I can't even describe it. Having them in my head when we—"

"You were right," Crank interjected. "It's none of my business. And considering I'm not getting any, it's also in piss-poor taste."

Horvan mimed zipping his lips. He gestured to his mug. "You want some hot chocolate?"

"If there's some going, sure." Crank sat on the stool facing Horvan on the other side of the breakfast bar, watching him. "You sure you only came down here to give them some alone time?" Horvan stiffened, and Crank knew he'd nailed it. "What's really on your mind?"

Horvan went about the task of reheating the pan on the stove. "Did Hashtag tell you what he and Dellan discovered at Dellan's office?"

"About the shipment of materials to other chemical companies? Yeah." Crank frowned. "That don't sound good. So it's not only Global Bio-Tech who are making this drug?"

"That's the way it looks." He took the pan off the heat and poured its contents into a clean mug, then handed it to Crank. "Here." Horvan retook his seat, wrapping his hands around his own mug. "Hashtag did a great job finding out about the shipments. It took him a week, though. At least now we have an address we can start looking into. He's seeing what he can find out: who owns the buildings, whether it's a person or a company…. About time we had some leads."

"That's not what's worrying you, though." After so many years working together, Crank knew his team leader well enough to recognize the signs. "What's wrong?"

Horvan took a long drink. "Three department heads are missing from Global."

"What does that mean?" It didn't sound as if they'd quit.

"That's what worries me. It could be one of two not very good options. Either the people running this show pulled 'em—assuming they were placed there by the bad guys to keep an eye on production—or they were 'vanished' to keep 'em quiet. And now that Dellan has stopped all production of the drug *and* all shipments of its components…."

Crank stilled. "You think Dellan's painted a big target on his back."

"It's possible. We're gonna have to be extra careful from now on. Safety in numbers. If you go out with one of the team, one of you carries." Horvan waved his hand. "But you know the drill." He locked gazes with Crank. "So… wanna tell me what's bugging you? Did you have a bad dream or something?"

Crank blinked. "Why do you say that?"

Horvan snorted. "Because you are *not* an insomniac. Hell, you once slept through that firefight we had with those Kurdish rebels."

Crank wrapped his hands around the warm surface of his mug. "Can we talk?" He had to tell *someone*.

"You're not okay, are you?"

"Not really." He hesitated. *This is nuts.*

"Hey, it's all right. I won't share anything you tell me with my mates, or with anyone on my team."

"I got your word on that?"

"I promise."

Crank gazed at him with wide eyes. "Yeah, right. There are two guys upstairs who can read every thought that goes through your head."

"Only if I want them to." When Crank gaped at him, Horvan nodded. "Not gonna go into this now, but… Dellan showed us a trick. It's sort of a mental safety deposit box. You lock stuff away you don't want anyone seeing. I'm still getting the hang of it, but yeah, it works. So if this is something you don't want me to share, I'll shove it out of sight. Okay?"

"Fair enough." Crank took a sip of his hot chocolate. "This is good."

Horvan's eyebrows went sky-high again. "Something *really* has you shaken if it's taking you *this* long to come out with it."

Crank took a deep breath. "I keep having these weird dreams."

Horvan smirked. "Tell me about these dreams," he said in a really bad German accent.

Crank gave him the finger. "Fuck off, Dr. Fraud. You doof."

Horvan chuckled. "Okay. I'll be serious. I can't interpret them, but maybe if you share, I can offer opinions."

It was better than nothing.

Crank took another drink, then stared into the dark-brown liquid. "Like I said, I keep having these… dreams."

"Wet dreams?"

Crank jerked his head up. "How—"

Horvan touched his nose. "Doesn't matter how much soap you use, a shifter can still tell."

Well, fuck. "You know what? Never mind." He got off the stool, but stopped when Horvan put a hand to his arm.

"Tell me." Horvan's voice was unexpectedly gentle.

Crank shivered and sat back down with a sigh. He really did need to talk about this. "Okay. I'm swimming. It's just me, in the middle of an ocean. There's no land in sight, and my arms are so fucking *tired*." Crank swallowed. "And I *know* I'm gonna die out there."

Horvan straightened. "Okay, this is definitely not a wet dream. Well, it *is*, but it's a very different *kind* of wet dream. Keep talking."

Crank closed his eyes, picturing the dream, so real that it felt as though he was still in it. "Then I see this fin coming toward me, and that's it, I fucking *know* I'm a goner." He could still see it, the small blue-gray speckled fin slicing through the water. "It slows as it gets closer, to the point where it's almost crawling beside me." Another swallow. "But then there's this voice in my head that says, 'Grab on.' So I grab hold of the fin, and the shark picks up speed."

"Then it *is* a shark?"

Crank opened his eyes and nodded. "The only shark I know about is a Great White—thank you, *Jaws*—and this one feels about the same size. But its skin isn't one color. It's kinda… speckled. It's hard to describe it."

"Then don't. Carry on telling me about the dream."

Crank took another deep, calming breath. "The speed always surprises me. I mean, something that big? It was really moving. And I have no idea how long we go on like that, but eventually, I see land." Okay, this was the part that freaked him out every fucking time. "Next thing I know, I'm lying on my back on warm sand, and…." His mouth dried up.

"And what?" Crank mumbled a reply into his mug. "I didn't get that."

"Someone is sucking my dick, okay? *That's* when I come."

The kitchen suddenly became very quiet.

Crank jerked his head up again to find Horvan staring at him. "What? It means it's been too fucking long since I got laid, that's all."

Horvan was clearly biting back a smile. "And *who* is sucking your dick?"

"I don't know, all right?" Crank lied.

Another waggle of eyebrows. "So an invisible woman was blowing you?"

Fuck him. "Okay, it was a guy. Happy now? And before you ask, no, I didn't see his face. I saw enough to know it was a guy, and yes, he was damn good at it."

To Crank's surprise, Horvan didn't react to that. He got on his phone again, tapped the screen, and scrolled. "The shark… did it look something like this?" He held it up.

Crank peered at the screen and gaped. "How the fuck did you know that? That's exactly what it was like. Not scary. Almost… I don't know… cute."

Horvan nodded slowly, his dark eyes sparkling. "*That* is a Greenland shark." He cocked his head to one side. "Ring any bells?"

"No." Except that was another lie, because *something* was resonating in Crank's mind.

"Then let me help you. What is it that can be a shark one minute—a *Greenland* shark, mind you; that's very important—and human the next? Think carefully now."

He was enjoying this, the bastard.

Then Crank saw the light, and he almost choked on his hot chocolate. "No. Fucking. Way."

"Are you seriously telling me you haven't had the same idea?"

He almost said no, but stopped himself at the last second. Because hadn't there been the tiniest inkling? Crank glared at him. "I don't even *like* him. Why the fuck would I be dreaming about him? He was the most aggravating, superior, know-it-all—"

Horvan burst out laughing. "Oh yeah. Sounds like a match made in heaven."

"Hey, don't even joke about it." If he never heard Vic Ryder's name again, it would be too soon. Crank had no idea why the guy had riled him so much. He only knew Vic had gotten under his skin, and it felt as if he was still there, like an itch demanding to be scratched.

"Okay. But joking aside… we could use him. He could help us find Dellan's dad."

Crank folded his arms. "No."

"Hey, he could be very useful. Doc put us onto him for a reason, right?"

"No."

Horvan set down his phone, his eyes suddenly flinty. "Fine. *You* go upstairs and tell Dellan there's someone who might be able to help us but that *you* would feel too uncomfortable." He eyed the ceiling. "I could get 'em down here right now, without even moving from my stool or raising my voice."

"Okay, okay." Crank knew when he was licked. "Fine. Call Vic."

"I'll do it tomorrow." Horvan glanced at the wall clock. "Later today," he amended. "I'll arrange a meeting." His lips twitched. "I could also mention how eager you are to see him again."

Crank gazed at him in horror. "You *promised*."

"Hey, I promised not to tell my mates or any of the team. But Vic isn't part of the team, is he? And you don't *want* him to be part of the team."

"I hate you," Crank ground out. *Jesus, what the fuck?* He had no idea why the thought of Vic being on the team should stress him out, but *Christ*, he was tense.

All trace of amusement disappeared from Horvan's features. "Look, I don't know what's going on here anymore than you do, but I agree, this is weird as fuck."

"Ya *think*?" He got up from his stool. "Fine. He can come, but I'm not gonna discuss this with him. Like *you're* not gonna discuss this with *anyone*, you got that?"

Horvan squared his shoulders and looked him in the eye. *Oh shit.* Crank knew that expression.

"We can't afford to have you distracted by this. A distracted Crank may mean one of us ends up dead. So either get your shit together or you're not going out into the field." Then Horvan's expression softened. "We *need* you."

"I hear ya." Crank sighed. "Maybe all I need is a couple of nights of uninterrupted sleep. Well, that and getting laid."

Horvan snickered. "If that's what it takes? You've got tomorrow night off. Go into town, find yourself a girl who likes the sight of all those muscles, and fuck like bunnies. But take one of the guys with you."

Crank snorted. "Why? If I find myself a girl, I ain't gonna share her with Roadkill or Hashtag. And I sure as shit ain't taking Brick. Too much competition."

Horvan waved his hand. "Bed. Fight it out between you in the morning. But you know the drill. Safety in numbers."

Crank knew. "See you in a few hours, boss." He headed back up the stairs. When he reached the door to his room, he cocked an ear. All was quiet above him. He smiled to himself. *Hey, maybe they wore each other out.*

He climbed into bed and closed his eyes. Getting laid was a great idea. That would solve everything.

The last thing he wanted was more dreams of Vic—even if he *did* give a good blowjob.

CHAPTER THREE

HORVAN KNEW Dellan was awake without even opening his eyes. *This takes some getting used to.* Nothing came from Rael, so he was probably still fast asleep.

We wore him out. He knew he shouldn't feel pride, but *go them!*

Then he caught a hint of something in Dellan's thoughts, but all too quickly, Dellan locked it away. That momentary surge of anguish had Horvan wide-awake in a heartbeat.

He rolled onto his side to face Dellan, who lay in the center of the mattress. After only a week of sharing a bed, they'd quickly taken to falling asleep most nights in that position, not that Horvan was surprised. They were protecting Dellan, surrounding him with their love. And that was the part that still rocked Horvan to his core. It didn't matter how little time had elapsed since he'd met the two men who lay beside him. He knew to his very *soul* that he loved them and they loved him. Horvan didn't know how such a thing was possible, but he wasn't about to question something that felt so fucking *right*.

Dellan lay on his back, his eyes closed.

I know you're awake. Horvan didn't want to disturb Rael. *Come here, sweetheart.*

A soft sigh escaped Dellan's lips, and he shifted closer to rest his head on Horvan's chest, his hand on Horvan's stomach. *Hold me.*

As if he had to ask. Horvan enfolded Dellan in his arms and kissed the top of his head. *You're thinking about your dad.* That accounted for the way he and Rael had pounded Dellan into the mattress, to provide him with something—anything—to take Dellan's mind off his worries. Unfortunately, it seemed the distraction, hot as it was, only lasted as long as they were fucking.

Another sigh. *I still feel as if I'm in shock. Finding out he's alive after all these years....* Dellan craned his neck to stare at Horvan, and Horvan tugged him higher to kiss the lips that called to him.

We will *find him.*

Dellan broke eye contact, his cheeks flushed. *But we have nothing to go on. No clue where they're keeping him. All we have is that photo, and we have no idea when it was taken. For all we know, he might be—*

Horvan claimed Dellan's mouth in a fierce kiss in a bid to silence the rising panic within him. Then Rael spooned around Dellan, his arms enveloping him as he pressed gentle kisses to Dellan's shoulders.

So much for telepathy.

Rael bit back a sleepy smile. "Hey, who knew thoughts could be as loud as words?" He brushed his lips over Dellan's ear. "Think about it for a second. Everything we've learned so far points to something huge, right? They—whoever *they* are—have developed a drug to force shifts. Your half brother was shipping it out in great numbers. This is no small operation. You think there's gonna be no information *whatsoever* out there? We'll find something."

Dellan opened his mouth to speak, but Horvan covered his lips with his fingers. "We'll have more manpower too, remember? The rest of the team, whenever I give the word. And here's something else to think about. I want to call Vic Ryder. He may be able to help us."

"I was thinking about him too." Dellan frowned. "But we know so little about him."

"Doc got us together, and I trust him, but I'll make some calls of my own, see what I can discover. If I'm happy, I'll ask him to come on board for this. He'll be useful. We can always use another gun." Horvan's first impression of Vic had been that he had a military background, not that the rifle he'd carried or his bearing hadn't been a bit of a giveaway. "And if he's in the same line of work…." He wouldn't break his word to Crank, but after that dream of his, Horvan was curious to know more about Vic.

Horvan didn't believe in coincidences.

"Do we have to get up now?" Dellan murmured, stroking Horvan's chest.

Rael reached over him and wrapped warm, slim fingers around Horvan's hard-as-fuck shaft. "Feels like Horvan already is," he said with a chuckle.

"You got an idea what you want to do with that?" Horvan inquired.

As if he didn't know.

It looked like breakfast was going to become brunch.

HORVAN WALKED into the kitchen to find Roadkill pouring himself a glass of water. "Are you finished already?"

Roadkill grinned. "One makeshift private enclosure, ready for inspection. Hashtag and I put the last fencing panel up about ten minutes ago. It's not all that big—it covers maybe an acre—but it means your neighbors and the folks across the lake won't be calling Animal Control because they've spotted one or all of you out there." He grimaced. "Although they *might* be calling Dellan to complain about the eyesore blotting their view. Once Dellan plants all those trees, the fence can come down."

Horvan patted him on the back. "Thank you. They're gonna love this. Dellan was only saying this morning that he wasn't getting enough exercise."

Roadkill almost choked on his water. "Seriously? How can you say that with a straight face? I think all three of you are getting in a lot of cardio."

This is amazing! Get out here.

Horvan beamed. "Dellan just inspected your enclosure. You did good."

"I don't know about you, but I am ready to kick back."

"Funny you should say that. I told Crank to take the night off. Maybe you should too. You know, head into Chicago, dinner, a bar...." Christ, when was the last time *he'd* eaten out? Then he remembered. It had been with Rael, the day they met.

God, it felt like a lifetime ago.

Roadkill's eyes lit up. "I like that idea. Pretty sure Hashtag will too."

"That settles it. I told Crank to take one of you guys with him. Two is even better. All of you stick together, okay?"

Roadkill frowned. "And what about you?"

"What about me?"

"Why don't you three come along? *You* could use a date night, right?"

Lord, that was tempting. Horvan shook his head. "Not a good idea. Not now."

"But why not?" Roadkill's expression softened. "Look, I know you're concerned for Dellan's safety, but you'll be there, right? *And* you'll be packing. Let's be honest here. No one's going to cross you." He put down his empty glass and patted Horvan's arm. "At least think about it." Then he grinned. "I'll go tell Hashtag the good news." He walked out of the kitchen as Dellan and Rael came in from the yard.

Rael's eyes sparkled. "I think we could do with a shift now we've got some place to go."

Horvan could smell the sunlight on his skin, along with newly mown grass and another earthy scent that went straight to his dick.

"I second that," Dellan added. "I feel like I've spent a week staring at a screen."

It took Horvan a second to come to a decision. "You know what? We need a change of scenery. How about I take you both on a date tonight?"

Dellan blinked. "You're kidding. In the middle of all this?"

"And that's kinda my point. You said it yourself. Ever since we got to Chicago, you've spent every minute on that computer." He grinned. "Well, *almost* every minute. We need a distraction. And before either of you says it, I don't mean sex. Besides—" He gave a shrug. "—don't you think a date would be good? We haven't done anything like that. There's been too much other shit going on."

Rael smiled. "A date does sound nice. Are we talking dinner, someplace… romantic?" His eyes gleamed. "Why, Horvan Kojik, do you *do* romance?"

Horvan had never felt so *seen*.

He coughed. "Okay. Maybe there hasn't been a ton of romance in my life." When both Dellan and Rael gazed at him with obvious disbelief, he rolled his eyes. "Fine. You got me. I don't do romance. But that kinda comes with the job. Who has time for romance when you're saving the world?" he quipped.

"I think a date sounds amazing," Dellan said in a quiet voice. "And it doesn't have to be romantic. Dinner with you two would be enough."

That did it. Horvan was going to ensure their evening was filled with as much romance as he could cram into it.

"So *now* do we get to shift?" Rael asked with a smile.

"How about you two go on out, and I'll join you in a minute or two? There's a call I have to make."

"You promise?"

Horvan walked over to Dellan and kissed him on the lips. "Promise." His voice sounded so husky. He waited till they'd headed outside again, then went into Dellan's office and closed the door. He sat in the wide chair behind the desk, pulled his phone from his pocket, and speed-dialed the number.

He hadn't been in contact with Duke since that call to alert him to the situation, not that Duke was about to haul him over the coals for that.

He might be the guy who coordinated multiple teams, sorted out funding for their operations—yeah, Horvan wasn't even going ask how Duke got as much as he did—and had more contacts than Horvan could count, but before Duke had taken on his various roles, he'd been a friend. They'd served together way back when, and they were solid. It had been Horvan's idea to set up the company, but he'd been more than happy for Duke to run it. *He got the desk job, I get the action.* It was a win-win.

"What do you need?" Duke was his usual calm self. "I've put the team on standby."

"Thank you. And I need information. Find out all you can about a Vic Ryder. Start with guys who've served in the military."

After a moment of silence, Duke chuckled. "That's it? That's all I get?"

"This is gonna sound weird."

"Coming from you? Yeah, right. I've known you for far too long. So *what's* going to sound weird?"

"I'm hoping you're gonna get back to me and say all you could discover is his military record. That he's not on our books. That we have no interest in him."

"Color me intrigued. Who is this guy?"

"Someone I met in Idaho who could prove useful." If Vic worked for a shifter organization, Duke would have no info on that. *Please, let him be one of the good guys.* Horvan's senses told him this was the case, but he wanted to back up his instincts with cold, hard facts.

"Okay. I'll see what I can dig up." Duke cleared his throat. "So what's this I hear on the grapevine about you getting hitched?"

What the fuck?

"Jesus, Duke."

He laughed. "I take it the rumors have been wildly exaggerated."

At that moment, Crank came into the office. He gave Horvan an inquiring glance, and Horvan gestured to the empty chair beside him. Crank came over and sat.

"Yeah, just a tad. But... I *am* off the market." Next to him, Crank stuffed his hand into his mouth, but even so his muffled laughter was way too loud. Horvan glared at him.

"No kidding. Wow."

"Don't *you* start. I'm getting enough shit from my team. I don't need it from you too."

"Saying nothing." A pause. "But reeling here. I thought you of all people…." Duke snickered. "I'll get back to you when I know something." He disconnected.

Crank exploded into a loud guffaw. "Off the market? I think having two mates is a little more than that. What did Duke say?" Horvan repeated his last sentence, and to his surprise, Crank's good humor fled. He nodded, his expression grave. "There are two main reasons why we stay single, y'know. One, distractions. You said it yourself earlier."

"And two?" Except Horvan knew exactly what Crank was about to say.

"Bad guys, dude. They work out we got someone at home we care about? They might see it as a weakness and exploit it. Remember Colby?"

Horvan wasn't likely to forget. Colby had been a member of the team seven or eight years ago. He'd gone to pieces during a vital mission. They'd discovered later that the network they were trying to take down had organized for Colby's wife and son to be taken. Thankfully, Colby's team leader had worked out what was going on and mounted a rescue mission to get them out. Once they were safe, it was back to the plan.

Colby quit, not that anyone was surprised.

"Change of plan about tonight," Horvan told Crank.

He gaped. "What? You said I had the night off."

"And you still do. Only we're coming too."

Crank squinted. "Who is *we*?"

"Anyone who wants to come along for the ride. Don't worry, we won't cramp your style."

Crank snorted. "As if."

Horvan ignored him. "Once we hit the center of Chicago, we'll leave you guys to your own devices. Watch each other's asses, okay?"

Crank folded his arms. "And what will *you* be doing?"

"Going on a date," Horvan mumbled.

"I'm sorry. I didn't quite get that. Could you repeat it?" Crank was grinning, the bastard.

"I'm going on a date." Horvan enunciated every word. "You know, where you wine and dine someone and make conversation, instead of coming out with lines like 'Hey, you've got a nice ass. Can I fuck it?'"

Crank's jaw dropped. "Okay, I take exception to that." When Horvan arched his eyebrows, Crank glared at him. "That is *not* one of my lines, all right? Give me credit for more subtlety than that." Then he preened. "Although I *am* shit-hot at anal, pardon the pun. So if you need any pointers…."

Horvan couldn't resist. "I'm sure Vic will be delighted to hear that." When Crank bared his teeth and growled, Horvan pointed to the door. "Out. Now."

Crank held up his hands. "Whoa there, Mama Bear. Someone's a little cranky this morning. Maybe *someone* needs to get his ass upstairs and mellow out a little."

That was the last thing Horvan needed. Rael and Dellan were like cats in heat, and all it would take would be a look and they'd be naked again. Then he chuckled to himself. *Technically they* are *cats in heat.*

Talk about a distraction.

He cleared his throat and squirmed in his chair, conscious of his dick, which clearly liked the idea of more naked time. "Make yourself useful. See who wants to come along this evening. In the meantime, I'm gonna find a restaurant for my *date* night."

"A date with your mates." Crank cackled. "Never thought I'd see this day."

"I'm gonna store all this up, you know." Horvan smiled. "I know I joke about all the women that come and go in your life, but it stands to reason one day *one* of them is going to crawl into that heart of yours and turn it to mush, turn *you* inside out and your life upside down."

Crank snorted. "Yeah, right. And who says I'm fool enough to let that happen?"

Horvan held up his hands. "Hey, who's to say you'll have a choice in the matter? Look at me. I never saw them coming. And I'd be the first to admit that yeah, they've rocked my world." He cocked his head. "Maybe *your* world needs rocking too."

Crank got up from his chair. "And maybe love has turned your *brain* to mush." He headed for the door. "I'll go find the others. I think I saw 'em outside, yakking with Brick. And speaking of Brick, is he staying on? As part of the team?"

Horvan nodded. "My gut tells me we're going to need all the help we can get for this one."

"And I trust your gut." Crank grinned. "Doing that has kept all of us alive so far." He left the office.

Horvan leaned back in his chair. He'd known Crank for more than a decade, and the intervening years had done little to effect any great change, except that now Crank seemed to have lost the few filters he'd possessed. Horvan didn't mind that.

I know where I am with Crank. What you see is what you get. Horvan had been around too many guys where he'd had no clue what was going on behind their eyes, and on one occasion, it had cost him dear. *Never gonna let myself fall into* that *trap again.*

Horvan wanted people on his team that he could *trust.*

His phone rang, and he smiled when he saw Duke's name. *Damn, that was fast.* "Okay, talk to me," he said as the call connected.

"You were right. Vic Ryder is ex-military. In fact, his record is exemplary. Want me to send it your way? For deletion after reading, of course."

"Yeah, thanks."

"But when you *look* at him? He doesn't look old enough to have done *half* this stuff."

"Guy's gotta have a painting in the attic for sure."

Duke laughed. "See, this is why I like you. You're as rough as they come when the occasion warrants it, and I've seen the air turn blue when you cuss, but you're cultured enough to know about Dorian Gray."

"Good to know I'm still an enigma. So, nothing in there that should worry me?"

"Clean bill of health from our standpoint. So what's next?"

Horvan was still thinking about that. "I'll give him a call, take it from there."

"Okay. Keep me in the loop. I'm sending the docs now."

His phone pinged. "Got it. I'll be in touch." He disconnected, then opened the email. Duke was right; Vic could certainly handle himself. What mattered more to Horvan was what lay between Vic's ears. Back at the cabin, Vic had admitted he knew more than he'd shared.

I want to know the rest. Then he pushed all thought of Vic from his head.

A lion and a tiger were waiting for him. He grinned. *Oh my.*

CHAPTER FOUR

CRANK'S STOMACH growled. "I don't know about you guys, but I'm ready to eat."

Roadkill snorted. "Then maybe you shouldn't have skipped lunch."

Crank knew it had been a mistake to drink on an empty stomach, but the place was jumping, they had to wait for a table, and the bar looked so damned inviting. He'd drunk the one beer, and it had gone straight to his head, so maybe the second had been a bad idea.

Come on, get us a table already. What he was really craving was a plate full of carbs, smothered in fat and cholesterol and topped with meat.

Ooh, meat.

Hashtag cleared his throat. "Don't look now, but someone over there is paying you a lot of attention."

"Please tell me it's a woman." After a week of those weird-as-fuck dreams, the last thing he wanted was for a guy to be lusting after him. Crank didn't think he could take that.

"Looks like a woman to me." Roadkill's eyes glittered. "Your kind of woman too."

Crank caught his breath. "Curves?"

"And then some."

Crank didn't even need to look. Roadkill knew his taste in women by now. He grinned. "I think this is a solo mission, boys. Why don't you go eat without me? I'll grab a bite when I'm done." He winked. "Whenever that is."

Roadkill snorted. "Yeah, right. We're going nowhere. Horvan would have my balls for earrings."

"Look, I won't tell Horvan you left me to my own devices. Besides, what are you gonna do? Hang around while we fuck?"

Hashtag rolled his eyes. "I can never work out if it's supreme confidence that makes you come out with shit like that or just sheer arrogance."

"It's confidence," Roadkill remarked. "Because you and I both know they *will* end up in the sack. It never fails." He narrowed his gaze. "What concerns me is where that sack might be. We're here to look out for each other, remember?"

Crank crossed his heart. "I promise not to fuck with my back to the door." He grinned. "She can ride me all night long."

Hashtag rolled his eyes again. "Fine. We're out of here."

"I'll see you back at the house." Crank waggled his eyebrows. "If I'm lucky, tomorrow morning." He picked up his beer, slipped off the stool, and turned to take a look at whoever was paying him such close attention. *Nice.* Long black hair, stunning eyes, a tight low-cut dress revealing considerable cleavage between ample bosoms….

He walked over to where she sat. "Can I buy you a drink?"

She gazed up at him, her dark eyes sparkling. "You sure can."

He gave the bartender a nod. "Whatever the lady wants." Then he joined her on the empty stool next to hers.

"Same again, please," she told the bartender. Then she smiled at Crank. "You called me a lady. You're already on a roll. What do they call you?"

"Crank."

Her lips twitched. "And is that what it usually takes to get you going? Or are you locked and loaded?"

His gaze met hers. "You know it." Even to Crank's mind, the flirting sounded corny as fuck, but he didn't care. His dick was on a mission.

Except it wasn't. His dick was asleep.

The bartender placed a cocktail glass in front of her, but she ignored it and swiveled on her stool to face him. "I'm Liz." Crank got an eyeful of slender legs, crossed at the knee, tanned and supple. Her toenails sparkled.

Oh yeah. Crank was a happy bunny.

He raised his bottle, she lifted her glass, and they *clinked.* "Good to meet you, Liz." He took a drink.

Liz stroked his bicep. "I do like a man with muscles." She leaned in close, and it was like she was breathing him in. "Damn, you smell good." Closer still, only now her lips brushed against his neck.

Do I have a sign on me saying Kiss my Neck? It was a major hot spot, one that never failed to get the blood heading south.

Only it wasn't. Not so much as a twitch.

Crank glanced down at his crotch. *Hey, buddy. Wake up.*

Liz leaned back. "Are you a shy boy? Because you don't *act* like a shy boy."

Crank gave a hopefully seductive smile. "I don't believe shy is in my vocabulary."

Her eyes gleamed. "Good to know." She leaned in and kissed his neck again, right below the ear.

Crank swore his dick gave a little snore. *What the fuck?*

"Want to come back to my place?"

Ordinarily, he'd have bundled her into a cab within minutes and been on the way to her bedroom, but Crank relied on his instincts. And right then, they were telling him something was wrong. He couldn't put his finger on it, but he knew to trust them. "I think I'm gonna pass."

Her eyes widened. "You're gonna *pass*? On *me*?" He nodded. She narrowed her gaze. "Are you gay or something?"

Crank wasn't turned on, but now he was pissed off.

"Hey, buddy. What the fuck you think you're doing with my girlfriend?" Fingers dug into Crank's bicep.

Crank swiveled slowly on his stool to find a big guy standing there, his cheeks flushed, one hand clenched into a fist, staring daggers at him. Crank glanced at the hand that only reached about halfway around his upper arm, then back at the guy. "Take your hand off me," he enunciated in a low, calm voice.

The guy jerked it back as though it had been burned.

"What are you doing here? You following me again? And what's this girlfriend crap, Wayne?" Liz flung at him. "We broke up, remember?"

Wayne glared at her. "No, we took a step back."

Liz was off her stool in a heartbeat, standing beside Wayne and matching him glare for glare. "I gave you your ring back and told you to shove it up your ass."

Crank blinked. "You were gonna *marry* this?"

Wayne squinted at him. "Hey, fuck you." He threw a drunken punch, which Crank easily sidestepped. He threw another, and Crank dodged it. When the third blow failed to connect, Wayne grabbed Liz's arm. "Come on, we're getting out of here."

"Let go of me, you son of a bitch." Liz struggled to free herself from Wayne's grip.

"Get your hands off her," Crank told him, still keeping his voice down. Around them, people at the bar and nearby tables were staring, and some of them were recording the altercation on their phones. And speaking of phones, the bartender was on his.

"This is none of your fucking business," Wayne told him. He moved away from the bar, pulling Liz with him, although she was clearly trying to pry his fingers from her arm. That only made him tighten his grip.

Crank had had enough.

"Hey, *buddy*?" When Wayne stopped and turned around, Crank pulled back, aimed, and laid him out with one blow. Wayne dropped like a stone, landing on his back. Then Crank saw Security heading their way. *Aw shit.* He pulled his phone from his pocket and speed-dialed Roadkill. "Dude, don't wanna interrupt your dinner, but I might be in trouble."

"Want me to get the boss?"

"Fuck no. I'll be in even more shit." Then a police officer came into the bar, and he groaned. "I think I'm about to get arrested. When I find out where they're taking me, I'll let you know. Do *not* tell Horvan, you got that?"

On the floor, Wayne was rubbing his jaw and pointing at Crank. "I want that guy charged with assault!"

Shit.

HORVAN HAD to admit, the restaurant had been an inspired choice. The high ceiling, red-and-gold theme, and candlelight everywhere gave it an opulent feel. A statue of some Eastern goddess with more arms than Horvan could count dominated the large space. Long tables filled the center of the room, and they'd been seated at a smaller round table toward the outer edge.

The server walked away to fetch their water, and Dellan turned to Horvan. "This is beautiful." Rael murmured in agreement.

"And after dinner? I thought we might let the guys go back to the house while *we* go to a hotel. Rose petals on the pillow, champagne, whirlpool bath...."

Dellan's eyes sparkled. "Wow. When you do romance, you really pull out all the stops."

When Horvan's phone buzzed, Rael's breathing hitched. "Don't answer it."

"You know I can't do that." He peered at the screen. *Oh fuck.* "It's Roadkill." He clicked Answer. "This had better be important." Except he already knew the answer to that.

"Crank just got himself arrested."

What the fuck? "Seriously? It hasn't even been an hour. What's he done this time?"

"They've taken him to the police precinct on West Harrison Street. He told me not to call you."

"Then why are you calling me?"

"To piss Crank off, of course."

Horvan bit back a growl. "You're not worried about pissing *me* off?"

"No, you're Mama Bear."

Horvan swore one of these days he was gonna kill Roadkill for coming up with that. He sighed. "We'll be right there." He ended the call and turned to his mates. "Guys, dinner might be on hold."

Rael bit his lip. "Don't they say it's the thought that counts?"

Horvan growled internally. "Don't look at my thoughts right now. They involve Crank and pain."

"You need to go. We'll come too. And if we have to go home?" Rael smiled. "I'm pretty sure we can come up with something equally romantic."

Horvan had the *best* mates.

Don't think romance—think pain. Crank's pain. It was only then that Horvan realized how much he'd been looking forward to his date.

CRANK COLLECTED his jacket and wallet. "So that's it?"

The police sergeant nodded. "The CCTV footage and the witness accounts all show you trying not to react to this guy. He threw the first punch. And you were clearly trying to help the woman. You're free to go." He pointed to the door. "The exit is that way."

Crank walked out the door, along a hallway, through another door… and came face-to-face with Horvan, Dellan, and Rael, who were sitting on a bench, their eyes focused on the door he'd stepped through. Horvan gave Crank a dark look that would have had anyone else pissing their pants.

That wasn't to say Crank wasn't a little nervous, though.

He turned to the nearest cop. "Can I go back in, please?" The guy smirked.

Horvan got to his feet. "Come on. We're going back to the house."

Crank trudged over to him. "Look, do we have to go right away? I didn't even get to eat dinner."

27

Rael glared at him. "Don't even go there. You ruined our date. *And* it was gonna be a fantastic date too." Dellan looked unhappy.

"Guys, I swear, it wasn't my fault. Some Neanderthal tried to get heavy with this girl, and—" He stilled. "Wait a sec. How did you know I was here?"

"Roadkill called me."

That little fucker.

Horvan glanced around the waiting area. "Where *are* Roadkill and Hashtag? I thought they'd be here."

"They went off to eat before all this went down."

Horvan's eyes bulged. "They left you alone?"

Crank nodded quickly. "After you specifically told them not to."

Horvan arched his eyebrows. "How old are you guys? Six?"

"Aw, come on, H. Can we go to a bar? Please? You know, drinks? Munchies?"

Horvan's eyes glinted. "No more bars for you. Not now, not ever. Food we can do. And I know just the place."

Crank wasn't going to ask. He was already in enough shit.

HORVAN WIPED his lips with his napkin. "That filled a hole." Across from him, Dellan belched, and Horvan grinned. "I guess you liked the burger too." He'd discovered the Palace Grill years ago. They cooked a mean half-pound burger, and their meatloaf plate was delicious. Plus, there were tables outside where they could watch the world go by, all the people on their way to or heading home from a night on the town.

Oh well. Date night would have to wait.

We'll make it up to you. Dellan's eyes sparkled.

Oh yeah? Got anything specific in mind? Then Horvan almost spat out his water when Dellan sent him a *very* graphic image of exactly what he wanted them to be doing when they got home.

Jesus... I think I'd need diagrams to get into that position.

"I never saw so much meat disappear so fast," Crank muttered, next to Dellan.

Rael laughed. "Do we have to remind you?"

"Yeah, yeah, I know, meat-eaters. But you're such a skinny dude." He glanced over Horvan's shoulder and stiffened. "Hey, H." The quietness and timbre of his voice alone was enough to have the hairs on the back of Horvan's neck stand on end.

"Talk to me."

"There's a guy two tables from us. I swear I saw him when we came out of the police station."

"Could be a coincidence," Rael suggested. "Maybe he was hungry too."

"Then why is he staring at our table?"

Rael grinned. "Maybe he thinks you're cute."

Crank didn't even break into a smile. "It ain't me he's staring at." His gaze met Horvan's. "It's Dellan."

"You sure?" Horvan was suddenly glad he was carrying.

Crank nodded. "He's staring holes through him."

Horvan got to his feet, and suddenly two voices erupted in his head.

Sit your ass back down. That was Rael.

Don't. That was Dellan.

"I'm only gonna have a quiet word." Horvan stepped away from their table, turned, and instantly spotted the guy in question. He was maybe in his midtwenties, dressed neatly, and staring at Horvan with obvious trepidation.

Horvan walked over to his table and sat in the empty seat facing him, his hands beneath the table.

The guy gaped at him. "Excuse me? I don't recall inviting you to sit."

"What's your problem?" Horvan demanded in a low voice.

"Excuse me?"

When Horvan got a good whiff of him, he froze. *This guy's a shifter.*

Up until a few weeks ago, that wouldn't have been a concern. Even in Rael's thoughts, Horvan could hear the note of panic.

That's what I was thinking too, Dellan cut in. *We don't know whose side he's on.*

They'd both nailed it. Until Vic's revelations, they'd had no clue there *were* sides.

Horvan cleared his throat. "Okay. I know what you are. So I repeat, what's your problem?"

The guy swallowed. "I don't know what you're talking about."

"My mates. You were staring at them, and I don't like it."

The guy blinked. "You can't stop me from looking at someone."

Horvan smiled. "My gun aimed at your balls says different."

29

The guy paled. "You… you wouldn't do anything stupid in front of all these people."

Click.

Fuck, his face was like milk.

"You'd be amazed what I'll do if I think my mates are threatened."

The guy caught his breath. "There's no such thing."

Horvan arched his eyebrows. "Says who?"

"Everyone knows that."

"Well, everyone is wrong. Now start talking. You followed us here. Why?" When the guy said nothing, Horvan gently rapped the underside of the table with his gun. "I can still blow your balls into itty-bitty pieces, remember."

The guy's Adam's apple bobbed. "I only came in here because when I walked past you by the police station, I caught your scent. Except…. The three of you seem to share a scent. I haven't come across that before."

Horvan studied him for a moment. There was something about the guy's face that seemed familiar. The hairs were still standing up on the back of Horvan's neck. There was a mystery here, and he didn't like it. Horvan's apartment in Chicago wasn't far, of course, but he wasn't going to run the risk of leading the enemy to it.

Especially an enemy he knew next to nothing about.

Horvan got out his phone and speed-dialed Duke.

"What do you need?"

Horvan gave their location, not once breaking eye contact with the guy. "I need the nearest safe house and the access code for entry."

"Give me a minute. I'll send it by text." Duke disconnected.

The guy's eyes were fucking *huge*. "Safe house?"

Horvan nodded. "I don't know who you are, but I trust my instincts. So you're going to come for a little ride with us, to a safe place where we can talk without being interrupted."

"And if I say no?"

Horvan rapped the table again. "I refer you to my earlier statement."

"Are you for real? I'm going nowhere with you. Not if it means I end up in a body bag."

Horvan couldn't miss the waves of fear that rolled off him. "You'll come to no harm if you do as I say." He locked gazes with him. "I swear it."

The guy was shaking. "Sure. As if I'm going to trust you."

Horvan took a deep breath. "I know you don't believe such a thing is real, but I swear it on the lives of my mates."

The guy stared at him for a moment, then shivered. "Okay."

Horvan's phone buzzed. "Crank," he called out. "Get over here."

Within seconds, Crank was standing next to the guy. Horvan picked up the man's check and handed it to Crank. "Pay both checks, then call for a cab. We're out of here."

He wanted to know what was going on... and why this guy's eyes seemed so fucking familiar.

CHAPTER FIVE

HORVAN KEYED in the access code, and the door clicked open. "Okay, get him inside." He stepped into the dark interior and flicked the light switch. Once everyone had entered, he closed and locked the door.

The open-plan room was sparsely furnished, with a couch and an armchair at one end, a kitchen at the other, and a small square dining table between. He pointed to the latter. "Sit him there."

Crank ushered the guy toward a chair, Horvan's gun in his hand. Rael peered at the kitchen. "You think it's got coffee?"

Horvan chuckled. "Go take a look. There's probably instant coffee and powdered creamer in a cabinet. Gotta have the basics, right?" He pulled out the chair facing the guy and sat, meeting his belligerent stare. "What's your name?" Crank stood behind Horvan, the gun aimed at the guy's head.

The guy looked right through him, saying nothing.

Horvan sighed. "I've been polite. I don't *have* to be polite. I could search you for ID."

"Getting this jerk to pat me down was polite?"

Crank scowled. "Had to make sure you weren't packing a concealed weapon. Now answer the man."

A pause, then, "Jamie Matheson."

Horvan smiled. "Thank you."

Dellan slipped into the empty chair beside him, his hands clasped on the table.

Jamie inhaled deeply, his eyes widening. "And there it is again. Strangest scent ever. Never smelled anything like it." He shivered, then recovered. "Okay. I've played nice. What's your name?"

"Horvan. That's all you get."

Jamie nodded toward Dellan. "And who are you?"

"You don't need to know their names," Horvan said brusquely.

Dellan laid a gentle hand on his arm. "Chill, all right?" He addressed Jamie. "I'm Dellan. The guy making what will probably be foul-tasting coffee is Rael. And the guy with the gun is—"

32

"I'm not talking while *he's* in the room," Jamie burst out, staring daggers at Crank.

"Oh?" Horvan folded his arms. "You got something against my friend?"

Jamie spat at Crank, then glared at Horvan. "How can you be friends with a human?"

"What's so bad about humans?" Dellan asked, his face tight.

"You have to ask? They're inferior. *We* are the dominant species, not them."

Crank laid the gun on the countertop and stepped closer to the table. "Get up." His voice was low and calm.

Horvan? Is this okay?

Horvan caught the edge of panic in Dellan's thoughts. *It's fine. Crank is about to teach Jamie the error of his ways.* Horvan wasn't worried.

Jamie gaped at Crank. "What? No."

Crank narrowed his eyes. "You say you're superior, don't you?"

Jamie's Adam's apple bobbed. "Yes."

"Then get the fuck up!"

Jamie stood, shaking.

Crank moved to his side. "I'm gonna make this easy on you. I want you to knock me down. That's it." His eyes gleamed. "And I'll sweeten the deal. You knock me down and I'll get on my knees and kiss your feet. I'll swear you're my master."

"Crank." Dellan sounded nervous, despite Horvan's assertion.

"Let this play out," Horvan told him. Rael stood in the kitchen, watching, and Horvan could feel his tension.

"Fine." Jamie's lips twisted into a sneer. He lunged at Crank, who sidestepped him, then pushed Jamie from behind, knocking him into the table.

Crank arched his eyebrows. "Oh, I'm sorry, did you trip? Here, I won't move this time."

Jamie straightened, wiped his mouth, and rushed Crank. True to his word, Crank didn't move, but as Jamie drew near, Crank leaned in, grabbed him around the chest, and flipped him over onto his back on the floor. Then he picked up the gun and pointed it at Jamie.

"Bang, motherfucker. Whatever the fuck kind of shifter you are, you're now a skin in front of my fireplace." He glared at Jamie. "Who's fuckin' inferior now?"

Jamie jerked his head toward Horvan, his face ashen. "You're gonna let him do this?"

Horvan hadn't even unfolded his arms. "I *could* stop him. You'd have to apologize to him first."

"Apologi—" Jamie stared at the gun barrel. "Okay, I apologize," he ground out. Crank hauled Jamie to his feet and shoved him roughly onto the chair.

Horvan studied him. "Let me run a few things by you. Shifters are the dominant species. Correct?" Jamie nodded, his lips pressed together. "Shifters should only mate with shifters, not with humans. Correct?"

Jamie's breathing hitched. "Yes."

"And the day will come when shifters will rule over mankind," Horvan concluded, recalling everything Vic had told them about the Gerans.

Jamie's mouth fell open. "Are… are we on the same side?"

"Fuck no. And regardless of what you've been told, mates do exist. You're looking at 'em."

"We thought they were so rare, they were a myth," Rael said as he walked over to the table, carrying four mugs. Dellan took them from him. "But when you start hearing someone inside your head, it's a bit hard to deny it exists." He gestured to the empty seat. "Crank, you want to sit down?"

Crank's eyes gleamed. "This *inferior* human will stay in his proper place and let the *dominant species* have the chairs." He leaned against the countertop.

Horvan chuckled. "You have *really* pissed him off."

"What do you mean about hearing someone inside your head?" Jamie demanded.

Rael sat next to Jamie. He pointed to Horvan and Dellan. "We hear one another's thoughts. I guess it's a mates thing, because none of us have ever heard of this."

"Bullshit." Jamie gaped at him. "Prove it."

Rael looked around. "Crank, pass me that notepad and pencil hanging up there?" Crank took them off their hook and handed them to him. "Okay." Rael placed the pad and pencil in front of Jamie. "One of us will go into the bathroom. *You* are going to write something on here."

"And you'll think it? Is that the idea?" Jamie's lips twisted. "Sounds like a cheap mind-reading act."

"That's why *you're* doing the writing, and *we* won't say a word," Horvan said. "Dellan, would you...?"

"Sure." Dellan got up and walked out of the room.

Horvan waited until they heard the *click* of the door shutting. He pointed to the pad.

Jamie picked up the pencil and stared at the white paper. He smirked and wrote, *This is all such bullshit.*

The bathroom door opened. "Doesn't matter if you think it's bullshit. It's true," Dellan called out.

Jamie's eyes widened. Then he narrowed them. "A good guess."

"Write something else," Horvan suggested.

Jamie chewed on the end of the pencil for a moment before writing, *I'm hungry.*

The door opened again. "Better make him a sandwich, then, guys, assuming there's actually food in this place."

"Fuck." Jamie dropped the pencil, and it clattered onto the table.

"Come on back, Dellan," Horvan called out. A moment later, Dellan retook his seat beside Horvan.

Jamie was still pale. "That... that wasn't a trick, was it?"

Horvan shook his head. "So if whoever told you mates didn't exist got *that* wrong, maybe there's a possibility that everything else you've been told is wrong too."

Jamie said nothing for a moment. "Is that why you three smell different? Because you're mates?"

"Possibly? We're still finding out about all this," Rael told him.

Dellan inhaled deeply. "You're a tiger."

Jamie froze. "How did you know that?" Before Dellan could answer, Jamie's eyes widened. "So are you."

Horvan's scalp was prickling again. "This doesn't make any sense. I've never known what kind of a shifter someone is. I've always had to ask."

"Me too," Rael confirmed.

"Up till now, I'd have said the same thing." Dellan leaned back from the table, putting distance between himself and Jamie. Horvan sensed the sudden unease rippling through him.

"There's gotta be *someone* who has the answer." Crank frowned. "This shit keeps gettin' weirder."

Horvan pulled out his phone and scrolled to Vic's number. He composed a quick text. *Horvan Kojik here. You available to take a call?*

Seconds later, a message popped back. *Sure.*

Horvan hit Call, and Vic answered immediately. "I was only thinking about you today."

Horvan wasn't about to waste time with small talk. "Hey, Vic. FYI, I'm sharing this conversation with my mates, okay?"

"Gotcha."

"Question. If you come across a shifter, can you tell what *kind* of shifter they are by their scent alone?" For all he knew, this was an ability he and the others lacked.

"No. No shifter can do that. Well, except when we reach puberty, of course."

Horvan frowned. "What do you mean?"

"Well, when you discovered what you were, did you have to ask your parents what *they* were?"

"I—" It had been on the tip of Horvan's tongue to say he'd assumed they were bears, but…. That wasn't true. Hadn't there been some innate knowledge? Some sense that revealed to him exactly what his parents were?

Not that the realization helped him.

"So if we've met a shifter for the first time, and he and Dellan know *without being told* that they're both tigers…?"

There was silence for a moment. "Okay, there can only be one reason for that. They're related somehow."

Excuse me? Dellan's jaw dropped.

"Okay, you've just shocked the hell out of Dellan."

"But how did he—oh. Yeah. Sorry. I forgot he hears what you hear. I take it he doesn't know this guy?"

"Like I said, first time we met was today." Then Horvan put the phone to his chest, a knot in his stomach. *Holy fuck. Now* he knew why Jamie's eyes had seemed so familiar. "Vic. Can I call you back in a sec?"

"Sure."

Horvan disconnected, and Crank didn't wait for him to take a breath. "When I said *someone* would have the answer, Vic wasn't the first person who came to mind."

"Well, he came to *my* mind, okay?" Horvan's head was still reeling. Dellan was staring at Jamie, as was Rael.

Oh my God. I can see it now. Rael jerked his head to look at Dellan, then back to Jamie, then to Dellan again.

"Want to tell me why you're all staring at me?" Jamie bit his lip.

Horvan wasn't sure where to begin.

"How old are you?" Dellan asked.

Jamie frowned. "Twenty-seven."

"Where were you born?" That was Rael.

"Boston."

"What are your parents' names? And are they tigers too?" Back to Dellan.

"Miles and Greta Matheson. Dad's a tiger, Mom's a panther. Look, why—"

"What do you do for a living?" Horvan interjected.

"I work for a private school. My job is to interview prospective students and their parents."

"Any siblings?" Dellan's voice shook a little.

"I'm an only child. Okay, what is this, Twenty Questions?"

"Which of your parents do you most resemble?" Dellan again.

Jamie blinked. "That was... random."

"Well?"

Jamie frowned. "Neither of them, to be honest. My mom always said I resembled my grandfather. I never knew him. He died before I was born."

"Any aunts or uncles?" Horvan was clutching at straws.

Jamie went quiet. "I'm not answering any more questions unless you tell me why you're asking them." He lifted his chin and looked Horvan in the eye. "What's going on? And don't bother lying to me. I might not know any of you, but right now my instincts are telling me something is up."

There was no way to sugarcoat it.

"You and Dellan could be related. That would account for you knowing about each other." Horvan paused. "And it would also explain why you look alike."

Jamie's lips parted. He stared at Dellan. "This is bullshit."

"I would agree. I had a half brother, but... he's dead." Dellan's face tightened. "My mom died a year or so ago. As far as I know, she and my dad didn't have any other children."

"We are *not* related," Jamie insisted with some vehemence.

"Then let's prove it, one way or the other." Horvan dialed Vic's number again. When he answered, Horvan didn't give him a chance to speak. "Doc told us there's a network of shifters. We're in Chicago, and we need someone to take blood and run a DNA test. Do you think you could find someone for us?"

"Give me five minutes. I'll call you back." He disconnected.

Jamie snorted. "Excuse me? And what makes you think I'm going to let anyone take my blood?" His face contorted. "Christ, all I did was follow you guys because I was curious. This is getting out of hand. If I hadn't walked past that police precinct at that precise moment—"

"But you did, and you *know* you'll agree to a blood test, because you need to know the truth, just like Dellan does." Horvan glanced at Dellan, who nodded.

"Don't DNA tests take weeks?" Jamie observed.

"They do for us humans," Crank muttered. "Who *knows* how it works with shifters?"

Horvan's phone buzzed. "I guess we're about to find out." He clicked Answer.

"Okay, I've found a phlebotomist. We can be there in the morning, hopefully. I'll be on the first flight out of here, and I'll pick him up and bring him to you."

"Whoa, slow down." Horvan's head was spinning, Vic was moving so fast. "First of all, you don't have to come."

"Yes, I do, and don't try to stop me. What's your next point?"

"How long is all this going to take?"

"He says he'll have the results in twenty-four hours, so sometime Monday. Where are you staying, and who is 'we'? You got the whole team there?"

For a second, what flitted through Horvan's mind was that what Vic *really* wanted to ask was if *Crank* was there. "We're in a safe house in Evanston, north Chicago. And it's me, my mates, Crank, and our guest." He could see Roadkill and Hashtag wanting to come over, once they knew what was going on, but Horvan had already told them to go back to Dellan's place. "You still sure you wanna come?"

"Text me the address. I checked—the first flight gets in after eleven. Warren, the phlebotomist, texted to say he'll meet me at O'Hare."

"You've already arranged all this? While we've been talking?" Horvan was impressed.

"Hey, I can multitask. And I *might* have someone sitting next to me, booking flights on my laptop."

Horvan chuckled. "That's handy. Okay, then, we'll see you tomorrow. I'll send the address once I've ended the call. *Some* of us don't multitask as easily as you." He disconnected, then typed the safe house's location.

"He's coming here?" Crank rubbed the back of his neck. "Why? What's he gonna do—hold Jamie's hand while some guy takes blood?"

"I'm not sure why he's coming, but he wouldn't be dissuaded." Horvan put his phone down on the table, then laced his fingers, looking Jamie in the eye. "I'm sorry if you had plans for the weekend. In the circumstances, you're going to need to cancel them. Because you do want to get to the bottom of this, don't you? As much as we do."

Jamie nodded. "I didn't have plans. I was going to relax a bit before my next trip, which isn't for a few days." He glanced at their surroundings. "I think I preferred my hotel, but I guess you're not going to let me go before you have answers, right?" He sighed. "Before *we* have answers."

Rael gestured to the mugs. "Drink your coffee. There's a TV. I'll check out the rooms and see where everyone is going to sleep." He gave Horvan a searching glance. *That's if you intend on sleeping tonight.*

Crank and I will take turns to keep watch. Horvan looked at Jamie. *We still know next to nothing about this guy.*

Jamie picked up his mug and went over to the couch. Crank switched on the TV, tossing the remote to Jamie before flopping into the armchair.

I've got a theory.

Both Horvan and Rael turned to Dellan. *Want to share?* Horvan inquired.

Well... up until last week, I'd have said it was impossible for me and Jamie to be related. But now?

Horvan knew where Dellan was going with this. The same thought had occurred to him.

We know my dad isn't dead—or at least he was alive when those photos were taken of him, whenever that was. But he's been missing since I was seven. Thirty-one years, guys. Who's to say what went on during those years? Maybe... maybe he had more children. It's possible, isn't it?

There's another possibility, Rael added. *One that I don't like very much, but we can't dismiss it.* He reached across the table for Dellan's hand. *When they had you in that cage, and they kept bringing in females....*

Dellan swallowed. *I've been thinking about that too. What if they were mating me with females to breed more shifters? It's the only theory that makes any sense. And suppose they're the ones who took Dad, and they've been keeping him someplace and... using* him *to breed more shifters too?*

But why him? Horvan demanded.

Doc said Dad was remarkable, even when he was younger. And that he was fast. Maybe they're choosing shifters with traits they want—speed, intelligence—and creating.... Oh, I don't know. A race of super shifters. Dellan glanced over to where Jamie was channel hopping. *He could be my half brother. The age would fit. And if we're right, what if there are* more *of Dad's children out there?*

How about we leave all the what-ifs till we have solid evidence that we're on the right track? Horvan followed Dellan's glance. *One thing is certain. We can't trust him.*

Why not? If it turns out he is Dellan's brother....

Horvan shook his head. *After all that stuff he came out with? He could've been fed nothing but lies his whole life. There are words for people like that.* He looked from Rael to Dellan. *Indoctrinated. Programmed. Brainwashed.*

And none of those words inspired Horvan to trust Jamie an inch.

CHAPTER SIX

SAUL'S HEARTBEAT quickened as Vic dragged a bag from the closet and began filling it. "Why you?" His stomach had been clenched all through Vic's phone call, and he was at a loss to know why.

Vic paused, his brow furrowed. "Excuse me?"

"Why are you going to Chicago? You've organized for this guy Warren to go. *You* don't have to be there."

Vic dropped a folded pair of jeans into the bag. "This is what I do, right? I'm an oral historian. I document whatever I learn about shifters. Maybe I'm about to learn something new."

"But you don't know that for certain." Saul watched as Vic reached into a drawer and removed a pile of underwear. "These the same guys you met in Idaho?" When Vic nodded, Saul's scalp prickled. "Maybe I should come with you. I could book another ticket."

Vic blinked. "Why would you want to do that?"

The fact that Vic would even question Saul's motives only added to his growing unease.

I thought we were solid.

But that had been before Vic had had a sex dream about another guy.

And what if that guy is in Chicago? Fuck. Saul wanted to ask Vic but was too fucking scared of the answer. *You don't know if there* is *a guy in Chicago.*

Maybe he was being paranoid. Maybe he was seeing things where there was nothing *to* see. Maybe he was hearing things in Vic's tone that weren't even there. Maybe he'd been wrong that night, and Vic hadn't moaned in his sleep or thrashed on the bed. And maybe that *had* been sweat on his chest.

Maybe.

"How long will you be gone?" Judging by the clothes Vic was shoving into the bag, this was no overnight trip.

"I don't know. I'll take enough clothing to last a few days."

"Will you call me?" Christ, he sounded so fucking *needy*. *What is the matter with me?*

41

"If I can."

It was as if someone had opened a door or a window somewhere, letting in an icy blast: the skin on his arms pebbled into goose bumps. "I'll take you to the airport in the morning." Saul had no clue what the fuck was going on, but he knew he had to do *something* to fight the irrational fear building within him.

"You don't have to do that."

"No, I don't have to—I *want* to. That's why I'm offering."

Vic didn't respond, and Saul's throat tightened. He wanted to yell "Don't go!" but he knew that would make no sense.

Vic zipped up his bag. "There. All done. One less thing to worry about when I wake up. Can you see to the gun case?"

"Sure. Which one are you taking? The Glock?"

Vic nodded. "I'm going to bed, seeing as I have to be up at stupid o'clock for the flight." He gave Saul a half smile. "You don't have to come with me. It's still early."

That icy blast chilled Saul to his core.

"You don't have to come with me." Words neither of them had uttered in all the years they'd been together. Even if Saul wasn't going to sleep, he could still hold Vic. And then there was the sex that always happened before Vic left on a mission. Vic joked about it, said it was his way of making sure Saul thought about him while he was away. It was their thing, and now Saul felt like he was being dismissed.

Well, fuck that.

Saul folded his arms. "Wow. You really don't want me around, do you? You don't want me to go with you to Chicago. You don't want me to take you to the airport. You don't want me to go to bed with you."

Vic gaped. "Hey, that is *not* what I said."

"No, but it's what you *meant*," Saul fired back.

Vic rolled his eyes. "If you want to come to bed too, that's fine. If you want to come to Chicago, that's fine too. Forgive me for not wanting to disrupt your days, especially as you'd probably be bored as fuck the whole time."

"It's okay. I won't go. Go to bed." The words came out terse even to Saul's ears.

"What are you going to do while I'm away?"

"What I always do—take care of things till you come back."

Vic walked around the bed and stood in front of him. "Think how happy you'll be to see me. Very happy, if my last 'welcome home' was anything to go by."

Saul arched his eyebrows. "Was that the time you came back and had a sex dream about another guy?" Even as he said the words, Saul regretted it. *Why am I being such a bitch? It was just a dream.*

Except something had changed.

Vic's visit to Idaho had opened the door onto a whole new world. One where there were mates, telepathy…. What if Vic's dream was somehow part of that world? What if it had greater significance than either of them imagined?

And therein lay the dilemma. Saul could imagine a *lot*.

He knew one thing for certain. If he carried on thinking like this, he was going to drive himself mad. Or worse, drive Vic away. With Saul's attitude, he might not have to worry about Vic hooking up with this dream guy, because Saul was going to push him right into his arms. A part of him knew without a doubt Vic loved him. The problem was, right then he was having difficulty believing it.

Vic winced. "I'll try not to disturb you too much in the morning."

Saul couldn't respond. His chest was tight, and it ached when he breathed. He left Vic in the bedroom and hurried into the guest room that housed their weapons and other mission gear. Saul opened the cabinet and took out the Glock. He removed the magazine and placed it in the small padded case along with the gun and some extra magazines. Then he pulled open a drawer to find a padlock for it. The whole time, his head was spinning.

I'm fucking this up, aren't I?

Vic was doing what he always did, so why did it feel so different?

He went around the house, switching off lights and checking locks, because hey, that was what *he* did, right? He crept back into the bedroom to find Vic lying on his side, facing the window, his back to Saul. From the sound of his breathing, he wasn't asleep.

Saul stripped off and climbed into bed. He deliberated saying something but dismissed the idea—he'd already said way too much. He lay on his side, his back to Vic, feeling cold.

Am I making too big a deal of this?

Then the mattress dipped and a warm body spooned around him, Vic's arm snaking over his waist. "You know I can't sleep without you." Vic's voice was soft.

43

The tightness in his chest eased. Saul turned in Vic's arms. "In case no one ever told you, you're the little spoon."

Vic chuckled and rolled over. "You're the only one who gets to say that."

I'd better be.

Saul curled around him, his hand pressed lightly against Vic's chest so he could feel Vic's heart beating.

I don't want to lose you.

SAUL DIDN'T recognize the house. It was big and dark, with cool marble floors and high ceilings. Noise came from behind one of the many doors in front of him—a very distinctive noise. Saul went from door to door, trying each handle, but they were all locked. The last door yielded to him, and he cautiously pushed it open, the soft cries from within suddenly louder. He peered into the dimly lit interior… and froze.

Vic was on a huge bed, his back to the door, and he wasn't alone.

Saul couldn't move, rooted to the spot as he watched Vic riding a guy whose face Saul couldn't see. But it was Vic, his lithe body undulating as he rocked back and forth, making low noises of pleasure every time the guy's thick cock slid into him.

Then Vic turned to look at Saul, and he stilled. "I wanted to tell you, but… I couldn't."

Saul's throat seized.

A large hand rested on Vic's waist, stroking him gently. All Saul had to do was take a couple of steps to the left and he'd see the guy's face, but he couldn't make his feet move.

"Tell me what?" he croaked.

Vic gave a leisurely roll of his hips. "I'm not coming back. I'm staying here. With him."

"No. No. Please, don't do this."

"I have to."

"Vic, please!"

SAUL SAT bolt upright in bed, his heart pounding, sweat covering his neck and chest, struggling to breathe. Beside him, Vic murmured and rolled over, unaware of the turmoil raging inside Saul.

It was a dream. It was a dream. It was a dream.

Saul lay back down, his heartbeat slowly returning to its normal rhythm.

Please, God, let it be just a dream.

SAUL WAITED while Vic checked his gun case at the ticket counter. Vic took the card he'd filled out, placed it inside the case, and attached the padlock before leaving it with the rest of his luggage.

He grinned as Vic walked back to him. "I guess that's one lesson you're not gonna forget in a hurry." There had been one time when Vic had forgotten to pack the gun appropriately, and there had been all kinds of hell to pay with TSA.

Vic chuckled. "Yeah, and the lesson was—let Saul pack the guns."

Saul glanced at the clock. "Wanna grab a coffee before the flight?"

"No, I want to get through Security, onto the flight, over to Chicago, and back to you before you have time to even notice I'm gone." Vic sighed. "But since time travel is *not* one of my gifts...."

Saul knew this was all because of him. "I'm sorry. I don't know why I said all that stuff last night. You'd think I'd be used to you going on missions by now. I'm not sure why I even reacted that way."

Vic's eyes sparkled. "Maybe because you love me?"

Saul stilled. "I don't say that enough, do I?"

Vic stared into his eyes. "You're not the kind of guy who's continually saying it. You've never sent me roses on Valentine's. You don't hold my hand in public. *But*"—his face seemed to glow—"you learned how to cook for me. You take care of our home. You take care of *me*. You're there for me when I'm tired and cranky and sore." His lips twitched. "You give the most amazing head massages."

Saul leaned closer. "I think you *meant* to say, I give the most amazing *head*." He bit his lip. "You also forgot the part about me having an enormous dick."

Vic whacked him on the arm. "I'm trying to say something meaningful here." Saul mimed zipping his lips. Vic took a deep breath. "I don't have to hear the words to know you love me. Like you know I love you, right?"

45

"I do. And because I do, I'm gonna step out of my comfort zone." Saul cupped Vic's face, moved in, and kissed him on the lips, a lingering kiss that he hoped said more than his clumsy words.

"Get a room," a guy murmured as he walked close by.

Saul didn't miss a beat. "We had one," he called after him. "They threw us out because the bed kept banging on the wall." The guy dismissed them with a wave and continued on his way, but Saul was certain he detected a smirk. Saul cupped Vic's chin. "Now, where was I?" He gave him one more kiss, resisting the urge to reach down and squeeze the tight little ass he knew was hiding in Vic's jeans. "Now get your butt through Security." As Vic pulled away, Saul grabbed his hand. "Be safe."

Vic nodded as Saul released him." I'll be back as fast as I can." His eyes gleamed. "If only to get some more of what we had this morning."

Saul huffed. "I wasn't even awake. God knows how I managed to find it in that state." Thankfully his cock had been on autopilot, gravitating to Vic's hole like a homing pigeon.

Vic grinned. "This morning was slow and sweet and sexy as fuck, and I loved every second of it. When I get back, we're going to do that again. Not that I'm complaining, you understand. I love it when you pound me. But this morning was something else." He cupped Saul's nape and drew him closer into a kiss. "Love you." And then he walked off toward the TSA check-in without a backward glance.

Saul wanted to call after him, to tell him not to board that plane. He wanted... what, exactly?

I don't want my life—our life—to change.

It didn't matter what his head said. Saul's heart told him something different.

It already had.

CHAPTER SEVEN

CRANK GOT up off the couch and wandered into the kitchen, reaching into his shorts to pull on his dick. He'd grabbed a couple of hours sleep while Horvan took watch, but it hadn't refreshed him.

However, it had been the first night for a while without the dream.

Is that it? I've got rid of whatever weird shit was rattling around inside my head?

Lord, he hoped so. At least he hadn't woken up smelling of cum. Horvan would have had a field day with that.

On autopilot, he set up the coffeepot, thankful Rael had discovered a packet of ground coffee in a cabinet. Life was too freaking short for instant.

Horvan came out of the bedroom, yawning. He gave Crank a nod, then smiled when he registered the coffee. "Good man." He peered at Crank's shorts. "You planning on getting dressed today?"

"Christ, give me a break." He grabbed his jeans from the back of the couch and squirmed into them. "How was the bed?" he inquired as he zipped up. The couch hadn't been lumpy, thank God.

"Too damn small for three of us."

He cackled. "It was probably too small for you on your own. Want me to go pick up something for breakfast?" He put on his shirt and buttoned it.

Horvan beamed. "You're a lifesaver."

Crank pointed to a cup. "I'll go *after* I've had some coffee. Trust me, you don't want me going out there without my caffeine." He went over to the table, grabbed his phone, and searched for somewhere nearby that did food at that hour. "A breakfast burrito do ya?" The place was about five minutes' walk from the safe house.

Horvan snorted. "I could eat three of 'em."

"Then I'd better tell them I'm feeding twelve." He inclined his head toward the bedroom where Jamie slept. "I suppose we have to feed him too?"

Horvan frowned. "Be nice. If our suspicions are confirmed, you might regret being an asshole." He held up his hands. "I know, he was a jerk, but what do you expect? He's probably been fed that bullshit his whole life." He

47

poured coffee into four cups. "I'll take coffee to Rael and Dellan. Then I'll be right back so you can go out." He disappeared into the bedroom.

Crank smirked. *In a pig's eye he'll be right back.* He estimated it would be at least twenty minutes before any of them surfaced. He picked up the mug and sipped, inwardly groaning at that first hit. Behind him a door opened, and he turned toward the sound.

Jamie shuffled into the kitchen, yawning. He froze when he saw Crank, and his face tightened.

Yeah, he's still a jerk.

Crank gestured to the coffeepot. "You want some?"

Jamie said nothing.

Okay, enough of this shit. Crank sighed. "I'm being nice. *You* gonna play nice? If I give you coffee, you're not gonna spit it at me?"

Jamie pulled out a chair at the small table and sat. "Coffee would be good… thank you."

Crank poured him a cup, then placed it on the table in front of him. "You're welcome." He pulled out the opposite chair and sat, his hands around the cup. "I won't be in your face for long. Once I've drunk this, I'm off to grab breakfast for everyone."

Jamie sipped his coffee. "Can I ask you something?"

Crank arched his eyebrows. Apparently hostilities had ceased. "Sure."

"How come you're working with shifters?"

He chuckled. "I didn't know I was until a few weeks ago. First I knew about shifters was when Horvan got a call to go rescue a tiger and brought us in. Except then we found out Horvan wasn't human, Rael was a lion, and the tiger wasn't really a tiger."

Jamie's eyes widened. "You rescued Dellan?"

Crank nodded. "He was being held in a glass cage at the top of a Chicago skyscraper."

"Who was holding him?"

Crank had to remind himself they knew nothing about this guy. "Doesn't matter now. Fucker's dead."

"I bet your services don't come cheap."

"Normally, no," Crank agreed. "We get paid a lot to get people out of tight spots by whatever means we can. *This* one we did for free."

Jamie blinked. "Why?"

Crank stared at him. "Dellan is Horvan and Rael's mate. He needed us."

"I see." Jamie drank some more.

"Look, I don't expect you to go all mushy and tell me you've got humans all wrong, because one, I don't think you're that kinda guy, and two, most humans suck, and not in a good way."

"Everything okay in here?" Horvan walked into the kitchen with a casual air that didn't fool Crank for a second.

Crank smiled. "Jamie and I are bonding over coffee." Then Jamie spluttered all over the table, and he grinned. "I'll grab the bathroom while it's empty. Then I'll go get breakfast."

He figured it would take more than one conversation over coffee to change Jamie's thinking. But maybe one conversation was enough to make him realize there were other possibilities out there.

"Do we know when Vic will get here?" Not that Crank was in any hurry to see him. The thought of being in the same room as him gave Crank a fluttery feeling in his stomach. He knew part of it was that freaking dream.

"He just sent a text," Horvan announced. "He picked up his bags, and Warren met him at the airport. They'll be here shortly."

"Bags?" Crank gaped at him. "How long is he staying?"

Horvan arched his eyebrows. "How should I know? Ask him when he gets here."

Yeah, no. That would mean *talking* to him.

"And then what?" Jamie demanded. He was sitting in the armchair by the fireplace, his arms folded. "We stay here and wait for the results?"

Horvan nodded. "That should be tomorrow, according to Warren."

"If you're bored, there are games in the closet," Dellan informed them. "Monopoly, Clue, a couple of packs of playing cards…." He grinned. "Most of the games even seem to have all the pieces. Except Monopoly is missing the car. I never get the damn car."

Crank held out his hand. "You're not getting it this time, either." He snapped his fingers. "I always get the car. Hand it over."

Dellan narrowed his gaze but fished the Monopoly piece from his pocket and smacked it into Crank's outstretched hand. "Dick."

Crank winked. "You know it, baby."

Horvan's phone buzzed, and he smiled when he saw the screen. "It's Hashtag. They've gotten into more files, Dellan."

"Excellent. Maybe by the time we get back to the house, they'll have some more answers for us."

Horvan walked over to where Dellan sat on the couch, bent over the back of it, and kissed the top of his head. Crank's throat seized at the intimate gesture. It was a side to Horvan he'd never glimpsed before. *He's so in love with them.* And yet they'd known each other for such a short amount of time.

"We're not playing Monopoly," Rael declared. "What if I discover another side to you two? What if Horvan turns into some power-hungry, land-grabbing, property-developing monster?"

"Then play strip poker," Crank suggested. "That way you know exactly what you're gonna get."

Rael chuckled. "I think that's a game for the bedroom." He cocked his head. "I hear a car outside."

"I didn't hear a thing." Crank got up from the table and went over to the front window to peer through the blinds. Vic was getting out of the passenger side. "It's them." And just like that, his heartbeat quickened.

Horvan went to the door and opened it. He shook hands with Vic and then with the skinny guy behind him. "You must be Warren."

He grinned. "That's me, your legalized vampire. Whose blood am I taking?"

"Mine," Jamie piped up. "Let's get this over with so I can prove we're not related."

Crank admired Warren's brisk, matter-of-fact manner. He opened his bag, removed a square package, and tore it open. He cleaned Jamie's inner arm with a sterile pad. "You're not going to faint on me, are you? Because if you're needle phobic or you hate the sight of blood, I'd rather know now."

"You're good to go," Jamie told him.

Vic was busy greeting Rael and Dellan—and ignoring the fuck out of Crank.

What the ever-lovin'...? What am I, chopped liver?

Finally Vic acknowledged Crank's presence with a nod of his head, then went over to crouch beside Jamie's chair and talk to him in a low voice.

That's it? That's all I get?

He couldn't explain the irrationality of his thoughts. Why should he give a flying fuck if Vic wanted to ignore him? It was no skin off Crank's nose, right? And it wasn't as if Crank wanted to talk to him, right?

Then why did it *burn* him?

Warren secured the vials of blood into his bag. "All done. Who do I call with the results?"

"Me," Vic and Horvan said simultaneously.

Warren grinned. "I'll email you the results," he told Vic. "You can pass them on, okay?" He inclined his head toward the door. "You ready to go? I can drop you off somewhere."

"Thanks, but I'm going to stay a while," Vic told him. He glanced at Horvan. "If that's okay?"

Horvan nodded. "If you want to stick around here until the results are in, you can have the couch." His eyes twinkled. "I'm sure Crank won't mind giving up the couch for you. He's told us so often how he can sleep anywhere."

Rael and Dellan chuckled. Warren gave one last wave, and then he was gone.

Crank wasn't in a chucklelicious kinda mood. *Vic's staying the night.* What he found most disconcerting was that he didn't know if that news pleased or horrified him.

"How about I sort out food for lunch and dinner, seeing as we're gonna be here a while?" He hated shopping with a passion, but at least it would get him out of the house—and away from Vic—for a while.

"You want a hand with that?" Vic asked.

Ice slid down Crank's spine as he recalled those exact words from a dream. Only then Vic's hand had been wrapped around his cock.

"No, I'm good," he croaked. "I'll be back soon." He grabbed his jacket and was out the door in a heartbeat.

What the fuck is happening to me?

CRANK AWOKE with a start, his heart hammering, his chest coated in sweat. He ran a finger through it. *Thank God. It really is sweat this time.* So much for being rid of that dream. He could still feel the coldness of the water pressing in around him, numbness crawling up his legs, his arms growing so weary….

"You okay?" Vic's whisper came out of the darkness.

Christ, I forgot he's here. And *that* was fucking weird, waking up to the guy who'd been jerking him off. "Fine. Bad dream." He rubbed his eyes. "Where's Horvan? He was supposed to wake me when it was my turn."

"I told him to let you sleep and that I'd do it instead."

"You armed?" Crank reached for the lamp beside the chair where he was sleeping beneath a blanket. The room was bathed in a dirty yellow light. Vic lay on the couch, a Glock on the floor beside him.

"Go back to sleep," Vic told him. "I'll keep watch. I'm not tired."

"Is that because you're an insomniac, or don't sharks sleep?"

Vic chuckled. "A bit of both?" He got up off the couch and headed for the kitchen. Crank got a glimpse of a broad, smooth back and narrow waist, white shorts tight across a round, firm-looking ass. Disconcertingly, Crank's dick twitched, but he told himself that was the remnants of his dream and nothing more.

Stop looking.

He heard the faucet. Vic came back carrying two glasses of water. "Here."

Crank took one, doing his best to ignore Vic's crotch that was right in front of him. "Thanks."

Vic returned to the couch and sat. "I feel guilty taking your bed, especially as you're sleeping and I'm not."

"It's okay." Crank drank half the water in a few gulps.

Silence reigned for a moment. *Is that it? Are we done?* He reached for the lamp switch.

"Have I... offended you in some way?"

Crank blinked. "Excuse me?"

"Just asking. You've barely said a word since I arrived."

What the fuck? "I could ask you the same question."

Vic bit his lip but said nothing.

Crank was tired of feeling off balance. "Look, why are you here?"

Vic's eyebrows went skyward. "Any reason why I shouldn't be? Horvan said he needed my help. And I want to know more about Jamie."

They were all valid reasons, and yet....

Crank was a mess, and he'd been that way ever since Vic had walked through the front door. Maybe longer. Maybe since he'd first met Vic? That sounded about right.

What if I'm to blame? He'd been hostile from the start to the idea of Vic getting involved, and Vic had to sense that, right? So what if the awkwardness that had been prevalent was down to Crank? And Vic was merely picking up on it, thrusting them into a circle of mistrust and discomfort.

If that was true, it was Crank's job to make the first move toward reconciliation.

"Look, we didn't exactly get off on the right foot when we met in Idaho."

Vic's eyes gleamed. "Was that when you told me I looked as if I was twelve years old?" Before Crank could respond, he held up his hand. "You're not wrong. It sucks to be me, especially when I have to buy clothes."

Crank didn't think there was anything wrong with Vic's build. He was slight, with a swimmer's body. That made him smile. *Well, he is a swimmer.*

"I'm sorry. Horvan says I put my mouth into action before I put my brain in gear."

"Yeah, but your heart's in the right place," Vic said in a quiet voice.

He blinked. "Careful, Vic. That almost sounded like a compliment."

Vic stared at him for a moment, and then they both laughed. "Want to start again?"

Crank could do that, especially when it hit him that his stomach had stopped churning and his nerves were no longer on edge. And all it had taken was to talk calmly with Vic. In fact, one look into those soft brown eyes and Crank was having a hard time remembering why he'd been so pissed in the first place.

"Get some sleep," Vic told him. "And when you wake up, I'll make breakfast for everyone."

Crank pulled the blanket up over his chest and stretched out his hand to turn off the lamp, plunging the room into darkness. "Vic?"

"Hmm?"

"I'm not tired anymore."

Vic chuckled. "Give it a while. Count backwards from one thousand."

"Nine hundred ninety-nine, nine hundred ninety-eight, nine—"

"In your *head*, Crank."

"We could play a game."

"Crank? I've got a gun."

He chuckled. "G'night, Vic." It wasn't long before a warm, velvety feeling crept over him, pulling him down into a dreamless sleep.

CHAPTER EIGHT

VIC GLANCED at his phone for what had to be the twentieth time that day, and Horvan chuckled. "You ever heard that phrase about a watched pot?"

Vic had no idea why he was so on edge. What did it matter to him if Dellan and Jamie turned out to be related? In fact, why was it such a big deal to Horvan, Rael, and Dellan?

Good question.

"Want to tell me why we're doing this?" he asked Horvan. "I mean, so what if they're cousins or something?" *Don't they have more important stuff to be doing?*

"I'd rather not say anything until we have the results."

Vic raised his eyebrows. "Why all the mystery?" He glanced across the room to where Jamie was channel hopping and Dellan was dozing on the couch. "Sure, I can see a resemblance, but—" His phone buzzed, and he grabbed it from the kitchen table. "I thought you were going to send a text?"

"I was," Warren told him, "until I saw the results. I'll email them once we've spoken."

"What did you discover?"

"Put him on speaker," Horvan demanded. "This is something we all need to hear." Jamie and Dellan got up and walked over to the table, and Rael came out of the bathroom to join them. Crank had gone on a food run.

Vic hit *Speaker*. "Okay, we're listening."

"First of all, I have to tell you this isn't conclusive. For it to be that, I'd need a sample of maternal DNA. But looking at the results, I *can* tell you… your two guys are half siblings."

Jamie's breathing caught, as did Dellan's.

"There's no doubt about that?" Vic asked.

"The test measures the amount of DNA. We're not talking about their profiles matching at every genetic marker. It simply determines whether they share a common parent. And they do." He paused. "You said they're both tigers?"

"Yes."

54

"Then the probability is that their parent was too."

"Thanks, Warren. Yeah, send the email please." Vic's skin prickled.

"Send him the bill too. I'll pay that," Horvan added.

"Thanks, guys." Warren disconnected.

Jamie shook his head. "No. No. Are you saying my dad had an affair with Dellan's mom? No. My parents were childhood sweethearts. You've never met a couple so into each other." He set his jaw. "I don't care what the results say. They're wrong."

"That's not what we're saying," Rael said gently. He pulled out a chair. "Sit down. We need to share some things with you."

Jamie stared at him, and Vic was convinced he was about to bolt. Then he shuddered out a breath and sat.

Dellan removed his phone from his pocket and placed it on the table. "You know I was held captive, right?" Jamie nodded. "Well, Hashtag—he's another member of Horvan's team—was able to hack their CCTV system. They saw shifters being brought to my cage. Our best guess is they wanted us to mate. We have no idea how many times this happened. I don't remember any of it."

Jamie frowned. "What does this have to do with me?"

"Dellan's dad disappeared thirty-one years ago, when Dellan was seven years old," Horvan told him. "His mom remarried when Dellan was sixteen, about a year after she'd had his dad declared legally dead."

"Only now we have reason to believe he's still alive." Dellan swallowed. "And there's a distinct possibility he's your dad too. It all fits. Us knowing we were both tigers, the DNA test results…."

"But I *have* parents," Jamie yelled.

Dellan picked up his phone and scrolled. He held it up for Jamie to see. "This was taken recently. This is my dad."

Jamie peered at the phone, then pushed his chair away from the table, his eyes wide. "Christ."

Dellan nodded. "You see it too, don't you? You told us yourself you don't look like either of your parents, but you *do* look like him. And me."

"We think the organization that kept Dellan captive is the same one that's keeping his dad someplace. And if they were breeding *Dellan*, then there's every possibility they've been doing the same with his dad."

"There's another possibility you haven't mentioned," Vic said. "Dellan, what if your dad's captors told him his wife had married someone else? Who's to say he hasn't had relationships that resulted in children? Dellan could have more half siblings out there that he knows nothing about."

"Wait a minute." Jamie was shaking. "Are you telling me you think I'm the result of this organization forcing Dellan's dad to breed with other shifters? What kind of stupid-assed idea is that?"

"How much do you know of shifter history?" Vic asked. "Do you know the tale of the two brothers?" When Jamie stilled, his brow furrowed, Vic nodded slowly. "That rings a bell, clearly. The story goes that one of the brothers, Ansger, thought men were weaker than shifters, and that therefore shifters shouldn't mate with humans."

Jamie blinked. "That's what I was taught."

"But who taught you?" Horvan demanded.

"My parents. The teachers at my school. All the students were shifters."

Rael gaped. "There's a school for shifters?"

"Sure. It's actually the school I work for now." Jamie gazed at the men around the table. "This is crazy. You're telling me I'm *adopted*? My parents have been lying to me my whole life? This is such bullshit."

Horvan sighed. "We've shown you the evidence, and we've shared our suspicions. There isn't much else we can do to convince you." He leaned back in his chair. "The door is right there. Have a nice life."

Jamie swallowed hard. "I can go?"

"Yup."

"Just like that? You're… you're not going to kill me?"

Horvan's expression was deadpan. "Not right now." Then his eyes twinkled. "You're my mate's half brother. *We* believe that, even if you don't."

"If you're going to leave…." Dellan grabbed the notepad and pencil from the countertop and scribbled on it. He tore off the top page. "This is my number. Call me, okay? If you have questions, if anything changes—"

"That's not procedure," Horvan interjected.

Dellan glared at him. "Well, that's okay, then, because I don't work for you, so your rules don't apply to me. But I'm not letting my *half brother* walk out of here thinking I'm happy to simply let him go. Because I'm not." His face tightened. "I've already lost one half brother. I don't intend losing another."

Jamie stared at the page in Dellan's outstretched hand. "You really believe that, don't you? That we share the same dad?"

Dellan nodded. "I also believe you're not the same man who walked into that diner. *That* Jamie Matheson had a closed mind. I think we've opened yours."

Jamie took the page, folded it, and pulled his wallet from his pocket. He slid the paper inside, then stood.

Horvan went into the bedroom and returned with Jamie's phone. "Here."

Jamie took it. "You thought I was like the people in that organization, didn't you? You thought I might be a danger to you." He glanced at the interior of the safe house. "Hence why you brought me here." At that moment, Crank walked through the door, and Jamie squared his shoulders. "Yes, I believe we're the dominant species, but I don't hold with keeping shifters—or anyone—captive, or breeding them. That... that isn't right." He held out his hand to Horvan. "Good luck. You're going to try to find Dellan's dad, aren't you?"

Horvan nodded as he shook hands. "If we can." Dellan and Rael were on their feet too.

Jamie walked around the table, his hand still outstretched. Vic's throat seized when Dellan grabbed it and pulled him into a hug. Then Jamie headed for the door, pausing for one last look at them before stepping outside.

Crank stared at them. "We're letting him leave? What did I miss?"

"We'll tell you while we eat those subs you're carrying," Horvan told him. "Then we're packing up. I'll get Roadkill or Hashtag to come pick us up. We're out of here." He removed his phone from his pocket.

"Where are you going?" Vic's heartbeat quickened.

"Back to Dellan's house in Homer Glen, about an hour's drive from here."

"Can I come too?" Vic blurted out.

Horvan grinned. "I was kinda hoping you'd ask. Sure. I wanted to pick your brains anyway."

"Then we'll need more than one car," Dellan told Horvan. "I don't have one big enough at home to take five passengers." He bit his lip. "Although given the circumstances, maybe I need to rethink that and go shopping. Mrs. Landon will show them where the keys are. Tell them to take whichever ones they want."

"I'll get them both to drive here." Horvan made the call while Crank went into the kitchen and unpacked the bag of subs.

"Anything I can do to help?" Vic asked him.

Crank inclined his head toward the refrigerator. "There's juice in there, and water. You can put them on the table."

Vic made himself useful, half listening as Horvan made travel arrangements. When he was done, Horvan smiled. "They're on their way." He gave Vic a warm glance. "Thanks for taking a shift last night. You won't be doing that at the house. Brick takes care of security."

When Vic frowned, Crank cackled. "Yeah, no one messes with Brick. I mean, who in their right mind would tackle a polar bear?"

"Another member of the team?" Vic inquired.

Horvan nodded. "We've worked with him before. He's a good guy."

Vic smirked. "Your team has the best nicknames. Why is he called Brick? I mean, I get Hashtag, Roadkill...."

"I wanted to know the same thing," Dellan said as he put the folded blankets into the closet.

Horvan snickered. "That one is down to Hashtag. The first day he met Brick, he stared up at him—Brick's a big guy—Brick grinned back, and then Hashtag said to Crank, 'Holy shit, he's a fucking brick shithouse!'"

"After that," Crank continued, "it was either call him Brick or Shithouse." His eyes gleamed. "He didn't seem all that enamored with the second option. Can't think why." That raised chuckles from everyone.

"You're sure I won't be in the way?" Vic inquired. His question prompted laughter, and he gave them a quizzical look. "Something I said?"

"You'll understand when you see the house," Dellan explained.

"There's plenty of room," Horvan informed him. "All the bedrooms are taken, but I'm sure *someone* wouldn't mind giving up their bed for you."

Heat flushed through Vic, catching him by surprise. It was on the tip of his tongue to tell Horvan he'd be okay with sharing a bed, but he reined in that thought. Because what came to mind was Crank, spooned around him, his body warm and his dick, hard, sliding between Vic's asscheeks.

Sweet Jesus. What the fuck is going on?

CRANK RECALLED his first impressions of Dellan's home, so he fully comprehended Vic's openmouthed stare as they turned into the driveway. "Ten thousand square feet, set on five acres. Home sweet home."

"Yeah, but it's home sweet home with a *lake*." Vic's wide grin and sparkling eyes were very attractive. Then Crank remembered he was sitting next to a shark.

"Ask Dellan if you can go for a swim," he suggested.

Roadkill laughed as he pulled up in front of the garage door and switched off the engine. "And you won't even need a bathing suit. You've got your own."

Before Crank could say another word, Vic had unfastened his seat belt, opened the car door, and was running over to the car Horvan, Rael, and Dellan had traveled in with Hashtag.

"I suppose it's like showing Dellan or Rael a box," Roadkill said with a chuckle. "He just wants to dive right in." Then he burst out laughing. "I guess Dellan said have at it."

Crank gaped as Vic ran full tilt toward the lake. "Oh my God, I think he's about to dive in now." His fingers fumbled with the seat belt as he struggled to free himself, and then he was out of the car and running after Vic, unable to stop himself. Horvan was doing the same.

By the time they reached the water's edge, Vic had stripped off his clothing and plunged beneath the surface, a streak of lean, toned flesh. Crank stared down into the clear waters, and the sight robbed him of breath for a moment.

The shark was fucking *huge*. The sunlight on the water produced a dappled effect on its skin, the shapes shifting and dancing as the water rippled.

"Holy fuck, and I thought the shark in *Jaws* was big."

"He looks as if he's at least twenty-five feet long," Horvan murmured. "Look at him. What a beautiful creature." He glanced at Crank. "Well? Is he like the shark in your dreams?"

Crank swallowed. "No. He's not *like* the shark. He *is* the shark." He crouched by the water, watching the small fin break the surface. "Why doesn't he swim farther out? It's a big enough lake. And it's not like any of the houses on the other side are close to the water. The people across there won't see him."

"Maybe he's waiting for someone to join him for a swim," Horvan suggested.

Crank said nothing, transfixed by the graceful shape that swam in circles. Then he realized Horvan had gone quiet. He glanced in his direction, and Horvan merely pointed to the lake. Crank goggled. "You're serious. You want me to go in there?"

"Why not? Don't you want to see if reality lives up to your dream?"

Crank snorted. "Swimming. With a shark. I'd freeze my ass off, for a start."

"Then wear a wetsuit."

Crank rolled his eyes. "Gee, why didn't I think of that? I *always* carry a wetsuit on me, just for occas—"

"Here's the wetsuit," Dellan said breathlessly, hurrying over to them with the dark blue neoprene garment over one arm and a pair of fins in the other.

"How did you…?" Crank narrowed his gaze. "You told him to."

Horvan shrugged. "I have no idea what you're talking about."

"It was my stepdad's," Dellan told him. "We used to swim in here all the time. I figured his would be more your size." He peered into the clear water. "I was *about* to say that's a freshwater lake, but then I remembered."

"What do you mean?"

"Greenland sharks swim in salt water, right? But he's not a shark— he's a shifter—so obviously the normal rules of nature don't apply."

"Now stop yakking with us, put on the wetsuit, and go swim with the fishes." Horvan grinned. "Only not in the Mafia sense." Dellan dropped the items onto the grassy bank, and he and Horvan walked back to the house.

Crank watched them go, then gazed out over the lake. Now and then the fin sliced through the water before disappearing from view, but never ventured too far.

What if he is *waiting for me?*

He peered into the distance at the houses on the other side of the lake. Sure, he could be seen, but only if they were watching with a telescope or binoculars.

Do it. You know you want to.

Crank shrugged off his jacket, kicked off his shoes, squirmed out of his jeans, and removed his shirt. It had been a while since he'd worn a wetsuit, and thankfully he could get into it with a bit of judicious tugging. He pulled on the fins and flapped his way to the edge of the lake.

This is nuts.

Then he realized the shark had swum closer.

Fuck it.

Crank dove in, the cold water shocking him for a moment as it enveloped his head, then rose to the surface. The shark drew closer, and he was awed to see the size of it in comparison to himself. Pushed by his recollections of the dream, Crank swam along the shark's back until he reached its fin, then grasped it with both hands.

He had to fight to catch his breath as the shark sped up, heading for the middle of the lake. It was exhilarating, cutting through the water, giving him the sensation of flying, the spray in his face. The shark—Vic—never dropped his fin below the surface of the water, and he slowed down several times. It took Crank a few moments to realize he was doing it to allow Crank to catch a breath before he sped up again. His heart rate picked up, a rush of adrenaline flooded through him, and he had never felt so energized, so *alive*.

Oh my fucking God, this is awesome.

He lost all track of time, exulting in the sensations that threatened to overwhelm him. But when the shark swam toward the far shore, slowing as they approached it, Crank wanted to yell "No!" He didn't want it to end.

His heart pounded as the shark shimmered beneath him and Crank found himself with his arms full of a lithe, toned man. He let go of Vic and scrambled toward the shore, his feet stumbling on the uneven bottom of the lake. He could hear Vic splashing behind him, and he couldn't turn around, not if that meant coming face-to-face with a *very* naked Vic.

"Wait!"

Crank came to a stop, the bank a few feet away, and slowly turned. Vic strode toward him, his hair falling into his eyes, his shoulders broad and muscled, his chest glistening, the water low enough to reveal the V over his hips that led Crank's eyes downward.

Fuck, he's beautiful.

The thought shocked Crank into stillness.

Vic didn't say a word but came to a halt in front of him, his chest rising and falling erratically, rivulets of water sliding down his creamy skin.

Unable to stop himself, Crank reached out and brushed the hair out of Vic's eyes. Vic's lips parted as he wet them with his tongue.

A single thought dominated in Crank's head. *Kiss him.* The urge powered through him, consuming him. "Vic, I—"

Vic's eyes widened, and his breathing quickened, his cheeks flushed. "Crank, we—"

Crank couldn't fight it a moment longer. So many women, so many kisses, but the need to lock lips had *never* been this primal, this... desperate. He slid a hand around Vic's neck and drew him in, until he could feel Vic's warm breath on his face.

"Crank."

His name on Vic's lips was heady as fuck, and heat barreled through him at the thought of those same lips begging Crank to take him harder, faster. Their mouths fused, and Crank moaned softly into the kiss. His heart pounded, his legs trembled....

And he came in his wetsuit.

Vic's nostrils flared, and he tore himself away, stumbling backward. "We can't do this," he hissed. "I have a boyfriend, for God's sake." He turned away, and suddenly he was gone and the shark had returned. Crank stood shivering as Vic sped across the lake, heading for the house. He watched as Vic climbed out of the water, his pale asscheeks like a beacon that called to Crank.

What the fuck just happened?

Crank's head was spinning, and he shuddered violently. As his heartbeat returned to normal, so too did his lucidity. His ride had run into the house, and it would be a long swim to the other side.

Maybe by the time I get back, enough of the cum will have washed away.

Not that it mattered. There were five shifters in that house who would know *exactly* what had happened.

Never done that in my life.

But then, he'd never kissed a guy before either. If that was what a *kiss* produced....

No. No. I don't kiss guys. I don't fuck guys. I don't do that.

It didn't matter how many times he repeated the words to himself, it didn't alter a thing.

He *wanted* to do that. With Vic.

CHAPTER NINE

VIC DIDN'T care that he was wringing wet. He hurried back to the house, his clothes clinging to him, but as he approached the door, a hulk of a man barred his entrance. The span of his shoulders had to be twice that of Vic's.

The guy folded his arms. "And who might you be?" He frowned. "Did you fall in the lake or something?"

Before Vic could introduce himself, Horvan pushed past the hulk. "Brick, meet Vic Ryder. Same line of business. Our guest. We okay now?"

Brick cackled. "Why are you suddenly speaking in short, choppy sentences?" He gave Vic a polite nod. "Hi, Vic. Come on in. Please excuse my reaction, only no one told me we were having company." He glared at Horvan. "I mean, I'm only Security. And ooh, listen to me, talking in complete sentences." Brick rolled his eyes and stood aside to let Vic enter.

"I'm sorry about that, but it's been ages since I shifted."

Horvan waved his hand. "It's okay. I get it." He aimed a meaningful stare at Brick. "And *some* people need to learn some manners."

"So which would you prefer?" Brick demanded. "The next bad guy that tries to get in this place, do I rip his throat out or ask if he'd like cream with his coffee? Or maybe some freshly made scones?"

"How about you detain him? Mrs. Landon doesn't want to be cleaning up the blood again."

Brick shrugged. "Whatever. I need coffee." Then he strode off.

Horvan's brow furrowed. "Where's Crank?"

"Swimming." He didn't want to think about Crank yet; his head was still spinning from that kiss. *What the fuck?*

Horvan picked up Vic's bags from the floor by the door and handed them to him. "Roadkill brought them in for you. We'll put your stuff in Crank's room for the moment, until we can sort you out a room of your own."

Vic's heart raced at the idea of him and Crank sharing. "I'd appreciate that." He followed Horvan through the marble-floored hallway and up the impressive staircase. "This is awesome. Now I know why everyone laughed

63

when I asked if I'd be in the way. This place is huge." They reached the second floor, and Horvan turned right.

"The guys sleep on this floor. Me, Rael, and Dellan are on the floor above." He opened a door. "This is Crank's bedroom. Look, I'd like to jump right into it. Put on some dry clothes, and then I'll show you what we've discovered so far." He paused. "But if you need some rest after your—"

"It's fine," Vic assured him. "I'm ready to go. Give me enough time to get into some dry jeans."

"Then I'll leave you to it." Horvan walked out of the room.

Vic glanced at his surroundings. *Why did I expect it to be a mess?* Crank, it seemed, was a neat individual. The bed was made, and nothing was out of place.

The only one who was a mess right then was Vic. The recollection of Crank's lips on his sent another wave of heat surging through him, and his dick pressed against the zipper of his pants. What came to mind was his dream—Crank balls-deep inside him and Vic loving every second of it.

He shivered. *Nope. Can't think about that.*

He reached into one of his bags and grabbed his jeans, then squirmed out of his damp clothing, hoping Crank wouldn't choose that moment to make an entrance. Except Vic couldn't avoid him completely.

We need to talk.

By the time he headed downstairs, his heartbeat had returned to normal. He followed the sound of voices and the enticing aroma of coffee and… cookies? When he found the kitchen, Horvan and his mates were in there, along with Roadkill and Hashtag, who raised their hands.

"Hey. Welcome aboard," Hashtag said with a smile. "Your timing is perfect. Mrs. Landon baked."

"Who is Mrs. Landon?" Vic asked.

"She's my housekeeper," Dellan explained. "She also makes the *best* oatmeal raisin cookies." He gestured to an empty stool at the breakfast bar. "Join us. We're just catching up with these guys."

"Coffee?" Roadkill headed for the coffeepot.

"Please." Vic sat next to Hashtag. "So what have you discovered?"

"I looked at the inventories for Global Bio-Tech, and I *think* I've worked out which chemicals make up the base for this drug they've come up with. All I had to go on were shipments."

"I'm impressed."

Hashtag snorted. "It only took me a week. Their security systems at the head office might have been total crap, but their encryption is top-notch. I've been looking for large shipments of these chemicals to factories, trying to spot where they've moved their manufacturing base to. I'm also tracking factories who've hired large numbers of employees within the last year. Employees with no designation."

"How many such factories, and where are they?"

Hashtag rubbed his chin. "Maybe five plants here in the US."

Vic stilled. "Have you started looking farther afield?"

"Not yet, but it makes sense to do that. We have no idea how big this operation is."

Vic sipped the coffee Roadkill had placed in front of him. "I know when you add everything up, right now it feels as if this all points to some huge, shadowy, evil master plan." He paused. "I told you back in Idaho that we didn't have much information on what the Gerans were doing, beyond snippets and rumors."

"You said nothing that was verifiable," Dellan commented.

Vic bit his lip. "Nothing wrong with your memory, is there?"

Dellan smiled. "Funny thing is, I can recall everything that's happened since I shifted back into human form with crystal clarity. It's as if my body has reset itself." He gave Vic a thoughtful glance. "Something has changed, hasn't it?" He held up his hands. "I know, you're an oral historian, and you won't stoop to spreading misinformation. But now we know my dad is alive, possibly being held captive, and *then* we learn that *somewhere* there's a school full of shifters who are being taught they're the master race. Anyone here think it's likely that where there's one such school, there could be others?" He shivered. "I'd say the situation has changed, wouldn't you? So tell us what you know, Vic." He locked gazes with him. "We're on the same side here."

Vic sucked in a deep breath. "Based on what you told me about shifters being forced to mate, and also the size of the chemical shipments, I'd have to say it points to one logical hypothesis. They're breeding an army."

Rael's eyes widened. "How can you make such a leap?"

"Look at who their group is named after, for Christ's sake," Vic remonstrated. "Ansger—that means Divinity and *Spear*, remember? Bit of a clue, don't you think? Why else do you think they're doing this? Because someone thought, 'Oh, wouldn't it be nice if there were more shifters in the world?' After what Horvan told me about that guy who had Dellan's half brother ripped apart, you can't think their purpose is benign?"

"I'm not *that* naive," Rael protested. "But what can we do about them?"

Vic met Horvan's gaze. "We hit them where it hurts. We raid the factories. We destroy the shipments. We take out any cells we find."

"Fuckin' A," Hashtag said with a gleeful note. "Horvan, does Duke have enough manpower to hit five plants at once?"

"He says he's got a huge list of ex-military guys who are always looking for a fight to join." Horvan got out his phone. "I'll give him a call." He nodded toward Vic. "I like this. I'd like it even better if I could be involved, but—"

"But you've got other matters needing your attention." Vic could understand that. "You want to concentrate on finding Dellan's dad."

"Yeah." Horvan glanced at Dellan before addressing Hashtag and Roadkill. "If you two wanna get in on the raids, that's fine."

Roadkill blinked. "Seriously? Hell no. We're sticking with you and your mates." Hashtag murmured in agreement.

"What raids?"

Vic froze at the sound of Crank's voice.

"See what you miss when you decide to go for a swim?" Roadkill said with a chuckle.

Crank walked over to where they sat. "Vic, why is your stuff in my room?"

Before Vic could respond, Horvan got in first. "Hey, play nice. It's only temporary." Then he added, with a gleam in his eye, "Unless you want it to be permanent?"

Judging by the look on Crank's face, he didn't like that idea.

Crank leaned in between Hashtag and Vic and grabbed a cookie. "So fill me in."

Vic's nostrils were filled with a scent that went straight to his dick, and he lurched off the stool. "I need to make a call." He hurried out of the kitchen and onto the patio. When he was a safe enough distance from the house, he dared to draw a breath. He stood by a rattan chair, shaking.

What the fuck is wrong with me?

"Can we talk?"

Jesus, the guy was a fucking ninja.

Vic turned slowly to find Crank standing there, his face tight. "What do we have to talk about?" Vic's mouth had dried up.

"Well, that kiss, for one thing."

Vic glared at him. "It never happened, you got that? And we're never going to discuss the fact that it never happened. Am I making myself perfectly clear? I have a boyfriend, and I love him."

"Yeah, you already said that part." Crank didn't move.

Vic struggled to breathe. All he could think about was Crank kissing him, stroking him, tugging on his dick. *Jesus.* "Why the fuck did you kiss me?"

"Apparently, I didn't." Crank's eyes gleamed.

"Fuck you, answer me."

Crank expelled a breath. "What can I say? Seemed like a good idea at the time." The words came out with all of Crank's usual confident swagger, but as Vic watched, he seemed to... crumple. "Look, I don't know why, okay? I just... I couldn't help myself. It felt as though there was a voice in my head yelling, 'Kiss him,' and I did." He swallowed. "Do you really need to make a call, or were you trying to get away from me? Because if it's the latter, that is *really* gonna piss Horvan off. Especially if we're gonna work together."

Vic knew Crank was right. "I can be professional about this." He shoved down hard on his libido. Whatever he was feeling was nothing one night with Saul wouldn't cure.

Crank shuddered out a breath. "Great. Now come back inside and grab a cookie before Roadkill eats them all."

He laughed. "You're right. I need to try one of these awesome cookies." They walked back to the house side by side. When they reentered the kitchen, Horvan was nowhere in sight, and Vic figured he'd gone to call this Duke character. He returned to his stool and picked up a cookie. They smelled amazing.

Not as amazing as Crank.

Vic pushed that thought aside.

None of the others made any comments, and his stomach finally stopped churning. He took another drink from his cup and smiled. "This is good." Then he bit into the cookie, relishing the hint of gooiness at its center. A burst of cinnamon hit his tongue, and he moaned. "These are better."

Crank laughed. "Told ya." He ate his in two bites.

"Your job sounds, I don't know, kinda boring?" Roadkill arched his eyebrows. "Oral historian? Sounds fussy and dry."

Vic bit back a smile. "Oh really?"

"You go places to collect knowledge. Doesn't really seem all that exciting."

He tried not to laugh, thinking about all the weapons in his house. "I'd have to disagree."

"Yeah, but—"

"You'd be amazed at the things I've learned," Vic told them. "As a for instance, cat shifters aren't big on fish, bear shifters love to have their nails—claws—done, and—"

"Wait." Crank's eyes bulged. "Bear shifters like their nails done?"

Vic nodded, his fingers crossed out of sight beneath the breakfast bar. "It's the colors. It soothes them."

Crank gave an evil grin. "You just gave me a fascinating idea, Poindexter."

Shenanigans were one way to banish anxiety.

HORVAN STIRRED on the bed. *Maybe Dellan was right.* He'd been dubious about the idea of napping in shifted form, but he had to admit, sleeping in fur with his mates had been amazing.

And speaking of his mates…. Horvan was alone. And it was quiet. In that house, between his mates and his team, such silence was highly suspicious.

He'd bounded off the bed and readied himself to shift back into human form when he heard the snickers on the other side of the bedroom door.

"What do you think he's gonna do?" Crank asked.

"Knowing Horvan, he's gonna bite your ass," Hashtag replied.

"I don't know how we let you talk us into this," Dellan moaned. "He's gonna kill us."

What the hell are they talking about? Horvan bowed his head and— *Holy fuck!* His claws sparkled as if they'd been dipped in a pot of rainbow glitter.

Those bastards.

First he was going to gut Crank, then Hashtag. As for his mates, he'd play that by ear.

He shifted, then grabbed a pair of jeans and a tee. He glanced at his fingers, rolling his eyes. The nail polish was even more pronounced against his lighter human nails. He crept to the door and flung it open. Four figures scampered away, and he could hear Crank's and Hashtag's laughter as they ran down the stairs. Horvan strolled to the kitchen, which proved to be empty.

He figured it wouldn't stay that way for long.

He poured himself a coffee and sat on a stool. Within minutes, the others filed in one by one, their expressions wary. No sign of Dellan, though.

Crank broke the silence. "Nice... nails, H. Guess you're taking this whole Mama Bear thing to heart."

Horvan arched an eyebrow. "Y'know, I'm secure enough in my masculinity to admit something that you're too juvenile to understand." He held out his hand. "I fucking *rock* these colors."

Crank's brow furrowed. "You're not mad?" Hashtag's gaze was equally disbelieving.

"Nah, I'm not mad. But I *am* curious."

"What about?"

Horvan grinned. "Whose was the nail polish? I'm dying to know. My money's on Crank."

Crank gaped. "Fuck no. We borrowed it from Mrs. Langford. It belongs to her daughter."

"*Sure* you did." Horvan wagged a finger. "But remember, karma will come for you. Maybe not today, might not even be tomorrow, but come it will." He stood. "And now, if you'll excuse me, I'm going outside so I can watch my nails sparkle."

He walked out onto the patio, and seconds later, an eruption of laughter shattered the quiet.

Let 'em laugh. We're gonna need all the laughter we can manage. Because if Vic was right, the battle was only beginning.

"WHERE'S HORVAN?" Dellan asked Rael, who was sitting beside Hashtag at the desk, peering at the monitor. Vic was at one end of the couch, his laptop on his knees, and Crank was at the other.

Dellan had deliberately stayed out of Horvan's way all evening.

"He said something about taking a shower." Rael grinned. "Why? Scared to face him?"

Dellan straightened. "As if." He bit his lip. "Nervous? Hell yeah."

Vic chuckled. "I gotta admit, I didn't think that would actually work."

Crank gaped at him. "What the fuck?"

"Y'all thought I was boring. I had to do *something*." Vic grinned. "I thought painting a bear's claws was inspired, though."

Hashtag glared at him. "And how are you gonna feel when Mama Bear decides to rip us all new assholes with those pretty painted claws?" Then he grinned too and met Crank's gaze. "I like him. Can we keep him?"

Dellan had put it off for long enough. He headed out of the kitchen, conscious of Rael's voice in his head.

Sure you don't want to wait a while? Maybe till he's had a chance to remove the polish?

Dellan walked into the bedroom and found it empty. He went into the bathroom to find Horvan naked, rubbing his head with a towel. One glimpse of Horvan's face made his stomach clench. *Oh crap, he's pissed.* He tried to reach out with his thoughts, but he couldn't get through.

Aw fuck, he's blocking me.

Dellan really was in the shit.

"What's wrong?" he asked in as innocent a voice as he could muster, his heart pounding, his mouth dry.

Horvan held up his sparkly nails. "Look familiar? Crank confessed you had something to do with this."

Dellan bit back a snort. "Oh, come *on*, you can't be *that* upset. It was just a joke."

There was no trace of humor in Horvan's expression. "I'm their leader. Do you understand that? This?" he said, fluttering his fingers. "This undermines my credibility with them."

Dellan swallowed hard. He hadn't even thought about that. "In my defense, I did say it was a bad idea." It sounded weak, even to his own ears.

Horvan's brows lifted. "I'm sure that makes it all better, right?" He wrapped the towel around his hips and strode past Dellan into the bedroom. Fuck, his voice was so *cold*.

There was no way Dellan could leave things like that.

"Horvan, I'm sorry," he called out after him, following him. "I swear it was meant as a joke. I thought you'd laugh. What can I do to make it up to you?"

Then he noticed the large empty cardboard box in the corner of the room. Written on one end in black marker were the words Free Cat. Nearly Housebroken.

Horvan pointed to it. "Get in." When Dellan gazed at him with incredulity, Horvan's grim demeanor vanished, replaced by a grin. "Gotcha."

"You...."

Horvan dropped the towel and curled his fingers around his erect dick. "Now, give me some head and we'll call it even." Then his grin turned decidedly evil. "And when you're done, we can plan what to do with Rael."

CHAPTER TEN

WHEN HE woke to another missed call from Saul, Vic knew he couldn't put it off any longer. He'd known texts wouldn't cut it, of course, but he hadn't been able to bring himself to do more than that.

Saul had to be going nuts right then.

Vic sat up in bed, rubbing his eyes. There was no sign of Crank's stuff; he'd moved everything out the day Vic arrived. When Vic had protested, Crank had shut him down fast, saying he was fine sleeping in the den and using the downstairs bathroom.

It didn't stop Vic from feeling guilty as fuck. Nor had it stopped the dreams, each one hotter than the last. *I wonder if he fucks like that for real?* His hole tightened at the thought, and Vic shuddered. *I'm about to call my freaking* boyfriend, *for Christ's sake.*

He leaned against the mound of pillows, took a deep breath, and hit Call. Saul answered within seconds. "You *are* alive, then."

"Sorry I missed your call. I had my phone switched off." It was a lame-ass excuse, and Vic knew it.

"Since when do you do that? And since when do you go for *a week* without calling me? Is something wrong? What's going on? I've been going out of my mind here." Saul's voice rose, becoming more strident.

"I know. I'm sorry. It's just that… we're organizing raids," he lied. Whoever Horvan worked with was doing that. "Life got a little complicated."

There was silence for a moment. "That's all I get? Your life got too complicated to *call* me?" There was a pause. "Okay, that's it. I'm on the first plane to Chicago."

"No," Vic protested. "This is not a good place to be." Not with Crank around. Saul was no idiot, and he knew Vic too damn well.

"So you're worried for my safety now? Gee, what a waste all that training was. I guess little ol' me can't take care of himself." He paused again. "Or is it more the case that you and that guy you had a dream about are getting to know each other, and you don't want me to interrupt?"

"What? No!" It came out a little louder than Vic had intended. "Saul, I really am sorry."

Something in his voice must have broken through. Saul let out a heavy sigh. "Look at it from my side. I stood in the middle of that fucking airport and told you I love you—well, as good as told you—and then we don't speak for a week. You can't blame me for worrying."

"I'm a shitty boyfriend. I don't deserve you." Vic meant every word.

"No, you don't." There was another pause. "Are you sure there's nothing wrong?"

Other than the fact that another guy kissed me—a guy I've been having the hottest dreams about—and I can't get him out of my head? Sure, everything's peachy.

"Honestly, I'm fine. Things got a little interesting around here, that's all. This whole business might be bigger than I previously thought. Scarier too. Please, stay where you are. I'll feel happy knowing you're safe." And far away from Crank.

"Fine. You know how much I hate flying anyway."

Vic chuckled. "Exactly."

"So you're getting on with the team?"

"Yes. You should see the house. It's enormous. We're talking five bedrooms."

"What's your room like?"

Vic didn't have to be a mind reader to know what he was really asking. "It's great. Got this huge bed all to myself." He swallowed. "I promise I won't leave it so long between calls next time, okay?"

"Okay. I feel better now that I've heard your voice." Saul paused. "And about what I said… I love you."

Vic's chest tightened. "I love you too. And now I need coffee."

Saul gave a wry chuckle. "Oh please, don't let me stand in the way of you getting your caffeine. I wouldn't wish a noncaffeinated Vic on anybody."

They disconnected, and Vic shuddered out a breath.

That went better than I expected. Except lying to Saul made him feel sick.

CRANK OPENED his eyes and stretched. The couch was comfortable, thank God. There was no way he could have stayed in that room. It didn't matter the bed was a king—sharing it with Vic was a step too far.

73

Why did I kiss him? That thought had never been far from his mind the past week. Only, it wasn't the most pressing thing on his mind. Another question had been plaguing him with frightening regularity.

Why do I want to kiss him again?

Crank wasn't a relationships kinda guy. With the work he did, he never had time to form any kind of bond with a woman, because he might be in her bed one night, and the next he'd be off to Saudi Arabia for six months. Sure, he'd had plenty of sex, but it was best to keep the emotions out of it. A few of his conquests had wanted more from him, but he'd been honest with them from the start. He didn't want anyone claiming he'd broken their heart.

The past week, he'd caught himself staring at Vic and had hastily averted his gaze. *Why can't I stop thinking about him?*

When he'd picked up all his stuff and moved out to the den, Horvan hadn't said a word, but there was a look in his eye that told Crank he was *thinking* about it.

What he needed right then was some action. A really tough mission to tax his brain and his muscles.

Anything to force Vic out of his head.

CRANK SHUFFLED into the kitchen in search of coffee and breakfast. The air was filled with the delicious aroma of bacon, and Mrs. Landon was at the stove, preparing eggs. Horvan, Rael, and Dellan were seated at the table, Roadkill was helping himself to coffee, and Hashtag was at the breakfast bar, peering intently at his phone.

Horvan smiled. "Morning." He narrowed his gaze. "You look like shit. Bad night?"

Crank hadn't had a good night's sleep in weeks. "Nothing a mission wouldn't cure. And have you looked in a mirror lately? You're no oil painting first thing in the morning either." He glanced around the kitchen. "Where's Brick?"

"Grabbing some shut-eye," Horvan told him. "He went to bed about an hour ago. And I don't know where Vic is." He arched his eyebrows. "Do you?"

Crank resisted the urge to give him the finger.

Horvan's phone buzzed, and he picked it up, pushed his chair back, and walked toward the patio doors, speaking in a low voice.

"Good morning."

Crank stiffened at Vic's voice, and he didn't turn around.

Dellan smiled at him. "Hey. The eggs will be ready very shortly, and there's bacon, english muffins, toast, and coffee."

"Coffee. Thank God." Vic ignored Crank and went to the coffeepot.

Crank was trying not to be pissed, until he realized he was just as bad. *I'm trying to ignore him, so why should it rile me when he does the same?*

Horvan came back to the table. "It's official. Operation Shutdown is a go. Duke's got enough men to carry out five raids simultaneously, in three days' time."

Vic's face brightened. "Great. That's gonna hit them where it hurts."

Dellan gave Horvan a speculative glance. "You want to be a part of the raids, don't you?"

Horvan huffed. "Yeah, but like Duke said, my efforts will be better employed elsewhere. Doesn't mean I like it, but he's right."

Vic sat at the table, his hands wrapped around his mug of coffee. "I don't know about you guys, but this inactivity is killing me."

Horvan bit his lip. "I have to be honest here. I'm usually on the go all the time, but this past week, it's been good to take a breather."

Roadkill chuckled. "This wasn't a breather. This was your honeymoon."

Rael laughed. "Many a true word spoken in jest." His eyes gleamed as he gazed at Horvan. Dellan made a choking sound and quickly took a drink from his cup.

Hashtag put down his phone. "I'm sorry. I'm no closer to finding out where they're keeping Dellan's dad. I thought I'd know by now."

Dellan got up from the table, walked over to Hashtag, and patted him on the back. "It's okay. I know you're doing your best. Maybe we need another source of information." He glanced at Vic. "There's nothing you can add? Nothing you can share?"

Vic shook his head. "I'm as much in the dark about this as you guys are. We didn't even know about the camp until you showed me those photos. I shared that information within the network of shifters that I belong to. Everyone is looking, but no one is turning anything up."

"We're gonna get a break," Rael said with confidence. "I can feel it."

Horvan leaned over and kissed him. "And that is why I love you. No matter how bad it seems, you hang on to that optimism."

Crank's throat tightened. Steering clear of relationships was all well and good, but after watching the three of them interact, he got the feeling he was really missing out.

The kitchen door opened, and Brick walked in, yawning. "It's no good. Can't sleep. I'm tired enough, but as soon as I close my eyes…."

Horvan nodded toward the coffeepot. "Help yourself."

A phone vibrated, and Crank chuckled. "You're popular this morning," he told Horvan.

"Except it's not my phone."

Dellan blinked. "It's mine." He gazed at the screen. "I don't know this number."

"Then don't answer it," Horvan barked out.

Dellan rolled his eyes. "It's probably someone calling about my new car's extended warranty." He answered the call. "Hello?" Then his eyes widened. "Jamie. Is everything okay?" He listened intently for a moment. "Okay, I'm with the others. Can I put you on speaker?" He placed the phone on the table.

"I need to talk to you," Jamie said. "It's really important."

Dellan bit his lip. "Come here. I'll send you the address." A low noise erupted from his side, and he glanced toward Horvan. "H? Stop growling. Jamie, do you have a car?"

"I'll rent one at the airport. I'll be there before the end of the day."

Dellan frowned. "Are you all right?"

"Not really, no. This has me so confused, but I'm not gonna talk about it over the phone. I'll tell you everything when I see you."

"When we hang up, I'll text you the address. See you soon." Dellan disconnected the call, and his thumbs flew over the screen as he typed.

"Something is wrong," Rael said with a frown. "You could hear it in his voice."

Brick scowled. "Who is this guy? Because going by Horvan's reaction, we shouldn't be inviting him here."

"He's Dellan's half brother," Rael told him. "And I know we didn't trust him when we first met him, but I think we opened his eyes to a lot of things."

Horvan's brow furrowed. "I still don't like bringing him here."

"But *you're* not," Dellan declared. "And he's my family. Maybe the only one I have left. Give him a chance, Horvan."

"He might have new information for us," Vic proffered. "After all, he works in a school for shifters. Maybe he's discovered something that could help us."

Horvan folded his arms. "Well, we'll see when he gets here."

Vic cleared his throat. "Dellan, would it be okay if I went for a swim?"

"You don't have to ask," Dellan remonstrated. "And you could've gone for a swim at any time this past week."

Vic's gaze wavered briefly in Crank's direction. "Thanks. I'll see you all later." Then he left the kitchen by the patio doors.

Horvan raised his eyebrows. "You look like you could do with a swim too, Crank. Wanna join him?"

Crank shoved down hard on the image of a naked Vic, water beading on his creamy skin, that luscious V leading down to....

Jesus.

"I'll pass." The words came out as a croak.

He was going nowhere near that fucking lake.

JAMIE ARRIVED that afternoon, and Horvan assembled everyone in the living room. He introduced the team, and Crank noted there was none of Jamie's previous hostility.

Something's changed.

Jamie sat on the couch with Horvan on one side and Dellan on the other. He was pale. "I'm not sure where to begin. A lot has happened since I last saw you."

"It's okay," Dellan assured him. "Take a deep breath and start at the beginning." Crank sat in one of the armchairs, Vic in another, and Brick, Hashtag, and Roadkill on the second couch.

Jamie gazed at them. "This is quite an audience."

"You said it was important," Horvan reminded him. "So I thought everyone should hear it."

Jamie nodded. He drew in a sharp intake of breath. "I guess what shook me up the most was the idea that my parents aren't my parents."

"You believed us, then?" Dellan asked in a soft voice.

He nodded. "I had to once I saw that photo of your dad. So I paid them a visit this week." He held up his hands. "I didn't do anything stupid. I didn't confront them with what I'd discovered. Instead I got out the old photo albums. I'd never really looked at those before. And it was amazing what I noticed."

"Such as?" Rael asked.

"When I looked at all the photos of the three of us, there was a kind of… disconnect. My parents seemed almost robotic. There was never a lot of hugging or touching between the three of us when I was growing up. I know they love me, in their own way. But the more I thought on it, the more I realized they were… detached." He swallowed. "Like I said, I'd never looked at the photos before, so I suppose I was seeing them with fresh eyes. Mom caught me looking at them, and I couldn't resist asking a couple of innocuous questions. Things like which hospital was I born in? She said I was born at home. Then I looked again at the photos of my grandfather." He frowned. "I don't resemble him. Not in the least." Jamie shivered. "And then I went to the school."

Dellan rubbed his knee. "It's okay. Take your time."

"I don't know why I got to thinking about the kids who didn't make it. My job is to interview each prospective student and their parents, to decide if they would be a good fit with the school. So I went back over my notes, looking for kids who didn't make the cut. Because not every kid does."

"What kind of things are you supposed to look for?"

Jamie took another deep breath. "The school is interested in kids who have certain strengths. If they're good at sport or particularly bright. But I interview the parents too, to see if they'd support the school's ethos."

"What did you find?" Vic asked.

"Like I said, I don't know why I did it. I called the parents with the excuse that I was following up, making sure they'd found a suitable school for their child. Maybe there had been a change in their circumstances and they wanted the child to apply again. What I *found* was a pattern." He swallowed. "I was told I couldn't speak with the child because they weren't there. On more than one occasion, the parents now had another child and were keen to have them assessed too. When I commented that the last time I'd seen them, I'd interviewed their only child, they replied that they'd recently adopted." He looked at them. "Do you know *how many* parents had adopted a child since I saw them? Too many to be a coincidence. And it got me thinking." He looked at Dellan. "If you're right and they're breeding shifters? All these pregnant shifters…. What happens to all the kids? And I also discovered how many schools there are."

"Tell us," Horvan said.

"There are five in the US, each one taking up to one thousand students. Three in Canada, twelve in Europe, three in South Africa, and two in Australia. That's as much as I was able to discover, because someone walked in at that point and almost caught me."

"Oh my fucking God." Vic paled. "So many? Where are all these kids coming from?"

"I think we now have the answer to that." Horvan's expression was grim.

Crank leaned forward, his hands clasped. "Let me get this straight. Are we hypothesizing that they're breeding shifters, and when the pregnant ones give birth, the babies are then farmed out to couples for adoption? That *is* where you're going with this, isn't it?"

Vic's eyes gleamed. "Smart man."

Warmth spread through Crank at Vic's praise.

"There's something else to think about," Dellan added. "If schools are actively seeking out shifter children, then shifters must be aware of the schools. But how do they find out about them? Because they seem to be a well-kept secret. And what do you suppose happens to those shifter children who don't make the grade? You know, the ones that Jamie can no longer talk to? Where do you think they go?"

"I can guess." Vic's face contorted. "Any army needs soldiers who are expendable. So what if those kids are sent to the same camps where they're keeping Dellan's dad?"

"Camps?" Dellan stared at him, aghast. "You think there's more than one?"

Vic arched his eyebrows. "There are how many schools? Think about it. Because that gives us an insight into their numbers."

Rael shivered. "All I can think about is schools full of shifter kids, all being indoctrinated. All being brought up to believe that it's their destiny to rule the world." His gaze met Horvan's. "We have to stop this."

Horvan blinked. "Were you listening? Jamie said there are twenty-five schools around the world. What do you expect us to do?"

"Close them down. One at a time. Until whoever is running them gets the message. We need to be one huge fucking fly in the ointment."

Crank had never heard such steel in Rael's voice, and it sent a shiver through him.

Vic nodded. "I agree with Rael."

"Look, you've got me on the inside," Jamie told them. "I have credibility. I work for them. Surely that's a start?"

"That's all well and good," Horvan declared, "but we need someone trained to get in there and find out everything we can."

Vic stilled. "I might know someone."

CHAPTER ELEVEN

HORVAN RAISED his eyebrows. "Who?"

"His name is Saul." Vic gave Crank a pointed look. "And he's my boyfriend."

Crank threw his hands in the air. "Oh, well, that makes it all right, doesn't it? Maybe I should ask my aunt Mary to go on a mission too. Hey, H? Want me to ask my aunt if she's available? Remember how much you like her cookies?"

Horvan narrowed his gaze. "Can it, Crank. And for the record, you don't *have* an aunt Mary."

Vic glared at him. It almost seemed Crank was jealous. But that made no sense. "Saul is as trained as you are. Maybe better."

Crank snorted.

"Is he ex-military too?" Horvan asked.

"Yes. He graduated with honors from his school, then immediately went into the Navy, where he scored high marks across the board. After, he asked to join 1st SFOD-D."

Crank's brows shot up. "He was in Delta Force?"

"He was." Vic puffed up his chest. He was fucking proud of Saul. "And he excelled there."

"Where did you meet him?" Rael wanted to know.

That memory was… not so pleasant. "I was in Bahrain, researching rumors of a shifter species we'd never heard of. It turned out to be bullshit, and I got caught in a firefight with the assholes who were after our repository of shifter knowledge. I caught a bullet in my left side, which pierced my lung."

"Oh my God." Rael shivered.

"So there I was, down on the floor, my blood pooling beneath me, when this man and his people stormed in. There was shouting and gunfire and screams. When the dust settled, Saul came to where I was lying, smiled down at me, and said, 'You need a keeper.' Like an idiot, I peered up into his gorgeous green eyes and asked if he was volunteering for the position. He pulled me out, got me patched up, and then asked me on a date."

"Ah, love on the battlefield," Crank groused. "Is there anything more precious?"

Vic ignored him, refusing to take the bait. "After I got home, I went to my organization and told them about him. They were impressed. So much so, they reached out and offered him a spot working with me. He took it, and the rest is history."

"Is he a shifter?" Horvan asked, his head cocked. "What kind?"

"No, he's human. My people agreed with him when he said I needed a keeper. He was the one I chose. And I've never regretted it for a minute."

Except for when memories of Crank's kiss won't leave me alone.

"Does he know about us?"

"Yeah. Kind of hard to hide the fact you're a twenty-five-foot shark, especially from someone who watches your every move."

"How'd he take it?"

Vic grinned. "Surprisingly well. He told me how amazing I was and asked a lot of questions, but he never questioned the reality of it. He told me he'd seen stranger things in his life." He gave Crank that same pointed stare. "So you see? He's more than capable of doing this mission. In fact, this is the kind of job he excels at. Infiltration."

"Wait a minute." Dellan gaped at them. "Do we *need* to send anybody in there?"

"I think we do." Vic counted off on his fingers. "There's so much we don't know about the schools. Who organizes them? Who pays for them? If we want to do as Rael suggests and take them out, then we need to assess them for weak spots. And another thing. I know it's a long shot, but these kids who got turned down? Maybe there's some information at the school that will tell us what happened to them. Because I don't know about you, but I find it a little disturbing that they're no longer with their parents. Where are they? If Crank's right and they've been sent to these camps, then maybe the school has information about where those camps are located."

Crank snorted again. "Wow. I think your boyfriend will have a real big job on his hands."

That earned him another glare. "I wouldn't have suggested him if I didn't think he could cut it."

"Hold on there." Horvan frowned. "I am not sending *anybody* on a mission like this without meeting them first. I want to go see Saul. That's if he even agrees to do it."

Vic's heart pounded. "Let me talk to him. If he says yes, we'll *both* go and meet with him."

"You'll need a cover story to get him into the school," Jamie suggested.

"But isn't everybody at the school a shifter?" Hashtag asked.

"The teachers are. But the custodians, the people who work in the kitchens… they're human."

Crank raised his eyebrows. "Is taking out the trash beneath the dignity of a shifter? Seems to me that humans are given all the menial jobs."

"That's because they are." Jamie looked him in the eye. "And before you start another argument, I didn't see anything wrong with that. I might be starting to change my opinion, however."

"We need information from you about the layout of the school," Horvan told him. "As much information as you can give us. And if you have any ideas for getting Saul in there, feel free to share them."

"I'm already thinking about that. I know the school goes through a lot of custodians. They don't seem to stay for very long."

"Gee, I wonder why that is?" Crank rolled his eyes. "Maybe because they get the feeling everyone is looking down their noses at them."

"That's enough." Horvan's voice was firm. He turned to Vic. "Make the call. We'll take it from there."

"I'll do it now." Vic got up and went to the french doors that opened onto the patio. He stepped outside, his phone in his hand.

I hope to God I'm doing the right thing.

Saul answered after three rings. "I know I said don't leave it so long between calls, but even I didn't expect two calls in one day."

"Something's come up. There's a mission that requires your expertise."

Silence ensued for a moment. "Okay, you've got my attention. Where's the job?"

"Boston. You'd need to infiltrate a school, assess its layout, and find vital information."

"What kind of a school?"

"The shifter kind."

"Is it dangerous?"

"We think so. You'd need to be armed." Vic smiled to himself. This was right up Saul's alley.

"Okay. Tell me more."

Vic gave him all the information they had so far and what they were trying to discover.

Saul chuckled. "You don't want much, do you?"

"I wouldn't ask if I didn't think you were capable."

"Oh, I can do it, but thanks for the vote of confidence. The question is, when do you want it done?"

"The first step would be for you to meet the team leader. He's one of those three shifters I told you about. I'd come with him, of course. And we'd bring Jamie. He works at the school. He's the one who's going to work out how to get you in there."

"Let me know when you'll be arriving." Saul's voice softened. "I've missed you."

"Missed you too. You sure you want to do this?"

"Let me think. Go on a mission that is potentially dangerous or sit at home twiddling my thumbs, waiting for you to call. Kind of a no-brainer." He chuckled. "I was so bored out of my skull the other day, I contemplated taking up knitting."

"Oh God. Seriously?"

"I said *contemplated*. Then I dismissed the idea and cleaned every weapon in the house. Again."

"I'll call you with travel details when I know them." Vic paused. "Thank you."

"To be honest, much as I've loved being your assistant, I've missed this. Now I'm glad I cleaned all the guns. Looks like I'm gonna need them. Sure you don't want me to come there? That would be simpler, wouldn't it?"

It would, but Vic didn't want Saul anywhere near Crank. And vice versa.

"This is the way Horvan wants to play it, so we'll go with that."

"Fine. In that case, I'll see you soon." Another pause. "Looking forward to it." He disconnected.

Vic headed back indoors to where everyone was still seated in the living room.

"He'll do it."

"Good man." Horvan glanced at Hashtag. "I need you to—"

"Check on flights and book 'em?" Hashtag said with a grin. "How many, for when, and a destination would be good."

"Me, Vic, and Jamie. And ASAP." Horvan blinked. "I have no idea where we're going."

"Duluth," Vic told him.

Roadkill grimaced. "Minnesota? You poor man."

Vic narrowed his gaze. "Ain't nothing wrong with Minnesota. Especially when you're a shark shifter and you live ten minutes from Lake Superior."

"Hey, don't badmouth Minnesota," Crank piped up. "Remind me again—where is it exactly that *you* hail from?" He glared at Roadkill.

Vic had to admit, Crank standing up for him was kind of sweet.

"Okay, three tickets for Duluth. I'm on it." Hashtag stood and walked out of the room.

Vic blinked. "I guess I need to pack." He didn't glance in Crank's direction as he left the living room.

Maybe this is for the best.

"I HAVE information."

The voice at the other end was cold and detached. "I'm listening."

"They're going to send someone to the school in Boston. With orders to infiltrate and find what information they can about the other schools and possibly the camps."

"Who are they sending? And when?"

"I don't know yet. All I have right now is a name—Saul."

"Then call us when you have more news."

"Please, can I talk to—"

"When this is over. When we decide you've done enough." The call disconnected.

VIC SHOVED his clothes into his bag and checked the room one last time.

I don't even know if I'm coming back here. Everything was up in the air at the moment. He wasn't worried about Saul—this type of mission was a piece of cake for him—but he *was* concerned about seeing him again. In all the time they'd been together, he hadn't so much as looked at another guy.

85

I'm not sure I can hide what happened.

There was a knock at the door. "You decent?"

Vic's heartbeat raced. "Come in, Crank. You can have your room back tomorrow."

The door opened and Crank stood there, his hands by his sides, his usual confidence nowhere to be seen. He shifted from one foot to another, continually glancing to his left and right.

Vic frowned. "Is something wrong?"

Crank took another glance down the hallway. "Can we talk?"

Vic nodded, his pulse quickening, and Crank stepped into the room and closed the door behind him. Vic arched his eyebrows. "I take it this is a private conversation."

Crank said nothing, but strolled over to the bed and sat on the edge, his elbows on his knees, hands clasped between them. He studied the rug for a moment. "I don't pretend to understand what the fuck is going on. I just know I can't go on like this."

"Like what?" Not that Vic didn't already have a fairly good idea.

"I don't *do* men, okay? I certainly don't kiss them. And yet that day by the lake, I couldn't help myself."

"You've managed to control yourself since then," Vic observed.

Crank's eyes flashed. "There was a reason for that. I stayed the fuck away from you."

"And do you still want to kiss me?"

Crank raised his chin and looked him in the eye. "Yes. You have *no idea* how badly. I've kissed plenty of women in my life, but never a guy. And one kiss from you? It was unlike anything I've ever experienced in my life. You know how they say the earth moved? Well, it did that day. That one kiss rocked me to my core. That's what's so fucked-up about all of this. I want to experience that again." He shivered. "I want to push you up against a wall and plaster our mouths together. I want to taste you on my tongue. I want…. But I'm not going to."

Vic didn't know which emotion was the greater, relief or disappointment.

"Why not?" he demanded. "What's stopping you?"

Crank was so still. "I don't cheat. You have a boyfriend. I didn't know that when I kissed you, but I do now." He lurched from the bed and paced up and down. "I can't explain it, but my fingers are itching to touch you. All

I wanna do is crush your body against mine, even though there's a voice in my head saying that this is fucking *nuts*. And what I need to know is this. Is it just me? Am I going crazy, or do you feel the same thing too?"

It would have been so easy to lie, except the torment in Crank's eyes was all too real.

Vic sighed. "It's not only you. I can't explain it either, but you're in my dreams, in my head, and I can't seem to shake you loose. I don't understand it. Maybe all I need is to get home to Saul. Maybe that will make everything right again."

"Do you believe it's that simple?"

Vic swallowed. "No. Because I was dreaming about you when I was there too."

Crank widened his eyes. Then he shivered. "I dreamed of you too."

Vic had to know. "In your dreams, were we...? Did we...?" He swallowed again.

Crank gaped. "Fuck, you too? What the fuck is going on?" He kept several feet between them, as if getting too close would burn him.

"I don't know. I don't cheat either. And right now, all I want to do is kiss you. But we can't."

Crank raked his fingers over his close-cropped hair. "Go home to Saul. Stay with him. Don't come back here." Crank's jaw set. "I mean it. Maybe if we keep distance between us, the dreams will stop."

"I have a feeling it's not that simple, but I'll stay away," Vic promised. *It might work.* Except he didn't believe that, and he didn't think Crank did either.

HORVAN DIDN'T need to see inside Dellan's head to know something was wrong, and it didn't take a genius to know what that was. All three of them had gotten ready for bed in silence, which wasn't like them. Horvan tried to ignore the tension in the air as long as he could, but by the time he pulled the comforter over them, he'd had enough.

"Hey." He curled up around Dellan, stroking his arm. "It's going to be all right."

"And you know that for sure?" The harsh edge to Dellan's voice took him aback. Then Dellan sighed. "I'm sorry. There's so much to take in. All those schools... shifters being bred and farmed out to adoptive parents...

the insane idea that someone out there is breeding an army." He shivered, and Horvan pulled him tighter against his body. "What frightens me most is that I think that last part might be true."

Rael kissed his forehead. "We *will* fight them. We'll do everything we can with all the resources we have. And if that's not enough, then we'll find *more* resources." He pressed his lips to Dellan's. "Don't give up hope, sweetheart. Hold on to the good stuff. You've got a half brother you never knew existed. We've got Vic and his network on board for this."

"And you've got us," Horvan murmured.

"Thank God for that." Dellan turned to kiss him. "Make it all go away? Even for a little while?" he whispered.

The pain that lay beneath that plaintive appeal tugged Horvan's heart. "You got it." He rolled Dellan onto his back and kissed him, and Rael moved in to lay a trail of sweet kisses from Dellan's collarbones to his navel. Soft moans escaped Dellan's lips, increasing in volume as Rael took Dellan's cock into his mouth.

Dellan shuddered. *Oh. Love it when you do that.* He reached for Horvan's dick and pulled gently on it, and Horvan knew what he wanted. He knelt at Dellan's head and fed him his shaft inch by inch, holding Dellan's head steady while he pumped into that warm mouth. *Love your dick.*

Horvan smiled. *I love your mouth.* More than that, he loved their connection, the ability to feel their emotions, the tumult of desire, lust, need, and utter joy that encapsulated every occasion when they joined like this.

I want you both. Rael broke off from his enthusiastic sucking, his lips shiny.

"You've got us. Want us to take turns?" Horvan arched his back as Dellan took him deep. "Fuck."

"That's not what I mean." Rael knelt up, his chest heaving. "I want both of you inside me—at the same time."

Dellan pulled free of Horvan's cock, choking a little.

Holy fuck. "Have you ever taken two dicks?" Horvan asked.

"No." Rael bit his lip. "I've seen it done, of course. Who hasn't these days?" He tilted his head. "Have *you* ever done that?"

"With another guy and a woman. Once." He peered at Rael. "That's gonna be quite a squeeze. You sure you wanna try it?"

Rael's eyes sparkled. "I'm sure. I want to know how it feels."

"Me too," Dellan added, scrambling into a kneeling position. He proffered his hardening dick. "Put your mouth on here while Horvan gets your hole ready."

Horvan chuckled. "Then I guess we're doing this." Rael was already on his hands and knees, ass tilted, Dellan's shaft between his lips. Horvan moved across until he was kneeling behind Rael, that tantalizing hole begging to be fucked.

Then fuck it with your tongue, Rael pleaded.

As if Horvan could ignore an entreaty like that.

He spread Rael's cheeks and dove in, licking a path from Rael's balls to the top of his crease before flicking the tight pucker with his tongue.

"Oh, he *really* likes that." Dellan placed his hands on Rael's head and fucked his mouth. "Don't stop."

Horvan had no intention of stopping. He probed and licked Rael's hole until Rael's moans were constant, adding a finger, then alternating between that and his tongue.

For God's sake.... Even in Horvan's head, he could hear the need in Rael's voice.

"And that's your cue." Dellan tossed Horvan the lube, and he slicked up a couple of fingers and slid them into Rael's warmth, Rael's body clinging to them.

Rael moaned around Dellan's cock, and Horvan added a third. Then when he couldn't wait a second longer, he wiped lube over his dick and slid into Rael's body with a sigh.

Oh yeah. Dellan and Rael's thoughts were simultaneous.

Horvan was home.

He fucking *loved* this, when the three of them were connected, not only in mind but in flesh. He loved how Rael rocked between them, shuttling between Dellan's shaft and his own. He loved watching his dick split Rael's ass, listening to the slap of flesh against flesh as he slammed into him. He leaned over Rael's back and pushed his head, feeling Rael's internal whimper as Dellan's shaft filled his throat. Horvan gripped Rael's shoulders and anchored himself, hips snapping forward as he drove his dick all the way home, Rael pushing back to meet his thrusts. Horvan slowed to a crawl, withdrawing almost all the way out of Rael, only to fill him to the hilt, then repeat the motion again and again, until noises poured from Rael's lips and Dellan was clamoring inside his head.

My turn.

Horvan eased out of Rael, and Dellan flopped onto his back. "Ride me, beautiful."

Rael straddled his hips, and Horvan slicked up Dellan's cock before guiding it to his hole. He pulled Rael's cheeks apart and watched Dellan's shaft disappear into his body, inch by inch. Rael rocked back and forth, Dellan's hands around his slim waist, helping him to rise and fall.

That's it. Sit all the way down on it, Horvan told him.

Rael put his weight on his hands and rolled his hips, taking Dellan deeper and deeper. Then Dellan tilted his hips and drove up into Rael's body, each thrust punching the air from Rael's lungs, until the room was filled with Rael's grunts.

Horvan squeezed lube onto his fingers and added one to the mix, easing it into Rael's hole alongside Dellan's dick.

More, Rael demanded.

He added another, and Rael sank down onto them until Horvan's fingers and Dellan's shaft were buried in Rael's ass.

Rael twisted his head to stare at him. "Now, Horvan, please."

Horvan swiped lube over his rock-hard dick, then knelt between Dellan's spread legs. Dellan pulled Rael down to him, and Horvan covered Rael's back with his body, his weight on one hand as he brought his cock to Rael's filled hole.

Horvan had never moved at such an unhurried pace, as slow as clouds drifting across a summer sky, as he eased his dick into Rael's body. When he was finally seated, Dellan's cock so hard against his, Horvan let out a sigh. "There you go."

"Jesus." Rael was trembling, but one look inside his head reassured Horvan that he wanted to feel this. Horvan shifted his legs to straddle Dellan's, and then they began, slowly at first, Horvan sliding in as Dellan pulled out, then swapping, until they'd gotten into a rhythm, Rael's body sandwiched between theirs.

Rael kept up a soft litany of "Oh" as they fucked him, both of them in motion, until Horvan picked up speed and Dellan's cries of "Oh yeah" mingled with Rael's. Dellan stilled inside Rael as Horvan rocked into him, propping himself up on his hands as he increased the pace.

"Gonna come," he gritted out, his hips in constant motion.

Inside me. Come inside me.

Horvan arched his back as he came with a growl, his body shaking.

Oh dear Lord, how that feels. Dellan's gaze met his over Rael's shoulder. *This is amazing.*

Horvan gently freed his dick from Rael's body, his cum pushed from Rael's hole, coating Dellan's still solid cock as it slid in and out of him. He stretched out beside Dellan and took Rael's shaft into his mouth, working it in time to Dellan's thrusts, until both Dellan and Rael came at the same time. Horvan swallowed every mouthful, then kissed his mates as they trembled with the force of their orgasms, until at last they lay in each other's arms, their bodies covered in a mix of sweat and cum. Horvan couldn't get enough of their kisses, and it was a long while before they moved off the bed toward the bathroom.

As they stood under the shower, three pairs of hands engaged in gentle cleansing, Horvan kissed them.

There might be shadows in our life together, but as long as we have each other, we can beat them back and let the light in to banish them completely.

Dellan locked gazes with him. *You truly believe that, don't you?*

Horvan *had* to believe it. No other scenario bore thinking about.

CHAPTER TWELVE

EVERYTHING WAS in readiness for the trip. The tickets were booked, and Roadkill was taking Horvan, Vic, and Jamie to the airport. The bags were already in the trunk of the car. Horvan had insisted he wasn't taking a bag because he didn't intend on staying.

And now Vic was about to leave, Crank wasn't sure how he felt about that. It didn't matter that he'd told Vic to go.

I don't understand this, and I really don't like it. The whole situation messed with his head, and for a man who needed to keep cool in tight situations, this was *not* good.

Dellan had made coffee, and everyone sat around the kitchen, drinking and snacking on Mrs. Landon's cookies. Except all was not well with Dellan. One glance at his face was enough to tell Crank something was up.

Finally Rael sighed. "Just come out with it. Thinking the same thought over and over won't make it any clearer."

Vic frowned. "Is there a problem?"

"Not with you, no." Dellan stared at Jamie. "Once you've met with Saul, what do you intend doing?" When Jamie didn't respond, Dellan's eyes widened. "You're going back to the school, aren't you? For God's sake, why? Why would you deliberately return to such a dangerous situation? Stay out of there. Let Saul go in, do his thing, and then *these* guys can go do *their* thing. And you stay safe."

"I have to go back," Jamie said softly.

Rael's breathing hitched. "Okay, now I'm with Dellan." He scowled. "Why?"

"Those kids are my responsibility."

Horvan arched his eyebrows. "How do you work that out?"

"I put them in this position. I have to do something to help get them out of it."

"But those kids aren't in danger," Dellan protested.

Jamie gaped at him. "Oh no? Do you know that for certain? Because *I* don't. I want to know where *all* those kids are, not only the ones who

92

made it to the school but the ones who didn't. I have to know what happened to them."

"Let Saul find that out," Rael suggested.

Jamie shook his head. "I'm sorry, you're not gonna make me change my mind."

Dellan lowered his gaze and stared at the coffee table. "I admire your integrity, but you have to know how scared I am. For you."

Jamie heaved a sigh. "I won't do anything stupid, I promise. I won't draw attention to myself. As far as they're concerned, I'm just a guy who interviews prospective students. They have no reason to suspect me."

"Then you'd better make sure it stays that way." Horvan leveled a hard stare at him. "Don't go taking any risks."

Crank was done keeping silent. "You're important to Dellan. You're family. So do what you feel you have to, then get the fuck out of there and get your ass back here."

Jamie swallowed. "After all the shit I threw at you, I don't deserve that. Because when Saul passes on what he knows, your group will go in there, and you'll be part of that."

"What of it?"

Jamie looked him in the eye. "Thank you."

"You can thank me when you walk through that door in one piece," Crank told him. He glanced at the clock. "Time is wastin', Horvan. You guys need to be out of here. You've got a plane to catch." He couldn't bring himself to look at Vic.

Horvan drained his coffee, then stood, his arms held wide. A heartbeat later, he was holding Rael and Dellan. No words passed between them, so Crank surmised whatever they needed to say was being kept private. Crank envied them that level of closeness. Their bond was intense and beautiful. Plus, he reasoned, it also had to make sex wicked hot. He bit his lip to keep from laughing, because Horvan would *not* appreciate such thoughts about his mates.

Jamie watched them. "Do I get a hug?"

Dellan's eyes glistened. "You're damn straight." He tugged Jamie to him, and they held on to each other for a moment.

Horvan cleared his throat. "Guys? We need to go."

Vic walked over to Crank. "I guess this is goodbye."

"I guess so." Crank ignored the irrational voice in his head that yelled, "Make him stay."

"This has been… interesting." Vic's lips twitched.

Crank saw the funny side too. "You can say that again." He held out his hand. "Good luck. Now get your ass back to that boyfriend."

Vic smiled. "Stay safe, Crank." Then he followed Horvan and Jamie out of the kitchen.

Crank dropped back into his chair and picked up his cup of coffee.

Stay safe, Vic.

Now maybe his life would get back to normal.

Whatever that was.

THE WHOLE time Horvan was talking, Saul kept resisting the urge to glance in Vic's direction. He figured the peck on the cheek he'd received when Vic walked through the door was down to the fact that they weren't alone.

After all that time apart, Saul wanted more than a peck. He estimated he'd have Vic naked and Saul's dick in his mouth within about three seconds of Horvan and Jamie's departure.

Who am I kidding? It won't even take that long.

Except something was up with Vic. Saul had no clue what, but he'd been with Vic long enough to trust his instincts.

"So what do you think?"

Saul realized with a start that Horvan was talking to him. "About what?"

Horvan's eyebrows went skyward. "If there's something else you need to be doing, please, don't let us stop you." His voice was heavy with sarcasm, but his eyes twinkled. "Although I don't think it takes much imagination to work out where your head is right now. I think I'd be the same if either of my mates walked in after more than a week apart." He cleared his throat. "But back to the matter in hand. You think you can do it?"

Saul nodded. "Piece of cake, except for the small matter of getting me in there." He turned to Jamie. "Have you given any thought to that?"

Jamie nodded. "I checked this morning. They need cafeteria workers and a custodian."

"That's a no-brainer then. A custodian will have better access. They're required to go through the whole school, and no one really looks twice at them. That's the one I'll go for." He winced. "You'd better hope I don't get any calls about puking kids. I can*not* handle barf."

"I'll find the details and email them to you. Of course, this all assumes they take you on."

Saul grinned. "I'll make sure I have all the right credentials. I'll get in there somehow. Do you want me to relay what I find to Vic or directly to you?" he asked Horvan.

"To me. I'll be the one organizing the raid."

Vic was *way* too quiet.

Saul dragged his attention back to the conversation. "So what happens now?"

"I go back to Chicago and wait to see what you turn up. Jamie, against my wishes and those of my mates, is returning to Boston to the school."

Saul frowned. "Seriously?"

Jamie held up his hand. "Before *you* give me the third degree too, I'm not changing my mind. Besides, you might need someone on the inside, ever thought of that?"

Saul shrugged. "I suppose. I'm not happy about it, though." He consulted the notepad on his lap, mentally ticking off the items as he spoke. "So... you want a layout of the school, with my assessment as to weak points of entry, notes on when best to plan an attack, and anything I can find in their records that will tell us where the camps are and the fate of those kids who don't make the cut. Is that everything?"

"Don't forget—any information you can give us about the schools. We still have no idea who started them, who funds them, or the exact number of kids," Vic added.

"I was only able to get the barest of details before someone walked into the office on me." Jamie's face was solemn. "If you can get in there at night, you'll have a better chance of learning more."

"Do the kids board there?" Saul asked.

Jamie nodded. "It's a huge site, set on fifty acres. This is why they need lots of custodians. The student accommodation is the newest part. The original school is the oldest building, but they've added onto it."

"I guess they need all those acres if the students are shifters. That must give them a degree of privacy."

Jamie's eyes gleamed. "And they are *all* about the privacy."

95

Saul cocked his head. "So I should expect a little… resistance? Got it." He closed his notepad. "I'll get my application in ASAP."

"You shouldn't have a problem getting the job," Jamie commented. "You've already got the most important qualifications nailed."

"And what're those?" Saul demanded.

"You're human. Plus you're strong. They'll expect to get a lot of work out of you. I *will* give you one piece of advice, however." Jamie's eyes glinted. "Don't go in there with an attitude. They want staff who are—"

"Meek? Servile?" Saul offered.

Jamie smiled. "Vic went through your bio for us. I think you could pull that off."

Vic snorted. "Saul servile? Not in this lifetime. I've got to wonder if he could turn in an Oscar-winning performance like that."

Saul turned to him and stuck out his tongue. "I'll pull it off just fine, thank you."

Horvan stood. "Then we won't take up any more of your time."

Saul blinked. "That was a short visit."

"Nothing personal, but I want to get back to Chicago." Horvan huffed. "First time I've been away from them since we got together, and it feels… itchy."

Saul didn't smile. "I know the feeling." He'd had it the whole time Vic had been away.

Horvan held out his hand, and Saul shook it. "Glad to have you on board for this, Saul. I can see now why Vic speaks so highly of you."

That brought a smile. He flashed a glance in Vic's direction. "Good to know he's appreciative of my… skills." Saul shook Jamie's hand. "So the next time I see you will hopefully be in the school. I'll blank you, of course."

Jamie nodded. "Good luck."

Saul smiled. "Like we used to say back in the day, luck is not a factor."

"But sometimes it helps," Horvan murmured.

Saul ushered them outside and waited until Horvan pulled the rental car out of the driveway. He closed the door and walked into the living room, where Vic was on his phone.

"Alone at last," Saul murmured. He took Vic's phone from him and tossed it onto the couch. "Nope. You won't need that where I'm taking you." Then he grabbed Vic and slung him over his shoulder.

"You don't think this is a little… Neanderthal?" Vic said with a laugh.

"And there you go, using big words again." Saul headed for the bedroom. "So you think you can be naked before I drop you on the bed?"

Vic chuckled. "I'm fast, but not *that* fast."

Saul kicked open the bedroom door, marched over to the bed, and dropped Vic like a stone. He stripped off his tee, unbuttoned his fly, and shoved his jeans to his ankles. "Assume the position." His dick jutted out, hard and aching.

Vic's breathing caught. His fingers trembled as he removed his own clothing.

Except he was taking too goddamn long.

Saul tugged at Vic's pants, freeing his legs, then tossed the garment to the floor. He bent over to finish taking off his own jeans, then climbed onto the bed, slowly and stealthily.

Vic swallowed. "If you were a shifter, you'd be a cat."

"We'd better not be talking about a house cat."

Vic laughed. "Oh, definitely not. Something like a panther or a jaguar. Sleek, sinuous, and dangerous."

Saul paused above him, his hands on the mattress, bracketing Vic's head. "Do jaguars have big cocks? Because if they don't, well then, that's just not me."

Vic brought his legs up to wrap around Saul's waist. "You know what? I never actually looked."

Saul stared into his eyes. "Miss me?"

"Fuck yes."

He rubbed the head of his dick over Vic's hole. "Missed this?"

Vic grabbed his head and yanked him down into a searing kiss. "How about you stop talking and fuck me?"

Saul could get behind that plan.

SAUL LAY on his back, staring at the cracks in the ceiling.

What the fuck is going on?

From behind the bathroom door came the sound of running water. Vic had claimed to be in dire need of a shower. Saul had no issue with cleanliness—what irked him was the speed with which Vic had launched himself from the bed.

What, no post-coital cuddles? Since fucking when?

He was trying to ignore the quiet voice in the back of his mind, the one that whispered in silky, slimy tones that guilt lay behind Vic's actions.

He wouldn't do that. He wouldn't cheat. Vic was no more a cheater than Saul was. *Then why couldn't he get out of the bed fast enough?* That was the million-dollar question, and Saul was determined to find the answer.

The water stopped, and a few minutes later Vic emerged from the bathroom, steam billowing around him. One towel clung to his slim hips while he rubbed his hair with another.

"That feel better?" Saul strove to keep his voice even.

"Much." Vic sat at the foot of the bed, gazing at his reflection in the mirror on the closet door.

Saul shuffled across the mattress on his knees, bringing his hands to Vic's shoulders and rubbing him there, digging his thumbs into the back muscles. "How about now?"

Vic dropped his head forward with a groan. "That feels amazing."

Saul kneaded the firm flesh, and beneath his fingers he felt the tension slipping away, melting into nothingness. "So. Wanna tell me what's wrong?"

Vic jerked his head up and stared at him in the mirror, straightening. "Who says there's anything wrong?"

Saul brushed his lips against Vic's ear. "I do. I *know* you. I can always tell—hell, *feel*—when something is wrong. So don't even bother lying." He locked gazes with Vic's reflection. "What happened in Chicago? Because *something* did. But what I want to know is, did that something have anything to do with your dream guy?"

Jesus. Vic was trembling.

Saul slowly withdrew his hands. "Talk to me. I have to know." His heartbeat raced, and sweat popped out on his brow.

Vic shivered. "He kissed me, okay?"

Saul didn't break eye contact. "Did you kiss him back?"

Vic's Adam's apple bobbed. "Yes."

"Was it good?" A sharp pain lanced its way through Saul's chest.

"Look… I can't explain it, but Crank is important to me."

"Oh, well, that's better. At least I have a name now." Saul arched his eyebrows. "Crank?" He got off the bed, walked over to the closet, and went inside. He grabbed a pillow and a folded blanket.

Vic's eyes were huge. "What are you doing?"

Saul came to a stop. "I'm gonna sleep on the couch. I'll go on the mission, all right? But I'm doing it for all those kids. And when I come back, you and I are gonna talk."

"A guy kisses me and you want to sleep on the couch?" Vic gaped. "You don't think maybe this reaction is a little excessive?"

Saul glared at him. "If it was only a kiss from *him*, then *maybe* I'd brush this off. But you kissed him back, so we both know it's more than that. This was brewing since before you left for Chicago." He shook his head. "You sit there and tell me some guy is important to you, then wonder why I don't wanna sleep in the same bed? Christ, we just made love." He froze. "Tell me you weren't thinking of him all the time I was inside you."

"And if I wasn't? Why should you believe me?"

Saul drew in a deep breath. "Get some sleep. I'll see you in the morning." And with that, he left Vic on the bed and trudged heavily into the living room. He switched off the lights and got under the blanket, gazing at the skylights above the dining table. The moon shone high in a velvet black sky.

He swallowed. *I want to fall asleep and wake up to discover this was nothing but a bad dream.* Except that was for fairy tales and that laughable drama from the eighties.

Reality was a much bitterer pill to swallow.

CHAPTER THIRTEEN

VIC DIDN'T think he could take much more silence.

In the three days since his return, he and Saul hadn't communicated beyond the bare minimum. Saul did what he always did—cooked, cleaned, shopped—but spent a large chunk of the first day putting together his application for the custodian's job.

In the moments when he wasn't busy doing practical things, he was perfecting the art of avoiding Vic. He wasn't cold or bitter—he just wasn't talking.

Vic hoped it wouldn't last, and he prayed the thaw would come soon. Of course Vic had never confessed feelings for another man before, so as to when that thaw might occur?

All bets were off.

I can't go on like this. Damn it, he missed Saul's laughter, his banter, his heated looks. Most of all, Vic missed that warm body curled around him at night, making him feel safe.

Saul had gone to the store, and Vic was glad of the break. It was amazing how draining silence could be. When his phone rang and he saw Horvan's name, he snatched it up. "Hey."

"Are you okay to talk?"

Vic resisted the urge to snort. "It's good to hear a friendly voice."

There was a pause. "Is everything okay?"

"Not really, but I can't talk about it now. Fire away."

"I have news."

"Good news, I hope."

Horvan chuckled. "Bad guys zero, good guys five."

Vic caught his breath. "The raids. They went off all right?"

"Well, I wouldn't say it was smooth running. We lost four good men. But they lost everything. Let's trust it makes as big a dent in their plans as we *hope* it does. How's Saul progressing? Any news on the job front?"

"He sent in his application. We're hoping to hear something soon— the closing date was yesterday, so he really did get his in under the wire.

The process is all online, so we'll see what transpires. I'll let you know if—*when*—we hear something. And in the meantime"—Vic had been pushing around an idea—"we agree there has to be more than one camp, right?"

"Yeah."

"Well, I've been thinking. There must be some reference to them *somewhere* in the records. I don't believe such places can exist in total secrecy. So I'm going to go through the archive and see what I can find. Maybe there's a clue in there, now that I know what I'm looking for."

"How big is this archive?"

Vic chuckled. "Big enough. It's all in the cloud."

"In the cloud?"

Vic snickered. "Let me guess. You were picturing dark catacombs with row upon row of ash bookcases, the air scented by moldy paper, the room buzzing with primal power…."

"Well, yeah."

"Sorry, but we're twenty-first-century mages, and all our tomes are on e-paper."

"But who has access to it? It can't be just you."

"As far as I know, there's me and the leaders of the Fridans. I'm not the only oral historian—I know that much—but anyone wishing to access the archive has to go through me."

Horvan whistled. "I had no idea I knew someone so powerful."

"Me? Yeah, right. I'm merely the gatekeeper. And I should have said *most* of the archive is accessible via the cloud. There are some files that are considered volatile, and those are kept locked away. The only chance a person has of accessing them is to meet with the Fridan leaders and convince them that their goal is noble and the information is vital to achieving it."

"I'm still impressed. But getting back to Saul's mission… I know you'd like to be on it when we finally raid the school, but I don't think it's a good idea."

"Why not?"

Horvan sighed. "Because of Saul. You're personally involved."

"He's not going to be there, remember? He'll get what info he can, pass it on, then get the hell out of there." He paused. "That *is* the plan, isn't it?"

"Yeah, it is."

"Then that's settled. I'm available. I'm trained. An extra body can't hurt, right?"

"Are you usually this stubborn?"

Vic chuckled. "You have *no* idea." Another pause. "Is everyone okay over there?" Except "everyone" was too broad a term. He only had one person in mind.

"*Everyone* is fine." The inflection in Horvan's voice suggested he knew exactly what lay behind Vic's casual question. *But he couldn't, could he?*

"I'll let you know if I turn up anything on the camps." Dellan had to be going out of his mind.

"Thanks. I'll let you get back to whatever you're doing. Say hi to Saul for me. We've got a lot riding on him getting in there. If this doesn't work, we'll need to think of an alternative."

"Understood. And I'll pass on the greeting." *When he decides he's talking to me again.*

"Hey, wait up. Someone wants to talk to you."

Before Vic could ask who, Crank's gruff voice filled his ear. "Hey."

Vic's heartbeat shifted into a higher gear. "You okay?"

"Hang on a sec." There was a pause. "Okay, I'm on the patio. I don't want the others hearing this."

"What's up?"

"I… I wanted to check you were okay."

Whatever the fuck is going on, he feels it too.

"Things are not so good here."

"What's wrong?" Vic couldn't miss the note of concern in Crank's voice, and for one irrational moment, it warmed him. Then he remembered he didn't want Crank to feel *anything* about him.

"I told Saul what happened."

"You mean that kiss you said never happened?"

"Christ, will you *listen*?" Vic swiped his fingers through his hair. "I told him that for some inexplicable reason, you're important to me."

"I bet that went down well." Crank made a growling noise. "Jesus, there have to be almost five hundred miles between us. What else does he want?"

"For you not to exist, I think would be a start. For you not to have kissed me, and *definitely* for me not to have returned that kiss. Which is the crux of the matter, by the way."

Silence.

"Crank?"

"You told him you kissed me back? *Why*, for fuck's sake?"

"Because I couldn't help myself!" Vic flung back at him. "We don't have secrets, and this one was eating away at me."

"Okay, okay." Crank sighed. "Well, it's out of the bag now. I take it he's pissed."

"I wouldn't know. He's avoiding me."

"Aw fuck." Another heavy sigh. "I'm sorry. That has to suck."

"In all probability he'll be going on this mission, and he'll be leaving with all this up in the air. My only hope is that by the time he gets back, he's calmed the fuck down and can talk about this rationally."

Crank snorted. "I don't know if this fact has passed you by, but there ain't nothing rational about any of this." A pause. "Fuck. I'm wanted. Look… if you wanna talk, vent, bite my head off, here's my number." He rattled it off twice in quick succession, and Vic grabbed a pen and scribbled it on the back of his hand. "But for Christ's sake, don't let Saul find it, all right? That really would stir up a shitstorm."

"Thanks. When I add it to my phone, I won't put your name." Vic stilled. "You have to have another name, right? I mean, you weren't called Crank at birth."

"Sure I have. I just don't use it, that's all."

Despite his roiling stomach, Vic was intrigued. "So? What is it?" Crank mumbled a reply. "I'm sorry, it's what?"

"For God's sake, it's Wendell, okay? And if you breathe a word to anyone…."

The fact that Crank trusted him enough to reveal his name meant more than it should. Vic took pity on him. "You know what? I'll keep on calling you Crank."

"You do that. And we never had this conversation, you hear? And now I really gotta go. Stay safe, all right?" Crank disconnected.

Vic was trying not to smile. *He is* not *a Wendell.* And seeing Wendell in Vic's phone would only arouse Saul's suspicions. On impulse, he tapped in the number and assigned it the name Dellan. Then he headed for the bathroom to scrub at his hand until all traces of the number had been removed.

Not for the first time that week, his stomach churned. *I hate this.* Trying to explain the situation was a nonstarter; how could he explain something that *he* didn't fully comprehend?

Keeping busy was the only option.

Vic reached for his iPad. *Let's see what's out there.*

SAUL HAD no sooner got through the front door than his phone pinged to notify him of a new email. He waited till he'd deposited the bags on the kitchen table before looking at it. When he saw the words HR, his heartbeat quickened.

Here we go.

"Honey, you're home," Vic called out.

In normal circumstances, the variation on Vic's habitual greeting would have raised a smile. *That was before Crank.* Saul had no idea what Crank even looked like, but he hated him with a passion. Then he reasoned that it took two to tango. *Vic kissed him back, remember?*

Saul wasn't about to forget.

Vic came into the kitchen as Saul was scanning the email. "Any news?"

"I've got an interview. Tomorrow."

"They don't hang around, do they?"

"They think I'm local," Saul told him. "I used one of the network's safe-house addresses in Massachusetts. So I guess I'd better haul ass over there." The sooner the better. Saul wanted to talk, but every time he tried to start the conversation, he choked up.

It can wait. Maybe a little space is a good idea right now.

"Where will you stay?"

"I'll find a hotel. The school isn't in Boston itself—it's near someplace called Easton. A whole lotta land to it, though." He smirked. "I'll leave my best suit here. Can't wear that to an interview."

"Remember what Jamie said about attitude."

Saul arched his eyebrows. "Of course. Relax, will ya? I've got this. I'll be in and out of there before you know it. And before anyone gets a chance to suspect a thing."

Vic's face tightened. "Saul, can't we just—"

He held up his hand. "This can wait till I get back. All right?" There was a knot in his belly and a lump in his throat, and neither of them would budge.

"But—"

"No buts. I can't deal with this right now. So let me go do my thing, and then we'll talk. But so we're clear?" He swallowed. "This is killing me." He gestured to the bags. "You can deal with the groceries. I'm going to book a flight and pack." And with that he strode out of the kitchen.

Jesus, this hurts.

Saul had to admit, at first glance the school was impressive. The taxi dropped him off outside the iron gates at the entrance. Saul gave his name and purpose of visit over the intercom, and they opened for him, shutting with a *clang* as soon as he was through. The driveway seemed to go on for miles until at last he reached the main building. It was constructed of red brick and beige stone, with a gothic-looking portico and a square tower topped by tall ornately carved spikes.

The overall impression was one of *age*, a place in history.

Saul walked under the portico to the solid wood doors. He rang the bell as requested by the sign, then waited, his heart pounding. A moment later, they opened to reveal a tall man in a smart black suit.

"Mr. Rosen? Step this way, please."

Saul followed him into a black-and-white tiled hallway lined with marble columns, on top of which sat classically sculpted marble busts.

"I take it the kids aren't allowed in this part of the school," Saul commented.

"No, they are not, and we refer to them as students." His words were clipped and precise.

"Of course. Sorry. I'll remember that." If Saul could have tugged his forelock without ruining his neatly combed hair, he would have. He kept his tone the right shade of subservient, and apparently that did the trick.

The man gave a thin-lipped smile. "That's all right. You know now." He opened a door and ushered Saul into a small office. Once the door closed behind them, he gestured to the chair in front of the desk, then sat facing him, his fingers steepled. "So. You're Hank Rosen, and you want to work here."

"Yeah. I think I'd be a good fit." Saul had prepared his whole spiel about why he wanted the job, but the guy cut him short with a wave of his hand.

"I should say at this juncture that this is merely a formality, a chance to see you in the flesh, as it were. On paper—virtual paper, at least—you're exactly what we're looking for, but a resume can only reveal so much. It is only by meeting face-to-face that it's possible to truly judge if a candidate is appropriate."

Saul nodded, careful not to meet the man's direct gaze. "Are you in charge of human resources?"

The man nodded. "I am Mr. Fielding, and you'll report to me."

Saul blinked. "That… kinda sounds like I got the job."

Mr. Fielding smiled. "Very astute, Mr. Rosen. I consider myself a good judge of character."

"But don't you need to run background checks?" Saul couldn't help himself. This was going way too fast for his liking. He knew his ID would stand close review, but he hadn't expected to get the job right away.

Mr. Fielding arched his eyebrows. "Already done. And if I didn't like what I found, you wouldn't be here. Now, shall we go over your duties? Then I'll have you sign a contract and show you around the place. Unless you can't accept the post without first seeing the site?"

Saul smiled. "I've worked as a custodian before, as I'm sure you saw on my resume, and in a variety of places—a hospital, a university. A school can't be that different, right?"

"Indeed. And I take great pride in our students. They are an exceptional group, as I'm sure you'll agree once you see them. We don't encourage familiarity between students and any staff beyond their teachers, by the way." Fielding proceeded with the description of the custodian's responsibilities and then said, "Now, why don't I give you a tour, and then I can show you your quarters. The ad for the post stipulated that you would be live-in, of course. You need to be on hand at all times."

"Thank you, Mr. Fielding." Saul managed to sound extremely grateful, but inside his head alarm bells were ringing.

I don't like this. I don't like it one bit.

"Do you have any questions?"

Saul had a whole heap of them, but he'd save them for when he got access to the files. Besides, asking too many questions gave the wrong impression.

"If I do, I'll know who to ask."

Mr. Fielding opened a drawer, removed a folder, and took from it a single sheet of paper. "This is your contract. Once you've signed it, I'll give you all the relevant documents and information you'll need." He plucked a pen from a container of them and handed it to Saul.

What shocked Saul was the supreme effort it took to keep his hand from shaking as he signed. When he was done, Mr. Fielding took it from him and examined it. Then he replaced it in the folder. He rose from his chair. "Let's show you our school."

Saul stood, his heart racing. He couldn't pull out now, not when he was being handed the job on a platter. And yeah, maybe this was all too easy, but there were all those kids to consider, not to mention the information he hoped to find to provide Horvan and his mates with something positive to go on in their search for Dellan's dad.

I've got to do this.

For once, he hoped his instincts were wrong.

CHAPTER FOURTEEN

"CRANK. CRANK!"

He stopped the treadmill and grabbed the towel he'd slung over the rail. "You don't have to yell, H. You're standing three feet from me." Crank mopped the sweat from his brow and neck, then realized his tee clung to his chest.

Horvan folded his arms. "For your information, I've been calling your name for the past minute. I don't know where your head was, but it certainly wasn't here. Now tell me what the fuck is going on."

Crank arched his eyebrows. "I'm getting in a little cardio, that's all."

Horvan snorted. "A little? You've been on that machine for the past two hours. You don't think maybe that's a bit excessive? But I'm not talking about this. Rael says you bit Hashtag's head off this morning, apparently for no good reason." He pulled the chair from its position against the wall and set it in front of the treadmill. Horvan sat, refolding his arms. "I'm staying right here until you tell me what's wrong."

Crank raised his eyes to the ceiling. "Who says there's anything wrong? Maybe I got up on the wrong side of the bed this morning, ever think of that? Maybe deep down, I'm a naturally cranky bastard. You know, hence my name?"

"And *maybe* there's something going on that you can't explain to yourself, let alone anyone else." Horvan cocked his head. "You still having those dreams?"

Crank shook his head, then expelled a breath. Running his feet off sure as shit wasn't helping. Maybe talking to a friend would. "Now I'm having a whole different set of dreams."

These were darker, more tense, and they scared the living shit out of him. What made it worse was that there was nothing he could point to that made them so terrifying, but each dream had him waking up in a cold sweat.

And then there was the constant itchy feeling, as if he had ants crawling over his skin. On occasion it felt like they were burrowing into it, tearing a hole, leaving his whole body on fire.

Something was coming, and he didn't have a fucking clue what it was.

Crank sat on the treadmill bed and put his head in his hands. "I can't shake it, H," he murmured.

Horvan was next to him in a heartbeat. "Can't shake what?" When Crank didn't respond, he gripped Crank's knee. "*Talk* to me, goddammit."

Crank shivered. "It's just this… feeling that something is wrong. I can't pinpoint it. I'm so fucking *antsy* all the time. I can't sit still for more than five minutes. And my sleep has really gone for a shit. You were right. I was the one that nearly slept through that firefight in Kabul. Now? I'm barely getting three hours."

"Tell me about the dreams." Horvan's voice was unexpectedly gentle.

Another shiver rippled through him. "I'm in this dark place, and I'm searching for something. Only I can't find it. And all the while, there's this feeling of… I suppose you'd call it dread. It lies so heavy on me, I can hardly breathe. And what's with the ants."

"Ants?"

Crank rubbed his hairy forearms. "Crawling everywhere. It's not all the time, but when it happens, it drives me crazy." He turned his head toward Horvan. "What the fuck does any of this mean?"

"I don't know," Horvan confessed. He patted Crank's back, then grimaced. "Dude. You need a shower."

"Thanks for that." He wiped the towel over his head. "Any news yet?" Vic had messaged them the previous day to say Saul had got the job and was starting immediately.

"Only that Saul did a quick recon of the school's office last night."

Crank whistled. "He doesn't mess around, does he?"

"He says there's a ton of stuff to go through. He's gonna send more info tonight, but it's looking promising." Horvan gave him a hard stare. "No more cardio. Grab that shower and then join us in the office. Mrs. Landon's made coffee."

"And cookies, right?"

Horvan snorted. "Does this bear shit in the woods? Of course she made cookies." His gaze grew steely. "And then you can apologize to Hashtag."

"Okay, okay." Crank got up and headed for the shower. Maybe the hot water would take away the itching. Not that it had worked the previous day, but he could hope, right?

By the time he strolled into the office, Horvan, Rael, Dellan, Hashtag, Roadkill, and Brick were sitting on the couch and on chairs, deep in conversation. The aroma of fresh coffee infiltrated Crank's nostrils, and he went over to the desk to pour himself a cup.

"I see Mrs. Landon's taken to brewing two pots," he commented.

Dellan chuckled. "She's getting to know us."

Crank glanced at Hashtag. "About earlier. I was outta line."

Hashtag stiffened for a moment, then relaxed. "S'okay. Next time I'll just tear you a new one."

"Fair enough." Crank grabbed a cookie from a nearby plate. "Sounds like I walked in on a high-level discussion. What's up?" He took a bite.

"I wanted to clear something up." Rael's brow furrowed. "This raid you're planning on the school.... I know when Jamie first told us about it, I said to shut it down, but I've been thinking. What exactly is the goal of this mission?"

"To find out what we can about the schools, the camps, whatever Saul turns up," Horvan told him.

"See, that's my point. If *he's* going to find all this information, why do you guys need to go in?"

"Because if Saul finds evidence those kids are being indoctrinated, we need to put a stop to that," Dellan said in a firm voice.

"Okay. So you march in there, grab the staff.... What happens to the kids?" Rael's expression grew somber. "Horvan, we're talking a *thousand* students. What are your plans for them? Supposing some of the staff run? You take the rest? What do the kids do with no one in charge? Hasn't anybody thought about that?"

"He's got a point," Roadkill observed.

Horvan nodded. "Okay. Then let's talk to Vic."

"How can he help?" Crank muttered. "He's just a historian." No sooner had he uttered the words than a pang of regret lanced through him. *He's way more than that, and you know it.*

"Vic controls access to the shifter-lore archive. And he can contact the leaders of the Fridan group. Maybe they have a solution." Horvan picked up his phone and scrolled. "Vic? You got a minute?" He listened. "Okay, gonna put you on speaker." He placed the phone on the desk.

"Who's there?" As soon as Crank heard Vic's voice, his skin erupted into goose bumps, and the itching followed. He resisted the urge to rub his forearms, knowing Horvan would notice instantly.

"All the team," Horvan told him. "Rael was asking about the students, and he raised an important point. If Saul gets back to us with enough evidence, then we go in there and grab what we can. But there's the issue of what happens with the kids. We don't have the manpower to walk in there with enough bodies to take care of all those kids. Plus these are shifters who've been brought up to believe humans are at the bottom of the evolutionary ladder."

"What this situation calls for is a team of shifters and humans who can be ready to go in there and deprogram those kids," Rael said. "If the students see shifters *and* humans working together, maybe that's a start." Rael gazed unhappily at Horvan. "And what no one's mentioned yet is that this is *one school* out of twenty-five worldwide. What about the others? You shut this one down and immediately the bad guys are on alert. So the next school you decide to raid, they're going to be ready for you."

"That won't prevent us from going in there." Vic's voice quavered slightly. "And as for a team? Let me talk to the leaders. They'll like the idea, but it'll need some organizing. Actually, I was about to call you. I've found something on the camps."

Everyone in the room straightened.

"What have you got?" Dellan demanded.

"It's not much, but it's something. I came across a report filed by a Fridan, about a year ago. It was dismissed at the time because no evidence was found to support it."

"Tell us?" Dellan's voice rose, and Horvan pulled him into his lap, holding on to him.

"Okay. It was a snippet from a conversation overheard in a bar in Bozeman, Montana. Two guys talking, and one of them was clearly drunk. They were also both shifters, the source said. Okay. The drunk one was doing most of the talking. Hang on and I'll read you what he said." There was a pause. "'I'm tellin' ya, you can't believe all shifters are on the right side. All I'm sayin' is, they had to have done something to end up in that desolate, godforsaken camp. And for shifters to incarcerate other shifters? That has to tell you something, right? So what if the place feels like a concentration camp, right down to the watchtowers? They have to have been dangerous dudes to be sent there, so I don't give two fucks for 'em. I just do my job. I drive up to those gates, show my ID, make my deliveries, then drive the fuck out of there.' The other guy then shushed him and told him to shut the fuck up. Not that they were talking loudly in the first place."

"The source had to have had great hearing to pick up all that in a bar," Crank remarked.

"I have two words for you—bat shifter. And as soon as he heard the word shifter, he started paying close attention. He said this account is as close to the actual conversation as he can remember. He also said it gave him the shivers, which was why he turned in a report."

"Do we have any idea where this camp is?" Hashtag asked.

"No, but at least we have a location. Sure, Montana is huge, but Bozeman gives us a starting point. We know the camp's in a desolate spot, it has gates and watchtowers, and there's vehicular access."

"This was followed up?" Dellan asked.

"Apparently yes, but after two months they turned up nothing, so they dismissed it as a drunken conversation that sounded way too farfetched to have any basis in reality. But we know different, don't we?" Vic paused for a moment. "I promise you, if they'd known then what we've learned only recently, they'd still be out there, turning over every rock, draining every creek bed, and sweeping away every tumbleweed to find answers."

"Vic's right," Horvan murmured. "It's a start."

"I'll keep looking. And maybe Saul will turn up something."

"How is he staying in touch?" Hashtag asked.

"Via encrypted messages. He'll be messaging me again tonight."

"Yeah, I get the same ones," Horvan told him. "Let us know if you find anything else. Is that all?"

"Yeah, that's all for now. I'll go back to the archive. Take care, guys."

"You too," Crank called out on impulse.

Horvan shot him a look but said nothing. The call disconnected, and Horvan whooshed out a breath. "Progress."

Hashtag got up. "Okay, I'm on this. I'm gonna grab a sandwich. Then I'll make a start."

"Doing what?" Crank asked.

"Scouring satellite images of Montana. If there's a camp out there, I'll find it. Unless they've got a Romulan-type cloaking device, which I very much doubt. They're shifters, not aliens." He walked out of the office.

Dellan got up from Horvan's lap, removed his phone from his pocket, and scrolled, his forehead scrunched up. He went to the window and gazed out.

"Is there something wrong?" Crank said in a low voice.

Rael sighed. "He's worried about Jamie. Dellan's sent voicemail and texts, but Jamie's not answering."

"I think I'll go and do a patrol around the perimeter," Brick announced. "All this talk makes me nervous." He went out the door.

Crank blinked. "I don't think I've ever seen Brick nervous."

"This situation is getting to all of us," Horvan commented. He gazed at Dellan. "And some more than others," he added softly.

Crank's stomach was in knots. *I just want this to be over.*

Unfortunately, he had the feeling it hadn't even gotten started.

SAUL CREPT through the silent hallways of the main building.

This place gives me the creeps.

The students—when their paths crossed his—acted as if he wasn't even there. Saul played his part, trying to blend into the background, and no one spoke to him unless there was a problem. Then it was a case of "There's a mess. Clean it up."

I don't count though, do I? I'm only a mere human.

He'd bided his time, waiting for the early hours of the morning when he was certain of not being discovered, then left his room, heading for the offices, his flashlight in his hand. Hidden beneath his overalls was his Sig Sauer revolver, not that he was expecting company, but he knew better than to underestimate the enemy. The previous night had gone off without incident, but he wasn't about to get complacent.

He went over to the filing cabinet, then reached into his pocket for the two paper clips he'd brought along. He straightened one end of both clips, then bent one into an L shape. Saul pushed it into the bottom of the keyhole and held it there before inserting the other pin into the top of the lock. He wiggled it, feeling for the lock pins. It took him a few times to find the right combination of tension on the bottom clip and action on the top to pop the lock.

Who needs hi-tech when they use ordinary filing cabinets?

Saul opened the top drawer as quietly as he could and scanned the folder tabs. Nothing leaped out at him, so he tried the next drawer, labeled Student

Records. He removed the first folder, opened it, and shone his flashlight on the documents inside. The first section was the usual info—name, DOB, home address, etc.—but the section at the bottom caught his eye.

Adoption Details.

He scanned it, but it seemed legit. The student's adoptive parents were recorded there, along with the agency used and the signature of the government official who'd signed off on it. Saul replaced the file, then pulled out the next one. When it turned out the second student had also been adopted, that made him look more closely. A different adoption agency, but....

The same government official.

Saul went through the first twenty folders, and in each case, the signature was the same. He was pretty sure there had to be more than one US government official assigned to adoption records. On a hunch, he removed his phone from his pocket and googled the official's name.

No such person.

Saul had a sudden case of goose bumps. At random, he removed folders to examine them. Not only had every single student been adopted, they had all had their adoptions signed off by the same person.

He pulled out a few of the folders, spread them on a nearby desk, then straightened. The building was silent. Saul clicked on the camera and took photos of the adoption sections of about five students, then sent them to Vic and Horvan. He held down the mic icon and spoke quietly.

"Vic, look at these records. These are just a sample, but every student I've looked at is the same. All adopted, but the government official doesn't exist. This isn't legal. So why not go through the proper channels? What are they trying to hide?" He released the icon, sending the recording on its way to Vic.

"A very astute question, Mr. Rosen."

The cold voice sent a shiver down Saul's spine, and he froze as the light snapped on. Mr. Fielding stood in the doorway, accompanied by three men, and all four were pointing guns at Saul, their expressions impassive.

Saul said nothing, his body tensing.

"We really underestimated you, Mr. Rosen. Or should I call you— Saul Emory?" Fielding came closer, his gun aimed at Saul's heart.

Oh fuck.

"We thought we were dealing with a stupid human, but you've proved more resourceful than we anticipated. Those records should have passed cursory examination, but you were *so* determined to discover the truth." He held out his hand. "Your phone. Give it to me." Saul handed it over. "And your weapon." Saul blinked, and Mr. Fielding narrowed his gaze. "I said we'd underestimated you, but even *you* are not foolish enough to come here unarmed."

Saul unzipped his overall and reached inside. The three men aimed at his head, and he carefully removed the Sig, holding it by the barrel as he handed it to Mr. Fielding. "So what happens now?"

"Now? We have a talk."

He stuck out his chin. "I'm not going to tell you anything."

Mr. Fielding's eyes glittered. "I think you'll find we already know everything. In fact we might be able to share information that would be of interest to *you*." He gestured toward the door with his gun. "After you."

Saul walked out of the office, flanked by the four men. He didn't believe in coincidences.

They knew I was coming. But how?

CHAPTER FIFTEEN

SAUL WINCED as the cuffs bit into his wrists, his arms pulled back behind the chair. All around him was darkness, and the air was cool. He couldn't see them, but he knew they were there. He'd said nothing as they'd escorted him to the basement, figuring he'd wait it out until he knew what they wanted. What worried him was how long they'd known his real identity.

Did they know when they hired me? Except why would they take on someone they *knew* had been sent to infiltrate them? The answer had to be they wanted something from him.

Well, they're not gonna get it.

Bright white lights snapped on, momentarily blinding him with their glare.

"I think we're ready." That was Fielding from someplace behind the lights.

Saul snorted. "Don't you people get new movies where you come from? I mean, really?" He nodded toward the lights. "The next thing will be, one of you goons is gonna say, 'We have ways of making you talk' in a really thick accent."

"You *will* give us what we need, Saul. Make no mistake about that." Then the harsh lights snapped off and the overheard lights came on. Fielding walked slowly to stand in front of him, his arms folded.

Saul rolled his eyes. "Is this your menacing look? Because I gotta say, it's not working. What, no gloves? You know, for when you work me over?" He didn't give a shit if he pissed them off. He'd taken plenty of beatings before this.

Beatings wouldn't loosen his tongue.

One of the others brought a chair forward, and Fielding sat. "I'm not going to lay a finger on you, Saul. I wouldn't deign to touch your human flesh."

Okay, Fielding is a shifter. Like he hadn't already guessed that.

"Do what you want. I'm not about to tell you a goddamn thing." His heartbeat raced, so fast that it sent pains shooting through his chest, and Saul strove to get himself under control.

"But as I said, we already know so much," Fielding said with a smile. "Your boyfriend, for instance. The shark shifter? We know all about him—and his role." He folded his arms again. "Very impressive, by the way. To have access to so much knowledge."

Cold trickled through Saul. "Well, if you know so much, what do you want from me? I don't know anything about any of that."

Fielding stretched out his legs. "Your friends are under the illusion that they've dealt us a serious blow. I'm sorry to disappoint you, but this is not the case. Those raids on our factories amount to a minor inconvenience, that's all."

Saul snorted again. "Yeah, right. As if you'd tell me anything else."

Fielding's eyes glittered. "You are not a shifter. You couldn't possibly understand why we're doing this."

Saul widened his eyes. "So it's not because you're all batshit crazy?"

Fielding's gaze narrowed for a second; then he relaxed his features. "The factories may be gone, but we have stockpiles of a variety of drugs. If we decide to resume those activities, we will need to procure new companies to produce it, but things have progressed nicely, and those needs have… evolved."

Saul didn't like the sound of that. "Why don't you get to the fucking point?"

"This issue of communication between mates interests us."

He feigned ignorance. "Mates? I don't have a clue what you're talking about."

Fielding's eyes darkened. "Don't insult my intelligence. We know about Horvan Kojik and his mates, Rael Parton and Dellan Carson. We know there is some element of telepathic communication between them. But how is this achieved?"

Saul stared at him for a moment, then burst out laughing. "You're nuts. You know that, right?"

"Telepathy. Now *there's* a weapon crying out to be developed. Infiltrating the mind of the enemy, speaking directly to the troops…."

"Sounds fucking crazy to me." Saul's stomach clenched. For Fielding to share such thoughts could mean only one thing: *I'm not going to be left alive to tell anyone about it.* For the first time since they'd dragged him onto that chair, icy fear surged through him.

"You're telling me you know nothing of this?"

Saul glared at him. "Not a goddamn thing."

"Not even about how they can appear in each other's dreams?"

He rolled his eyes. "Sounds more like a fantasy novel to me."

"And speaking of dreams—" Fielding leaned forward, his elbows on his knees, his eyes bright. "—we know all about your boyfriend and his mate, Crank."

What the ever-loving fuck? Saul's throat tightened.

Fielding nodded. "Vic has been appearing in Crank's dreams, did you know that?"

Saul couldn't swallow. *How the fuck can they know that?* Then his heart stuttered. Vic was dreaming about Crank too. *Oh God.*

"Very graphic dreams, by all accounts. And how do *you* feel about this?"

Saul managed to find some spit. "They're not mates," he croaked. "Crank is human."

Fielding arched his eyebrows. "But that's not how it works, Saul." He tilted his head to one side. "Have they bonded already?"

Saul gazed at him, perplexed.

Fielding waved his hand. "Stupid question. Of course they've bonded. They were in the same house. I doubt they could keep their hands off each other." He snapped his fingers, and one of the men stepped forward to hand him a sheet of paper. Fielding gazed at it, smiling. "Yes indeed. Who would be able to resist such a magnificent specimen?" He turned the sheet around and held it for Saul to see.

It was a photo of Vic and another guy, whom Saul assumed to be Crank. They were standing on a patio, their heads close together, apparently deep in conversation. *Fuck, he's built.* His heart sank. *And Vic loves muscular guys, doesn't he?* Saul couldn't help but notice how close they were to each other, the intimacy of their body language.

It all added up to Fielding telling the truth.

And it's not gonna matter to me, because I'm not getting out of here alive. Saul knew that, balls to bones.

With a supreme effort, he dragged air into his lungs. "I'm gonna ask again, because I still don't have an answer. What exactly do you want from me, if you already know all this?"

"Vic has access to the largest archive of shifter knowledge."

"So?"

"We want access too."

Saul raised his eyebrows. "You're telling me your side isn't doing the same thing? Or are you too busy trying to take over the world?"

That earned him another flash of Fielding's eyes. "We have our own files, but they're incomplete. And knowledge *is* power, make no mistake."

Saul had heard enough. "Okay. One, why should I tell you anything? And two, what makes you think I know how to access the archive?" He did, but he wasn't about to tell them that. Saul had seen enough over the years he and Vic had been together.

"We'll make it worth your while."

Saul didn't trust that silky-voiced fucker as far as he could throw him. "You have nothing I want." Except his freedom, and Saul knew he wasn't about to be handed that.

"Are you sure about that? I'd be willing to bet you're wrong."

Saul said nothing.

"As I said, it won't take us long to set up new companies, new factories. The drug we used on Dellan? That's only one of our more recent… achievements. We have a drug that helps us alter minds, bend them to our will. Another—and I'm *immensely* proud of this one—that enhances shifters while they are still in the womb. And then there's our drug to break the mate bond."

Saul tried to keep it in, but he couldn't help the gasp that escaped him.

Fielding cocked his head once more. "Did they tell you mates are rare and that only shifters mate?" He tut-tutted, wagging a finger. "That was naughty of them. They lied. Mates are commonplace. But now we can break that bond." He leaned closer until his face was inches from Saul's. "We can inject Vic and Crank," he said in a voice barely above a whisper. "It would be as if their mate bond had never existed. And one last point which I'm sure you'll appreciate." His smile was cold. "It will hurt Crank far more than it will hurt Vic. And when it's all over, your boyfriend would be all yours again." Fielding sat back. "So are you going to tell us what we need to know, in exchange for this drug?"

It didn't matter that Saul would never see Vic again, or that he'd betrayed Saul with Crank. He would *never* put Vic in harm's way, and that went for every shifter Vic strove to protect too.

"You can take your drug and go fuck yourself with it." Saul lifted his head high, his pulse rapid. "I'm telling you nothing."

One of the men cleared his throat. "Sir? This is a waste of time. We're going to get nothing out of this one."

"I fear I agree." Fielding let out an exaggerated sigh. "Has there been word of their plans?"

"Not yet, sir."

"Well, by the time they realize there's been no contact with our friend here, we'll have already made our move." He glanced at Saul. "Your people are much more astute than we gave them credit for. They'd be smarter if they chose the right side, of course, but alas, we can't have everything."

"So now what?" As if Saul didn't know the answer to that.

"Now? Oh well, those plans have already been altered and are moving in a different direction. The schools are a wash, thanks to your people. We don't have the resources in place to move *all* the students, so we're going to take the best and brightest and move them to a new location." He gave Saul a patently false smile. "Consolidate our assets, if you will."

"But what about the other kids?"

Fielding arched his eyebrows. "Those who don't make the cut?" He shrugged. "Oh, they'll probably be okay. They're smart and tough, but not so much that they're irreplaceable."

Saul didn't believe what he was hearing. "You're going to abandon children?"

Fielding laughed. "Do you think these will be the first ones we've culled? Survival of the fittest means doing whatever is necessary. For the strong to survive, the weak must perish."

Saul swallowed. "Why are you telling me this?"

"It might take your group a few days to get their act together, but I'm certain they'll be here eventually, and we don't relish the idea of wasting our time with them. Plans are already in progress to deal with them, and soon. For now, we need you to deliver a message to them."

"What kind of message?" Saul demanded. "I won't hurt them."

Fielding sneered. "No, of course you won't. *You'd* rather your boyfriend ran off with his new mate. Forget what I said earlier. You're *exactly* the weak, pathetic human we expected. And you needn't worry. You don't actually need to say anything to them."

The door to the basement opened, and two men entered, ushering in a slight figure. As they drew closer, Saul saw it was a boy, maybe ten years old. Fielding beckoned him, and the boy stood in front of Saul, his green eyes betraying no emotion.

Fielding placed his hands on the boy's shoulders. "This is such delicious irony. Saul, allow me to introduce Alec. He's one of our most gifted and promising students."

Alec stared at Saul, and a wave of dread swept over him as he looked into Alec's eyes. It was as if the lights were on, but no one was home.

Fielding stroked Alec's bronze-brown hair. "I'm sure you're dying to ask what Alex's particular gifts are, but only one of them need interest you."

"And what's that?"

Fielding locked gazes with Saul. "Inflicting pain."

With that, Alec held up a clawed hand and slashed Saul across his chest, ripping through his coveralls.

Fire roared through him, spreading as blood seeped from the wound. "I'm still not... telling you anything," Saul gasped.

"We don't care. If they find you, you're welcome to tell them whatever you want, because we will be long gone. Assuming Alec doesn't kill you, of course. That would be regrettable."

Alec stepped behind him, and Saul screamed as Alec raked his hand over Saul's back and neck. It was a pain like no other. Then Alec came into view and slashed once more from collarbones to navel, and Saul's scream rebounded off the walls.

Fielding's cackle reached Saul's ears. "Oh, I *do* hope you survive this. You see, there *is* one thing I want you to tell Dellan when you see him." Fielding laid his hand on Alec's shoulder. "Tell him we're taking very good care of his son."

Saul's mind fought against the pain, racking his brains for the details of Dellan's captivity that Horvan had shared with him. "That's not possible." His voice cracked.

Fielding twisted his lips into a cruel smirk. "I agree. For human science, it isn't even a remote possibility. However, *we* don't have the limitations that humans do. There are no moral and ethical debates. We do what we must in order to achieve our goals."

121

"I still call bullshit," Saul gasped, thankful that as long as Fielding was talking, Alec wasn't slashing. Every wound felt hot, as if something was infiltrating his body.

What if it is?

Fielding gave him an indulgent smile. "Aw. Are such advances not dreamed of in your philosophy, Saul? When your people were crowing about discovering penicillin, *we* were already on the cusp of implanted pregnancies. When your James Gamble was realizing the importance of electrolytes, *our* scientists were perfecting RNA sequencing. Throughout history, humankind has slogged to get the most basic things accomplished, while *we* pushed every boundary." He snorted. "And you wonder why we think the human race pathetic."

"Says the man who thinks nothing of culling children."

Fielding's eyes gleamed. "But they make for such great distractions."

Saul struggled to keep from crying out. He gazed at Alec, noting how the boy's blank stare hadn't changed. "He can't be more than a year old, and yet he looks as if he's nine or ten." His focus snapped to Fielding. "How long will he live?"

Fielding's face hardened. "He'll live long enough to fulfill a purpose."

"And then you'll discard him? How many others have you done this to? And what about those who didn't make the cut? Stupid question. Forget I asked." His gaze went back to Alec. "Why doesn't he speak? *Can* he speak? Or did you turn him into an automaton who does as he's—"

Fielding backhanded him across the face, his cheeks dark with anger.

Saul squared his jaw, aware that the pain was increasing. "Hit a nerve, did I? I guess I must have. I thought you wouldn't deign to touch human flesh."

Fielding straightened. "This conversation is at an end." He patted Alec on the shoulder. "Do what you do best. Try not to kill him, but if it happens, no one will shed a tear. When you're done, meet us at the helicopter pad." His gaze met Saul's. "Goodbye. I doubt we'll meet again." And with that, Fielding turned and strode from the room.

Alec stepped close, his arm raised, and Saul knew no more.

CHAPTER SIXTEEN

CRANK SAT bolt upright in bed, his sweat-slicked chest cold. He could still hear Saul's screams, still feel the pain that shot through him. Then he froze.

Wait one fucking minute.

He'd never seen Saul, so how could he know, with every cell, nerve, and fiber, that it *was* Saul? Yet somehow he did know. What shook him most was the strange nature of the dream. One minute he was watching Saul's head jerk back, his eyes glazed with pain, and the next, Crank could *feel* that pain, as if it was coursing through his own body.

He shivered, tugging the sheet to wipe the chill from his torso. For a nightmare, it had felt so *real*.

His phone vibrated on the nightstand, and he grabbed it. As soon as he saw Vic's name, cold sweat popped out on his brow, and he clicked Answer.

"Bit early for a call?" A glance at the bedside clock showed it to be three in the morning.

"Horvan needs to know. Saul's in trouble."

And just like that, Crank's heartbeat shoved into high gear. "How do you know? Did he call you?"

"No, but…. Look, I can't explain this, but I had a-a dream, okay? In it, Saul was in agony, and someone was torturing him."

Oh my fucking God.

"He was bound to a chair in some dark, cool place," Crank whispered.

Vic's breathing hitched. "How do you know that?"

"But I'm right, aren't I?" When silence fell, he groaned. "You want details? Fine. He's got black hair, swept up on top at the front. Thick dark brows. Green eyes. A full beard with tiny flecks of silver in it. Broad, muscular shoulders. Wide chest. Oh yeah, and he's in fucking *agony.*"

"But how the hell can you know all that?" Vic croaked.

"Because I had the same fucking dream, that's why!" Crank yelled into the phone. "Now what the fuck is going on? Why are we both dreaming about *your* boyfriend, a guy I've never even laid eyes on, yet I *know* it's him? And why call me? You could've called Horvan directly." When Vic didn't respond, Crank lost it. "Answer me, goddamn it. How could we both have the same dream? And if we did, does that somehow make it real? Is Saul *really* being tortured someplace?" He hit Speaker and tossed the phone onto the mattress, then threw back the sheets and lurched from the bed. Crank grabbed his jeans from the chair and squirmed into them. "You're not talking, Vic." He yanked up the zipper.

"I-I have a theory, but you're not going to like it."

"Try me, because I'm getting dressed to go wake Horvan the fuck up."

"Good. We need to get to the school before… before it's too late."

"You're telling me you think Saul's gonna die?" As soon as the words left his lips, pain speared through Crank's body, and he doubled over. "Christ."

"Crank? You okay?"

He gasped, pulling his tee over his head. "You said you had a theory. Start talking."

Another pause, and Crank was verging on losing it. Then Vic spoke, his voice quieter. "He-he's our mate."

That brought Crank to a dead stop. "Hold the phone—*our mate*? He's human. *I'm* human. And I am *no one's* fucking mate."

"Will you just stop and think for a second? It's the only theory that makes sense. The dreams? The kiss?"

"But I'm not a shifter!" he shouted. Except something in Crank's gut told him Vic might be right. It explained so much of what had been going on.

No. No. There has to be another explanation.

"Neither is Saul, but that doesn't seem to matter. I don't understand it either, okay?"

They were interrupted by a *thud* on Crank's door, and a moment later it was flung open and Horvan charged in, wearing a pair of shorts and holding a gun. "What the fuck is going on in here?" He scanned the room, then lowered the weapon. "Why are you yelling at this hour?"

"Call Duke," Crank snapped. "We need urgent transport, and we need it, like, yesterday. Whatever he can lay his hands on. We have to go rescue Saul."

Horvan gaped. "What the fuck? Has Saul been in contact?" Rael and Dellan appeared in the doorway behind him, rubbing their eyes.

"Kinda." Crank swallowed. "He's my mate." Even as he said the words, he wasn't sure he believed them. *No fucking way.*

All three men's mouths fell open.

"Say that again?" Rael's eyes widened. "You can't have a mate."

"You're right. I don't." Crank shivered. "I have two. Now, can we stop talking and get Duke on the phone?"

Horvan drew in a deep breath. "Okay. Calmly. One thing at a time. How do you know Saul needs rescuing?"

"Because we both had the same dream about him, that's why." Vic's voice burst from the phone on the bed. "And we're wasting time."

Horvan blinked. "You expect me to call Duke at three in the morning because you and Vic shared a *dream*?"

"Do you believe Dellan and Rael connected in a dream?" Vic demanded. "You know such things happen, right? So how else are you going to explain Crank being able to describe Saul, right down to the flecks of gray in his beard? And both of us knowing they're torturing him?"

"Someone's torturing Saul?" Roadkill stood behind Dellan and Rael. "What the fuck is going on here?"

"Is there a party in Crank's room and I wasn't invited?" Hashtag's voice came from the hallway. "Because you're all making way too much noise."

"I want everyone dressed and downstairs in five minutes," Horvan ordered. "Vic, I'll call you back in a minute, when I've grabbed my phone."

"Fine, as long as it *is* a minute. Saul needs us." Then he was gone.

Crank picked up his phone, his heart pounding.

This is fucking nuts. His mind was fighting the idea, but with every breath he took, Crank grew more convinced that Vic was right. It was the only hypothesis that made sense.

Rael was the first to join him in the kitchen, followed by the others. Rael went to the coffeepot. "I think we need this." Dellan grabbed cups from the cabinet. Everyone else sat at the table.

Horvan came into the kitchen, dressed in a pair of jeans, his phone in his hand.

"H, what's going on?" Hashtag yawned.

"In a nutshell, it appears Crank, Vic, and Saul are mates, Saul has been taken by the bad guys, and they're torturing him."

Hashtag blinked. "Okay, I'm obviously still asleep and this is a dream."

Crank shuddered. "If it is, I wanna wake up right fucking now." He gazed imploringly at Horvan. "H... make the call. This will take time to set up, and we don't know how much time Saul has left." He might not be rock-solid sure about the mates business, but he knew in his gut Saul was in deep shit.

"You're serious, aren't you?" Horvan's face was grave.

"Serious enough that it feels like my fucking *soul* depends on it." He swallowed again. "That pain…. Christ, I don't know what they're doing to him, but it was so bad."

Horvan studied him for a moment, then tapped the phone's screen. He held it to his ear, his gaze on Crank. "I hope you're wrong." Then he stilled. "Duke, before you start bawling me out, this is urgent. How fast can you scramble transport for us? … Duke, I don't fucking *care* what time it is. I've had your back more times than I can count, right? Well, now I need *you*. … When do we need it? Now would be great, but I'll take whatever you can get. … Destination is somewhere near Boston. A place called Easton. … No, I don't know where we'd need to fly from—"

"Waukegan airport," Hashtag called out, looking up from his phone.

"Did you get that? Good. I'll leave the logistics to you." Horvan glanced at the men huddled around the table. "I'll be taking Roadkill, Hashtag, and Crank. I'll leave Brick here to watch this place."

"We're going too," Dellan piped up.

Horvan's eyes bulged. "Duke, I'll call you back. See what you can rustle up? And thanks. You gotta know I wouldn't be doing this if it wasn't urgent." He disconnected, then glared at Dellan. "No, you are *not*. This is gonna be fucking dangerous."

Dellan drew himself up to his full height. "Great. So while you're dealing with whoever's got Saul, what happens with the students? They're going to be out of their minds with worry if suddenly there's gunfire everywhere. You *need* Rael and me to keep them calm, make sure they stay out of it."

"And you said it yourself," Rael interjected. "I'm a good shot. Crank's seen to that. I can protect us if I need to."

"Waukegan is over an hour's drive from here," Hashtag observed. "So can I suggest we all stop jawing and get our gear together so we're ready to go ASAP? We can be on our way while Duke's still working out the details."

"Good thinking." Horvan fired a hard stare at Rael and Dellan. "And my answer is still no."

"Horvan, you know we're right." Dellan locked gazes with him.

126

"That look might not work on you, H, but it sure as shit works on me. Let 'em come," Crank implored. "Rael's right. They can take care of the kids."

Horvan put his hands on his hips. "And what makes you think a whole lotta shifter kids are gonna listen to you?"

Rael tapped his chest. "King of the beasts, remember?"

Horvan narrowed his gaze. "Not in *our* bed."

"What is going on?" Brick stood by the french doors. "This a secret meeting or can anyone join in?"

"We've got an emergency," Horvan told him.

"H, you need to call Vic, remember?" Crank's stomach was still in a twist, so Vic had to be in the same tormented state.

Horvan dialed again. "Vic, we're organizing transport from Waukegan. ... Yeah, I figured that, but you're— ... Okay, but how long will it take you to— ... Fine. Let me know." He hung up. "Vic's coming too. He says he'll meet us at Waukegan, though how he's gonna get there, I have no idea. I'll leave that up to him."

"He'll be there," Crank announced. "He's got connections too, hasn't he? He'll probably be out the door by now." Which is exactly where Crank wanted to be, but he told himself they'd be on their way soon enough. *We'll get there.*

What sent ice flooding through his veins was the thought that they might arrive too late.

"Someone wanna tell me what's going on?" Brick demanded.

"We have to rescue Vic's boyfriend, Saul," Roadkill told him. "And both of them are apparently Crank's mates." Brick's eyes widened, and Roadkill nodded. "Yeah. We still haven't gotten our heads around that one. So we're going to that shifter school ahead of schedule."

"What happened to Saul?" Brick's voice was quiet.

"We don't have anything concrete to go on," Horvan told him. "But according to both Vic and Crank, he's being tortured."

Brick froze. "What? That's barbaric."

Roadkill snorted. "I keep forgetting, you weren't around when we listened to a gorilla tearing Dellan's—" He clamped his lips together.

Horvan glared at him. "Yeah, I don't think Dellan needs reminding, do you?" He expelled a breath. "Fine. Rael, Dellan? You're going too. But you stay away from where the action is, do you hear me?" Both men nodded.

"Am I included in these plans?" Brick asked.

"Yes. We're gonna need all hands on deck."

"So that's seven of us. How are we getting to the airport?" Roadkill asked.

"Take the Chevy Suburban," Dellan told him. He snuck a glance at Horvan, and Crank caught a glint. "Now, *who* was it who said, 'Oh, we're never gonna need anything *that* big' when I bought it?"

Rael snickered. "You know Horvan. Everything's about size."

From the way they kept glancing in his direction, Crank got the sneaking suspicion they'd put on that whole conversation to draw him out of his head.

You can give me all the openings you want, guys. Doesn't mean I'm gonna step through 'em. His mind was locked on Vic and Saul.

In the space of less than an hour, one nightmare and one phone conversation had turned his life upside down.

THE SUV sped along the 294, Roadkill at the wheel and Horvan beside him. Crank sat between Rael and Dellan, twisting his hands in his lap. Hashtag and Brick were behind them, and Brick was in charge of the weapons.

Crank was a mess. He had a feeling there was no way Horvan would put him in control of any aircraft; he didn't have a cool enough head for that. He dropped his chin onto his chest and closed his eyes.

I hope you're okay, Saul.

He jerked his head up at the sound of Horvan's phone. Horvan grabbed his notepad from the console and touched his earpiece. "What have you got for me, Duke?" He scribbled furiously, his head nodding now and then. "Okay. … Yeah, got that. … Right. … Okay, that's great. I'll keep in touch." He disconnected the call, then turned to look at the other occupants of the car. "There'll be a military plane waiting for us at the airport, and as soon as Vic reaches us, we can leave. Duke's filed a flight plan for Wappingers Falls, New York, where a Kaman Seasprite helicopter will take us the last two hundred miles to the school." He gave Crank a warm glance. "Hold on, buddy. We're gonna get there in time, you hear me?"

Crank nodded, his throat tight.

Dellan patted Crank's thigh. "Close your eyes again. You must be exhausted. Try to turn off your mind, all right?"

Easier said than done.

Nevertheless, he closed his eyes, and warmth stole over him as he slipped into a light sleep… and a dream.

HE WAS in the same room as before. Saul lay on his side on the floor, still bound to a chair, his breathing labored. Light came from a single bulb above them, and there was no one else in sight.

Crank crouched beside Saul and gently laid his hand on Saul's shoulder. His dark blue coveralls were shredded in places, and there was a lot of blood. His right eye was swollen shut, his cheek bruised. As Crank gazed at him, Saul opened his good eye and peered up at him.

"Crank… please keep Vic safe." The words came out as a whimper.

Crank cupped Saul's cheek with as much tenderness as he could muster. "Don't be stupid. He's our mate, and we can't be complete without you. Hold on, okay? I'm coming for you." He leaned in and brushed a kiss over Saul's lips. "We're both coming for you."

CRANK SNAPPED awake at the sound of Horvan's phone ringing once more. He was shaking. *Dear God. I didn't imagine that, did I?* Then he heard Vic's voice coming from the phone, and he was suddenly alert.

"Where are you?" Horvan asked. Crank could hear the drone of engines in the background.

"Military plane, en route to Waukegan. I pulled some strings. I should be there within the hour. Listen, I've been thinking. Saul is too good at his job to let himself get caught so soon into a mission. And even if they did catch him, he'd find a way to get out of the situation."

"So? What are you saying?" Horvan demanded.

"There's only one explanation," Vic said after a pause. "They knew he was coming."

Crank stiffened. "What? But how could they?"

"Someone told them. Someone who knew our plans."

"But there *is* no one," Rael called out.

"Yes, there is." Cold spread through Crank's body. "Think about it. Who hasn't been in touch for days? Who's not answering calls or texts?"

Dellan's breathing caught. "No. He wouldn't."

"Who wouldn't?" Vic shouted over the engine noise.

"Jamie." It all made perfect sense.

Dellan shook his head. "No. No. I'm not buying it."

"We know nothing about him," Crank protested. "And we all saw what he was like. You don't think we *deprogrammed* him, do you? Fuck that. His loyalty lies with that school."

Horvan gave Dellan a sympathetic glance. "I know you don't want to believe it, but as a theory, it does make sense."

"I'm sorry, but I can't. I *won't*." Dellan frowned.

"For God's sake, it wasn't Jamie, okay?" Brick blurted out.

Crank twisted in his seat to stare at him. "You don't know that."

Brick's face was pale. "Yes, I do. Because it was me."

CHAPTER SEVENTEEN

CRANK POPPED his seat belt and was out of his seat in a heartbeat and lunging over the back of it to seize Brick by the throat. Both Dellan and Rael grabbed him, and Hashtag thrust his arm in front of Brick to block Crank.

"Lemme at him. I'm gonna fucking *kill* him." Blood pounded in Crank's ears, and his fingers ached to squeeze Brick's neck until the fucker wasn't breathing.

"No, you're not," Hashtag exclaimed hotly. "Wait till we've got some answers—*then* you can kill him, but you're gonna have to get in line." He glared at Brick. "Start talking or I tell Dellan and Rael to let him loose. Crank may not be a shifter, but I guarantee he'll make a mess of you."

"And I'd deserve it, okay?" Brick yelled.

"Wait till I get my hands on you." Vic's voice burst from the phone.

"Be fucking grateful I'm driving right now," Roadkill gritted out. "Because you'd be a—"

"All of you, sit the fuck down and shut up!" Horvan's steel-edged voice cut through the air like a scimitar. Dellan tugged Crank back into his seat. "Vic, if you wanna hear this, then you listen without interruption, you got that? Or else I disconnect right this second."

There was nothing but engine noise for a moment. "I got it. I want to hear this. Don't cut me off."

"I won't." Horvan twisted to stare at Brick. "Talk to me, starting with why."

Crank had to see Brick's face. He turned in his seat, his fingers digging into the padding.

Brick swallowed, his face pale. "Because aside from those kids and Saul, there are two other innocent lives on the line here, that's why."

"Whose?" Crank demanded.

Pain flitted across Brick's stern features. Crank had always thought him unflappable, but right then he was the epitome of extremely flapped. "They've got my parents, all right? Three weeks ago, I was talking to my

131

mom. I call her and my dad every week to see how they're doing. While we were talking, she screamed, and I heard my dad yell to get their hands off his wife. Then there was a gunshot. I nearly broke my phone I was squeezing it so hard while yelling for them." His eyes glistened. "They said if I didn't help, my parents would die. So tell me—what would you do in those circumstances? Any of you?"

Crank's stomach clenched, his white-hot rage reducing to a simmer.

"How much have you told them?" Horvan asked in a calm voice, and Crank's admiration for him went up several notches. Horvan's ability to keep a cool head had kept them alive on several occasions, and Crank was never more thankful for it.

"Everything I could." Brick sagged into his seat. "They know about all of you guys, for one thing. They know about Vic and Saul. Jamie too. I told them Jamie had shared stuff about the schools, and that you knew about the camps. I also told them about... Vic appearing in Crank's dreams."

Vic's gasp was audible over the plane's engines.

Crank gaped. "How the fuck do *you* know about my dreams?"

"I was on patrol, it was late—well, early—and you and H were in the kitchen. I-I heard you talking."

Crank clenched his fists. "Fuck listening to any more of this—I *am* gonna kill him." Dellan gripped his upper arm, holding him in place with surprising strength.

"Do they know we're coming?" Horvan demanded.

Brick swallowed, his color returning. "No. I was supposed to inform them when you were ready to make a move."

"But you didn't. Why not?"

Brick's eyes held such pain that Crank winced. "Both Crank and Vic said they tortured Saul. They... they promised me no one would be hurt if I cooperated. They lied."

Crank stared at him with wide eyes. "And that fucking *surprises* you?"

"You mentioned Jamie." Dellan's voice cracked. "And now he's not answering calls or texts."

"It might not be as bad as you think. There could be any number of reasons why he's not responding." Rael's voice was gentle. "There must be another way to contact him. Maybe his parents are in touch with him? He told us their names, where they live."

"No!" Brick paled. "They won't help you."

"Why not?" Dellan asked.

Brick's chest heaved. "Because if they're like all the others, they won't give a shit about him."

"Tell us what you know." Horvan's voice was firm. "How did they know to target you in the first place?"

"That's a long story."

"And we've still got a way to go to get to the airport, so keep talking," Roadkill called out.

Brick shivered. "Okay. The thing is, I've always been upfront with my parents about what I do. I mean, not the details, because those are top secret, but the fact I work for an organization that goes everywhere to protect people and property." He paused. "So once all the screaming stopped, this guy came on the phone. He tells me my parents have been lying to me all these years."

"About what?" Horvan demanded.

"He figured I wouldn't know I was adopted, but I did. My parents told me that years ago." Brick's Adam's apple bobbed. "What I didn't know was the rest of it, and there was a lot—"

"Adopted?" Vic interjected. "Saul sent me an audio message about adoptions. Something about the kids at the school."

"Let him finish," Horvan instructed. He locked gazes with Brick. "Keep talking."

"What I didn't know was that my parents were part of that group. You know, the Gerans? The ones who are all about shifter superiority? It seems someone from the group brought me to them as a baby, to be adopted."

"Brought you from where?" Rael asked.

Brick shuddered. "A camp, they said. My parents were given instructions. They were to bring me up, send me to a special school where I would be… trained. Only they were supposed to remain detached. Their job was to see that I grew up knowing who I was, *what* I was, that I had a role to fulfill."

"They were supposed to program you," Dellan murmured.

Brick nodded.

"I'm guessing something went wrong," Horvan remarked.

"Yeah. My parents did the one thing they'd been told not to do—they grew to love me." His face tightened. "When Jamie was talking about his parents and remembering how they brought him up, that's how *my* parents were supposed to have been. But I *knew* they loved me. Anyway, this guy said they'd run away, taking me with them, and that they'd somehow managed to keep under the group's radar for years, until something went wrong and the group located them."

"Why was this guy telling you all this?" Hashtag asked.

"I think at first he'd hoped to sway me into going against my folks. Fat chance of that. So when his first plan failed, he had a backup." Brick shivered again. "He'd taken them hostage, threatening to kill them if I didn't do what he said. It wasn't until you guys brought me into this that all the pieces of the puzzle slotted together."

"But if you wanted to keep them safe, why didn't you tell the group about this mission?"

"Because I'm between a rock and hard place, all right?" Brick's face flushed red. "They won't let me talk to my parents, and after what I learned about Saul, I don't even know if they're still alive. My orders were to report back on what you were all doing, in detail. They said if I didn't call, they'd kill them. But—" Another hard swallow. "—this is different. I'd be letting you walk into a trap. I had to ask myself, what would my folks tell me to do?"

"And what did you come up with?" Crank knew all about that space Brick found himself in. Crank was in a similar tight spot. On the one hand, he wanted Brick dead for putting Saul's life in jeopardy, but on the other....

Is Brick right? Would I react the same way? Maybe. Who knew until they were faced with that situation?

"If they're still alive, I think they… they'd tell me to sacrifice them and save you. That they've had their lives. That what you're doing is important." His face contorted. "But I hope to God we find them." Brick stared at them, misery written across his face. "I'm sorry. I put Saul in danger, and Jamie. And if… if anything's happened to them, I'll never forgive myself."

"Let's see what's waiting for us at that school, okay?" Horvan's eyes were filled with compassion.

"If they don't know we're coming, we have an advantage," Vic declared. "They won't be expecting us to make a move until a day or two has elapsed with no word from Saul. They don't know what *we* know." There was a pause. "Crank, we're going to find him, all right? And he'll be okay. He has to be."

"You don't know that." The words came out as a croak, but none of the car's occupants reacted.

"Yes, I do. And so do you."

"What do you mean?"

Vic's sigh filled the car. "Because now I can *feel* him, inside my head, where I couldn't before. And if I can do that, then you can too. Focus. Let your thoughts go to him."

Crank was about to tell him such a thing wasn't possible, until he remembered that brief snatch of a dream.

But was it a dream?

His stomach churned, and his palms grew damp. "I-I can't." Part of his mind still resisted the notion of mates. *He can't be right. Things like this don't happen.* It was way too... mystical for his brain to cope with.

"Then wait till we're together, and we'll both try it. Maybe there's strength in numbers."

"Me, Dellan, and Rael think more clearly when we're together," Horvan confirmed.

"You see? Not such a farfetched idea after all." Vic's voice grew warm. "I can't wait to see you. We have so much to talk about."

Horvan cleared his throat. "Did you make any progress with the Fridans, Vic? Our idea about sending a team in to take care of the kids? Because it's kinda urgent now, don't you think?"

"I agree. I contacted them as soon as I got off the phone with you and told them to make this a top priority. They're assembling people as we speak. They'll contact me when they have more information, but the plan is to send a team in ASAP. For all I know, someone could already be there."

"Great. Then we'll see you at the airport, okay, Vic?" Horvan glanced at Crank. "I think Crank needs a minute right now."

"Gotcha. See you there." The call disconnected.

Rael squeezed Crank's knee. "You doing okay there?"

"Yeah, sure. Yesterday I was an ordinary guy, helping to save the world. Today? Who the fuck knows *what* I am anymore?" It messed with his head.

Dellan leaned in and whispered, "You're still you, Crank. There's just two other parts to you. Two really special parts."

Crank turned to gaze incredulously at him. "You believe all this? That I have mates? I mean, have *you* ever heard of humans having mates?"

"No, but until Rael turned up at that cage, I'd never heard of shifters having mates either. I'm not going to say something can't be true when I don't know that for sure. What I *will* say is both you and Vic dreamed the same dream. I don't believe in coincidence. So that would indicate there's a… connection between the three of you."

"Is everyone around here forgetting one tiny important detail?" Crank stared at him. "I'm straight. As in, I don't do guys. Even if I *did* kiss Vi—"

Oh shit. He could feel their eyes on him.

"Oh, well, that's all right." Horvan rolled his eyes. "I mean, if you're straight then we don't need to go rescue Saul, because he can't be your mate. Let's turn the car around and go back home."

"No!" Crank's heart felt as if it were about to explode.

"You know he won't do that," Rael murmured. "He's only trying to show you how strong that connection is."

"And as for being with a guy, it isn't *that* much different, apart from the plumbing," Hashtag commented. "Guys give better head, for one thing. At least, that's what every guy I've ever sucked off has said. Ask Horvan if you don't believe me." He bit his lip. "Oops."

Rael waved his hand. "Relax. Horvan let that particular cat out of the bag before we rescued Dellan. That thing you do with your tongue, remember?"

"Oh yeah."

Dellan gaped. "What thing with his tongue?"

"It's called Ancient History, okay?" Horvan declared. "So ancient it happened before he was even in my unit, so let it go."

Hashtag grinned. "Hey, Crank, if you want any pointers, I'm available."

"I think Vic and Saul might have something to say about that," Dellan observed.

"And I'm just trying to lighten the mood, all right?" Hashtag's eyes twinkled. "Although I can teach you the tongue thing, if you wanna try it out on your mates."

Crank couldn't believe they were talking about him being with Vic and Saul as if it was a totally natural occurrence.

"Don't worry about this now," Rael said in a low voice. "We've got much more important stuff to occupy us. Let's get Saul out of there and then see what we can do about those kids, all right?" He squeezed Crank's arm. "But I do understand a little of what you're going through. I still remember how I felt when my mom told me I could hear Dellan inside my head because he was my mate." His eyes glistened. "My whole world changed with one conversation. So if you ever need to unload, I'm here, okay?"

Crank's heart had never felt so *full*. "Thank you," he whispered. He still had to figure out how he was going to act when he came face-to-face with Vic.

Don't think about it. Let it just... happen. His throat tightened. *Hold on, Saul. We're coming.*

He hoped they'd make it in time.

Vic GRABBED his bags and thanked the pilot, then descended the steps to the tarmac. Dawn had yet to break, and the morning air was cold.

Off one military transport and onto another. He scanned the planes lined up at the terminal, looking for any sign of Horvan's team. Almost three and a half hours had elapsed since he'd awoken from his dream. It had been a minor miracle to get a seat on the plane to Waukegan, so he figured the gods were with him.

I hope so.

Then he caught sight of a figure standing alone in the middle of the tarmac, and even at a distance, he knew it was Crank. Vic ran toward him, his heart thumping, his pulse rapid, more energized than he'd felt in ages. When Vic was within ten feet of him, Crank simply held his arms wide, and Vic ran into them. Strong arms enfolded him, and for the first time since he'd had that fucking awful dream, peace trickled through him—not much, but it was way better than the panic that had engulfed him all morning.

"We're gonna get him back," Crank murmured.

Standing there held so fucking tightly against Crank's broad chest, and against all rationale, Vic believed him. "I can't lose him," he whispered. "I love him more than my own life."

"Is it too much to hope that in time you'll feel the same way about me?" Crank released him. "Don't answer that. Because right now, we need to focus on getting him out of there." Crank's voice dropped to a low rumble. "And kicking the shit out of anyone who laid a finger on him."

"Vic. Crank. Come *on*." Horvan waved them toward the plane.

Vic expelled a shaky breath. "Let's go find our mate."

CHAPTER EIGHTEEN

"THIS STILL makes no sense," Crank murmured to Vic as the helicopter headed for the school. "This whole thing about us being mates." He couldn't deny having Vic beside him was comfortable and nothing like the way he'd felt back in Homer Glen. And as for how it had been to hold Vic? Crank couldn't explain the emotions tumbling and colliding within him, but it seemed like....

Coming home.

"Why are you fighting this?" Vic said quietly.

Crank was about to fire off one of a half-dozen explanations why he couldn't possibly have one mate, let alone two, but he stilled. "When I got off the plane to look for you? I thought I knew what I was going to say. I was going to tell you you'd got it all wrong. And then I saw you, and all the words flew right outta my head. Because all I wanted to do was hold you. And I can't explain that reaction."

"I can't explain so much of this, so join the club. But I will say this. Once I thought about it, it was like a weight had been lifted off me," Vic confessed.

"Why?"

Vic sighed. "I love Saul, okay? You know that. And the idea that I could love him and yet be attracted to you felt so *alien*. I-I didn't like it. But now I know better." His gaze met Crank's. "The reason I was drawn to you was not because I was attracted to you, but because the mate bond was pulling us together. I mean, Saul and I already have a bond, but...." His eyes widened.

The hairs on Crank's arm stood on end. "What is it? What just occurred to you?"

"Gods, could the answer be that simple?"

"What answer? Stop talking in riddles and tell me what you're thinking." A rush of adrenaline spiked through him, and Crank's heart raced. The others paid them no mind, which was fine by Crank. Brick stared

138

through the window, his expression somber, and it didn't take a genius to work out where *his* head was.

Vic drew in a deep breath. "What if mate bonds are so rare because no one ever knew it took *three* people to complete it? Yes, two people can get together and recognize their bond, but what if it takes a third to *stabilize* their relationship? What if having that third is what triggers the telepathic connection?"

"*We* don't have that," Crank remarked. "And Rael heard Dellan in his head before he even knew Horvan existed."

"Well, that blows *that* theory all to hell. I was hoping we'd have that—once we have Saul."

Holy shit. Then Vic's words sank in. "Wait, you're not attracted to me?"

Vic arched his eyebrows. "I expound my momentous theory and *that's* all you pick up on? Can we discuss this another time? Say, after we've rescued our mate?"

"But we *are* gonna come back to this, right?" Having a mate who wasn't attracted to him—how the fuck did that work? *And what if Saul's the same? Has some otherworldly dickhead saddled me with two mates who don't even* want *me?* It didn't matter that he'd never been into guys—his ego got bruised just *thinking* about rejection.

"Okay, I see the school," Horvan yelled. "We're gonna circle once to get the lay of the land. Guys, get ready for some heavy resistance. Once they realize we're there, they're probably going to mobilize a group to drive us out. You must keep the fight as far away from the student buildings as possible. I won't have kids getting hurt."

Crank expelled a breath. *And if the bad guys decide to use the kids as human shields?* How would they get the students out safely in those circumstances? "H...?"

Horvan turned to look at him, his face grim. "We'll cross that bridge when we come to it."

Of course he'd know what was on Crank's mind. Horvan wasn't a born leader for nothing.

Horvan addressed the helicopter's passengers. "Make sure you're ready. This could get ugly very fast."

Crank checked his weapons, and Vic did the same. No one spoke, and the air crackled as if electrically charged. Rael and Dellan were solemn, and

Crank noted for the first time the holster Rael wore. "You've got the safety on, right?"

Rael narrowed his gaze. "No. I forgot everything you taught me. It went in one ear and out the other. Of *course* the safety is on. I'm hoping I don't have to use it, but if I do… I'm ready."

"Rael, Dellan, you stay in the chopper until I say otherwise, you got that?" Horvan twisted to stare at them. "And Brick, you stay with them."

"What? I wanna help you look for—"

"Stay with them. No arguments. And when they go to find the students, you stick to them, you hear?"

"I hear ya." Brick didn't look happy about it, though.

Horvan's features softened. "Look, I know things are raw between us right now, but you've never given us reason to doubt you before. Hell, you took a bullet for Hashtag in Kabul that one time."

Hashtag sighed. "H is right. This whole situation is fucked-up, but I have to tell you, if they had *my* parents, I doubt I'd be able to think at all. I don't know how everyone else feels, but for me this mess is on them, not you."

Horvan nodded. "Exactly. That's why I want you to stay with Rael and Dellan. I'm trusting you with the two most important people in my life. What does that tell you?"

Brick's eyes widened. "I…. Thank you, H. I swear I'll keep them safe. I'd die before I let anything happen to them."

Horvan arched his eyebrows. "Yeah, well, don't let it come to that."

Crank stewed. He wanted to rip chunks off Brick, but he couldn't deny Horvan spoke the truth. Brick had always been there for them. He'd come running whenever someone needed him. If this was going to be the last time he saw Brick, did he want there to be anger between them?

Say something.

Crank shuddered out a breath. "Hey, Brick? I don't hate you."

Brick stiffened. "I appreciate that."

Crank wasn't done. "Don't go thinking I've forgiven you, okay? But I… I needed you to understand that."

"Fair enough." He was quiet for a moment. "Crank? Vic? I know it doesn't help, but I have to tell you how sorry I am. I only saw my parents, not how this could hurt anyone else. I swear to God, I never thought they'd hurt Saul."

Vic tensed, and Crank reached out and put a hand on his knee. Vic sagged against Crank. "We know. Not that it makes the situation any easier, but… it helps. Thanks."

"There's a helipad," Horvan called back to them. "And there's a chopper on it. Looks like we've got company."

"Can you see anyone down there?" Roadkill hollered above the noise of the blades.

Horvan shook his head. "Not a soul. It's eerie. Surely there should be—"

"What is it?" Crank didn't like the sudden silence.

"There are two people down there, but whoever they are, they're not aiming at us. Weapons at the ready, guys. We're going in."

Within a matter of minutes, the chopper touched down, and Roadkill slid open the door, his Glock in one hand. He stared at Rael and Dellan. "Wait here like Horvan said until we say it's safe to come out."

"Stand down!" a voice bellowed from outside. "Stand down."

Vic froze. "I know that voice." His face lit up. "It's okay, guys." And before Crank could stop him, Vic was out of the helicopter and running toward the figures on the helipad.

"What the fuck?" Crank launched himself from the chopper and raced after him. "Are you nuts?" Horvan, Roadkill, and Hashtag followed, their weapons still drawn.

Vic reached the two men and turned to face Crank, his eyes shining. "It's all right." The taller of the strangers beside Vic smiled at them. His long dark hair was tied back, and he wore jeans and a black leather jacket.

Whoa. Who is this guy? Crank had an overwhelming urge to bow his head. The man exuded power.

Horvan strode across the helipad. "And just who is telling us to stand down?" Roadkill and Hashtag flanked him.

Vic gestured to the man at his side. "This is Aelryn. He's one of the Fridan leaders." He turned to Aelryn. "I don't think I've ever seen you outside of an office before."

"These are exceptional circumstances." Aelryn's voice was deep. He held out his hand to Horvan. "I've heard a great many good things about your organization, Mr. Kojik."

Crank scowled. "Look, I'm really happy we've got such a kickass rep, but can we save the introductions for later?" Aelryn raised his eyebrows.

"We need to search for our mate," Vic explained.

"Of course. You're safe to look for him. The main building has been deserted. Only a few teachers and cafeteria staff remain."

Horvan blinked. "Where *is* everyone?"

"We have yet to discover that," Aelryn informed him. "But your colleague is correct. Talk can wait."

"Can we come out now?" Rael sounded pissed.

"My mates are here to help with the students," Horvan told Aelryn.

"Your…?" Aelryn's face broke into a huge smile. "Then they are most welcome."

Horvan beckoned, and Rael and Dellan climbed out of the chopper, Brick following them.

"Come with me." Aelryn pointed off to the left. "The student accommodation is the farthest building on the site. Some of my team are already there."

Dellan came to a stop in front of him, and his breathing hitched. Crank could understand that reaction. He was having a hard time resisting the urge to kneel.

Whoever Aelryn was, he was Someone.

Then Crank's skin started itching, the sensation of ants crawling over it worse than ever. "We have to go. Now."

Horvan nodded. "Roadkill, Hashtag, you're with us. Let's go find Saul."

Aelryn gestured to the other man, who so far had remained silent. "Take Scott with you. He has medical training. It might come in useful."

Crank couldn't wait a second longer. He raced toward the largest building, constructed of redbrick and sandstone. "Let's start in there." Another rush of adrenaline spiked through him, and his pulse quickened.

Vic was at his side in a heartbeat, the others behind them. They crossed the lawn, heading for the doors. Crank pushed them open and ran into the cool interior. Once everyone was inside, Horvan took control.

"Hashtag, Roadkill, go to the top floor and work your way down. Search everywhere."

"I'm gonna start in the basement," Crank informed him. "Wherever they had him, it was someplace dark."

"You and Vic check it out. Scott, go with them. Stay in touch."

Crank didn't wait to hear another word. He pelted through a large hallway filled with marble columns and busts, searching for an entrance. Vic kicked open every door they encountered, but all they found were offices and meeting rooms, and not a soul in sight. By the time they found the stairs that led down to the basement, Crank's chest had tightened so much that he was fighting to draw breath.

At the foot of the stairs were three doors, and Vic made short work of the first one. "Closet!" he yelled. Crank kicked down the second, and they found themselves in the empty furnace room.

"Where is he?" Crank growled.

Vic froze. "Wait." He sniffed. "He was here! I can smell his... scent."

Crank was no fool. "You mean you can smell his blood." Rage surged through him.

Vic nodded, his face ashen. "A lot of it too."

Pain lanced through Crank's chest. "He's not dead, okay?" He wouldn't even entertain the thought.

"This last door leads to a tunnel," Scott called to them. "It looks as if it stretches for miles, and there are a ton of doors leading off it."

"Then we kick down every door until we find him," Crank gritted out.

"Wait. Looking for Saul blindly is useless. We're going to try something." Vic held out his hands. "Come here."

"We don't have time for—"

"Crank. Take my hands, now." The urgency in Vic's voice pierced through the layers of fear and panic that smothered him. As soon as their hands touched, a little of the anger that filled him ebbed away. "That's it. Close your eyes."

Crank did as he was told, ignoring the blood that pounded in his ears.

"Okay. Now, what do you see?"

Saul's image was right there, only his face wasn't bloodied and swollen. He was smiling.

"I see him," Crank whispered. His heart fluttered. "He's taller than you, but a little shorter than me. Green eyes."

"Take his hand."

In his head, Crank extended a hand to Saul, laced their fingers, and held on to him.

"Now... talk to him. Not out loud, but in your mind."

It should have felt ridiculous, but Crank was past caring. *Saul. Where are you?* Saul's lips didn't move, and a fresh wave of panic flowed through Crank.

"Again."

Crank focused on the man before him. *Saul. Please, answer me. Help us to find you.* Then he shivered as another figure stepped into view.

It was Vic.

"H-how are you doing that?"

Vic laid one hand on Saul and the other on Crank. *Saul. Can you hear us?*

Crank took a step closer, until he could feel warmth radiating off Saul's body. *Saul. We're here. Help us find you.*

Then his heart hammered as two words filled his head. *Vic? Crank?*

Vic's grip tightened on Crank's hands. *Yes, babe. I'm here. Crank's here too. Bring us to you. Where are you? What do you see? Tell us anything that'll help us find you faster.*

There was a long pause, but before Crank could ask him again, Saul's voice was in his head. *Poison makes it… hard to focus. There's a door. Red. There's a… barred window. I think it's barred from the outside.*

Crank tugged Vic by the hand and charged out of the furnace room to where Scott waited for them next to the open door that led to the tunnel. "Look for a red door with a barred window in it!" he yelled to Scott. The three of them ran along the dimly lit passage until Vic stopped.

"Here!" He peered through the window. "Fuck, I see him."

Crank yanked at the handle, but it wouldn't budge. Vic aimed his gun at the lock, and Crank grabbed his arm. "No, that won't work." He delivered a mule kick to the bottom corner of the door, then repeated it until the door gave way. When it finally opened, Crank lurched through it, his heart racing.

Saul lay on the stone floor, his coveralls dark with blood. He appeared to be barely conscious. Scott knelt beside him, two fingers at Saul's neck. "His pulse is thready."

"He said he's been poisoned," Crank blurted.

Scott blinked, then recovered. "Okay. He needs urgent medical attention."

Crank touched his earpiece. "We've found him, H. He needs to go to a hospital right the fuck now." Then he eased his arms beneath Saul's limp body and lifted him, cradling him against his chest. Saul stirred, and Crank heaved a sigh of relief.

"Crank," Saul moaned.

"I've got you. *We've* got you." Crank staggered to his feet, not letting go of his precious burden. Scott ran ahead, and Vic didn't move from Crank's side as they left the room and headed toward the light.

Hold on, Saul. Hold on, baby.

CHAPTER NINETEEN

Horvan stood on the helipad, watching the chopper as it rose into the sky.

Christ, he looks bad. Horvan wasn't usually a praying kinda guy, but he couldn't help sending up a silent entreaty. *Save him, okay? They need him.* Horvan had never seen Crank in such a state. His clothing was covered in Saul's blood, and the sight of it made Horvan's heart ache for Crank. *If Saul dies, does part of Crank die as well? Vic too?*

It didn't bear thinking about. Horvan couldn't imagine how he'd feel if anything happened to Rael or Dellan.

"We can do nothing more for him," Aelryn murmured beside him. "I assure you, he'll be in the best hands."

"Thanks for letting us use your helicopter." Aelryn had insisted, and Scott had gone with Vic and Crank.

"Scott will keep me informed." Aelryn studied him for a moment. "Your care for your men is touching. Think positively." He patted Horvan's arm. "Walk with me. We have much to discuss." He pointed to a nearby building with gables. "That is the dining hall. We've assembled all the students in there, and my team is putting together a meal for them. It won't be anything gourmet, but it will be nutritious. Most of the kitchen staff have fled, but those who've remained, we've informed them we'll cover their wages. And from now on, we don't give *anyone* access to the students until they've been vetted by us."

"You've commandeered the school? How big a team did you bring?" Horvan asked.

"We are nine in total, but plans are already in progress to bring in more people. I've called in our best operatives, which includes counselors. They'll be needed." Aelryn glanced at Horvan. "Your mate is impressive."

Horvan smiled. "Which one? I think they're both awesome."

"Rael—is that his name? When we walked into the accommodation halls, we found utter panic. The teachers who'd stayed were as confused as the students. They couldn't believe the school authorities had simply abandoned them. We were surrounded by the children, some as young as ten, and all clamoring at the same time to have their questions answered. Rael checked there were no humans present, shifted, let out one mighty roar—and there was total silence."

Good for Rael. Then he froze. "They… they just walked away and left over a thousand kids to fend for themselves? What kind of bastards are these people?"

Aelryn shook his head. "We've done a head count. There are nine hundred and ten students. At first, we feared the others had run away, but we've since talked with the those who remained." His serene features tightened. "It seems the rest were taken in the early hours. A number of students reported hearing vehicles, apparently for transporting the missing children."

"But why take ninety or so kids?"

"That we have not yet discovered. Some of my team are talking with the older students as we speak. Those who remain are safe. That is the main thing. We will take care of them."

"But for how long?" Horvan wanted to know. "Surely their parents must be informed."

Aelryn paused at the door to the dining hall. "No phones are allowed here among the student body. We can only assume those in power wished to control the flow of information. Each student will be given access to a phone, to call their parents. Those parents who wish to collect their child can make arrangements to do so."

"Be prepared. Some parents might not want their son or daughter back." Horvan could still recall Jamie's revelations.

Aelryn's expression hardened. "Then we will find homes for all those in that situation, with people who will care for them." He pushed the door open, and they walked into the hall. Tables filled the space, and along each sat rows of kids aged from under ten to maybe in their late teens.

Horvan had never been in one place with so many shifters before, and for a moment it shocked him into stillness.

"It's an impressive sight," Aelryn commented, "until you remember why they are here. Or rather, the intentions of those who created this place. A seat of learning? But to learn what, exactly? To look upon man as a substandard creature? To plan for a future that makes me shudder to think about it?"

Horvan had expected the air to be filled with chatter, but few spoke.

"They're stunned, and I can't blame them," Aelryn murmured. "It must be a hard pill to swallow."

Horvan scanned the tables and soon found Rael. He was sitting with a group of ten or so kids, and he was talking earnestly to them. Most regarded him with blank expressions, but some were clearly agitated.

Hey. Everything okay there?

Rael's head snapped up, and he sought Horvan out. *Hey. Oh God, Horvan, this is such a mess. They're totally bewildered. I'm trying to calm them, but....*

At one end of the nearest table, a tall, gangly boy rose and approached them. His eyes widened at Horvan's holstered weapons. He addressed Aelryn.

"Sir, what will happen to me? My parents... they...." The boy swallowed, his chest heaving.

Aelryn laid his hand on the boy's shoulder. "Don't be afraid. If for some reason you can't go home, we'll find you a place with someone who will care for you."

The boy nodded, shivering. "Thank you." He returned to his seat.

Horvan's breathing caught, and Aelryn touched his arm. "You feel it, don't you? Sorrow overwhelms me too. That child already senses that whatever bonds he shared with his parents, they are dissolving, so fast that he cannot prevent it. And what one feels, others must also." His face tightened. "We have much to do here."

One of Aelryn's team strode toward them. "Everyone has been fed, sir. And I've been informed three choppers are about to land, with reinforcements. We've also conducted a search throughout all buildings. All have been emptied. Everyone left behind is now in here."

"Thank you." When the man didn't move, Aelryn stilled. "What is it, Niall?"

"Sir, we've been talking with the students, asking about the missing children. There's a pattern to those who were taken. The same comments keep occurring." Niall expelled a breath. "I think they took the cream of the crop with them and left the rest. It's as if they thought them expendable."

Aelryn's face tightened once more. "I see."

He's not here. Horvan, he's not here!

147

Horvan jerked his head to see Dellan hurrying toward them, Brick at his side. Dellan came to a halt in front of him, and Horvan was dismayed to see he was shaking.

"You're sure?" Horvan cupped his cheek.

Dellan nodded. "We went with Aelryn's men who were searching. There's no sign of Jamie." He shivered. "This is not good."

"We've looked everywhere," Brick added. "We didn't find my parents either, but then there's no reason why they should be here."

"Who is Jamie?" Aelryn asked.

"My half brother. He works for the school."

"He's the reason we learned about this place," Horvan added.

"And they know it." Brick's face was a picture of misery. "Because of me."

Aelryn nodded. "Then they've taken him also. And I have an idea where."

Horvan felt the shock ripple through Dellan before it registered on his face. "One of those camps Hashtag is searching for? The ones Vic told us about?"

Aelryn blinked. "You're looking too? Then perhaps we should combine forces. We need to find them as soon as possible—before it's too late."

Horvan frowned. "What do you mean?"

"Just this. Rather than confront us and waste time and manpower, they abandoned this school. What if they do the same with *every* school? Take a select number and leave the rest? They might also reason that if we can find the schools, we can find the camps. And what will they do with all those they hold captive?"

Dellan's face was white. "My father. And now Jamie too."

Aelryn nodded. "We can deploy our people to take care of the schools, wherever they are, but the camps must be our focus."

Horvan couldn't make Aelryn out. He seemed Horvan's age but endowed with such gravitas that Horvan felt cowed before him. "Who are you? You're not just a leader of the Fridans, are you?"

Aelryn smiled. "I am a direct descendant of Ansfrid."

Dellan's eyes grew wide. "Wow. That kind of makes you… shifter royalty."

Aelryn laughed. "I suppose it does. Although *your* lineage is equally impressive." When Dellan's brow furrowed, Aelryn continued. "Your father, Jake Carson? We've traced his line back almost as far as Ansfrid. But enough of such matters. We should go to the main building and see what information we can still find there. If they haven't destroyed everything."

"Two of my team are already there." Horvan had left Hashtag and Roadkill in the main building, with instructions to search for anything that could help them.

"They won't find anything," Niall told him. "We checked. All paper records have been shredded, and they wiped the hard drives of every PC."

Horvan tapped his earpiece. "Hashtag, you got a sec?"

"Sure. What's up?"

"I've been informed the hard drives have been wiped."

Hashtag cackled. "Yeah, but they didn't physically destroy the drives. And as you well know—'cause I've told you often enough—it's possible to recover data from a wiped hard drive. As long as it's plugged in, data is continually being written and read to the hard drive. Wiping it doesn't directly erase the data from it." There was a cracking sound and another cackle.

"You cracked your knuckles, didn't you?"

"Lemme get to work on it, H. I'll let you know what I find." Hashtag disconnected.

Horvan smiled to himself. *I have a damn good team.* He placed his hand on Dellan's shoulder. "Come on. Standing here won't find them. Let's go see what the guys turn up." The waves of misery rolling off Dellan tugged at his heart.

Dellan nodded. "A more suspicious man might think those bastards really have it in for my family." *Because I'm still not happy about Mom's death. I think they got rid of her to get her out of the way so she wouldn't provide an obstacle to their plans.*

Horvan had reached the same conclusion, but he'd kept it locked out of sight.

I'm coming too. Rael got up from his place at the table and hurried over to them. *We need to make sure Saul is going to make it.*

Horvan intended staying until he was certain there was nothing more to be gleaned; then he'd be on a chopper with the group, heading for whichever medical facility Saul had ended up in.

We're going to be there for Crank.

VIC STARED through the glass at Saul lying in bed, surrounded by monitors, tubes, and wires going everywhere, against a constant soundtrack of *beeps* and *whirs*. White bandages covered his wounds. Saul's eyes were closed, and there was only a confused, muddled response when Vic tried to reach his thoughts.

He had no idea if it was still day. There were no windows in Saul's room or in the hallway, and the passage of time was marked by the rhythmic *chirps* and *clicks* of the machinery around the bed and the slow *drip, drip, drip* of the IV. Farther off he caught a muffled voice as someone was paged over the intercom, and farther still was the soft *whoosh* of automatic doors sliding open and closed.

Saul's color had returned, which was no bad thing, because his pallor had shaken Vic to his core. He had no idea how much blood or painkillers they'd pumped into Saul, but they'd obviously worked wonders. He was now breathing without the aid of a ventilator, with only an oxygen tube under his nose.

Crank sat in a chair beside the bed, his head resting on Saul's blanket-covered leg. He'd fallen asleep holding Saul's hand, and the sight sent warmth spreading slowly through Vic.

"Mr. Ryder?"

Vic turned toward the soft-spoken doctor. "Yes? Do you have the test results?"

Dr. Martinez nodded. "We got there eventually, but I'll admit, it had us baffled."

"Why? Did you discover what the poison was?"

The doctor consulted his tablet. "The toxin in his bloodstream comes from the saliva of an animal. The northern short-tailed shrew, to be exact, which paralyzes and subdues its prey with a bite. The toxin's strong enough to kill small mammals, but it usually only produces pain, swelling, and muscular problems in humans who attempt to handle the shrew. Mr. Emory doesn't appear to have any bites. In fact, his wounds are more consistent with those inflicted by claws. But the amount of toxin in his body is considerably larger than would be expected from a bite." He cocked his head to one side. "Do you have any idea how he came to be in this state?"

"None, I'm afraid." Vic's heart pounded. "Will he... will he survive?"

Dr. Martinez smiled. "Now that we've identified the toxin? Yes. He's strong, and his body is fighting it. He'll be here for a few days at least, though." He patted Vic's arm. "Try not to worry. He's going to pull through this." He glanced at Saul and smiled. "Now you should wake your friend and tell him the good news." And with that he walked off.

Vic entered the room and walked over to the bed. He pulled another chair closer and sat, taking Saul's other hand in his, trying to ignore the machine noises. Crank showed no sign of waking, and Vic let him sleep.

"Vic?" Saul croaked.

He snapped to attention, his gaze focusing on Saul's face. "Hey," he whispered. "Welcome back." He picked up the plastic water cup and placed the straw between Saul's lips. "Here, have a sip."

Saul sucked on it, then stopped, slowly turning his head to stare at Crank. He said nothing for a moment; then his gaze flickered back to Vic. "I-I know him. Not like from a picture, or…." He looked at Crank. "I know his voice, his eyes." Saul blinked. "I had a dream. He was in it, and you were there too."

"If you find a little dog called Toto, let me know," Vic quipped. Inside, he was buzzing. *He's awake. And he's going to be okay.*

Saul's forehead creased. "Huh?"

"Never mind."

Saul started to pull his hand from Crank's grasp, but Vic reached over and stopped him. "Don't. He's been by your bed almost every second since they brought you in. I had to force him to get up and go to the bathroom."

Saul's frown deepened. "Why?"

"I admit, I don't know Crank very well, but I know fear when I see it." Vic gazed fondly at their sleeping mate. "He's been terrified, watching you lying there. He wanted to do something—anything—to make you feel better, so he took your hand."

Saul stared at Crank. "That dream…. He said we were mates."

"We can talk about this when you're stronger," Vic said gently.

"Excuse me?" Saul's gaze met his, and something flickered in his eyes. "Tell me now."

Vic bit back a smile. "That doctor said you were strong. He has *no* idea." He sighed. "It wasn't a dream. Well, not exactly." Saul arched his eyebrows, and Vic relented. "We *are* mates. All three of us. And no, I can't explain it, so please don't ask me to. All I know is, he's ours, and that's why he's being so protective of you. He doesn't want you hurt more than you've already been."

"Ours," Saul echoed. He touched his lips. "In my dream he kissed me. Told me you were both coming for me." His gaze grew blank, as if he was trying to get his head around the situation.

Vic got out of the chair and perched on the edge of the bed. "I think if you told him to go away, he would."

Saul gaped. "But if he's our mate, why would he do that?"

"Because he doesn't want to take me away from you."

Saul looked at Crank. "It's the weirdest feeling."

"What is?"

"None of this makes any sense, and yet...." Saul brought his hand to his chest. "It's as if he's in here, in a space that was made for him, a space I wasn't even aware of—until that dream." His breathing hitched. "He's waking up."

Crank hadn't moved a muscle. "How do you know?" Vic demanded. Then he gasped as a voice filled his head.

God, you two are noisy.

Saul gave a hard swallow. "How... how did you do that?"

Crank raised his head from the bed. "I thought Vic already covered that part. Mates, remember?"

Saul's mouth opened, but then he narrowed his gaze. "Wait. No. I'm not a part of this." He tugged his hand free of Crank's, and Vic couldn't miss the hurt in Crank's eyes.

A sharp pain lanced through Vic's chest. "What?"

"How do you make that out?" Crank demanded.

Saul stared at him. "I know, okay? Fielding told me everything."

Vic struggled to breathe. "Who the fuck is Fielding, and what did he tell you?"

CHAPTER TWENTY

SAUL WAS having difficulty knowing what to believe.

The shock of hearing Crank's voice in his head had been overtaken by the recollection of Fielding's revelations. *But was he telling the truth?*

There was only one way to find out.

"Fielding was the one in charge. The one who had me shredded like I was nothing more than waste paper." He could still feel Alec's claws slicing through his coveralls, his flesh. Flesh that still hurt, though not the way it had, with a pain that had rocked through him.

"And? What did he say?" Vic demanded.

Saul strove to breathe evenly, aware of the cool flow of oxygen into his nostrils. "He told me you and Crank had... bonded while you were in Chicago. That you were mates."

Vic blinked. "Yes, we *are* mates. All three of us, like I told you."

"But how could he know that when *you* didn't?" He stilled. "You didn't, did you?"

"Not until Crank and I shared the same dream when they were... torturing you. That was when I first got the idea."

"And as for *how* he knew, someone told him about Vic being in my dreams," Crank added. "He couldn't have known we were mates. He was lying, playing on your fears."

"And he used that. He wanted access to the shifter archive. He said if I helped him... he said they had a drug that could break the mate bond." Saul's throat thickened.

Vic picked up the cup again and fed the straw between his lips. "Drink."

Saul took a long pull on it, swallowing the cool liquid. When Vic removed it, he sighed. "I didn't, by the way. I wouldn't tell him a thing. That was when he got really pissed." He paused. "He *was* lying, wasn't he? You haven't bonded, have you?" Then he froze. "Wait. I had a dream too." He stared at Vic. "You were in some house, and you were.... You two were fucking. You told me you

153

weren't coming back, that you were gonna stay with him." The memory of the pain created by that awful nightmare flooded back.

Vic frowned. "When was this?"

"Before you left for Chicago."

Vic cocked his head to one side. "And Crank was in this dream too? You saw his face? I said his name?"

"Yes. Wait—no. Maybe? And no, I didn't see his face. I just saw you riding his dick." Saul's body heat rose.

Vic held Saul's hand. "Then I think it was only a dream, not one of 'those' dreams," he said, air-quoting. "I know that makes no sense, but when you've had a few of them, you get a sense for the ones that mean something."

"Like the one you had about Crank?"

Vic nodded.

Saul pondered for a moment. "I think you're right. When they'd gone, leaving me in that room, I…. Crank *was* there. I could feel his presence. And before you found me, you were both there, touching me."

Crank sat on the bed, both men bracketing Saul. He retook Saul's hand. "Okay. I kissed Vic before I even knew you existed. That's on me. I-I couldn't help myself. It was like my whole body was yelling, 'Kiss him!'" He swallowed. "Like it's doing right now." Before Saul could get a word out, Crank leaned in and brushed his lips against Saul's in a kiss that bordered on sweet.

"Hey. No fair." Then Vic was there, his lips joining theirs, and they shared a kiss that started out as tender, but it wasn't long before tongues got involved and blood surged through Saul's body in a southerly direction.

Need a little help with that? A firm hand stroked his dick through the blanket, but it was Crank's voice in his head, Crank's hand giving his cock a leisurely massage.

Jesus, that feels good. Saul broke the kiss, gasping as Crank slowly worked his shaft. *It would feel even better without the blanket.*

Vic laughed. "Excuse me? Can I remind you we're in a hospital? And you're supposed to be recovering."

Crank chuckled. "Part of him recovered faster than the rest." Then he withdrew his hand, and Saul wanted to snarl at him to put it *right the fuck back.*

Vic grinned and moved in closer, nuzzling Saul's ear. "When we get you out of here, *then* we can play. But until then, get comfy, mate. We'll give you a taste of what's coming." He locked gazes with Saul. "Your world is about to be rocked."

Before Saul could ask what that meant, an image slammed into his head with such force, a gasp tumbled from his lips. It was Crank, on his knees, sucking Vic.

Oh my God. They looked amazing together. And far from resenting the sight, it was turning him on. Saul watched Vic's glistening dick sliding in and out of Crank's mouth. Vic's belly was taut as he leaned back on his hands, rocking his body as he thrust between Crank's lips. *Christ*, the noises Crank made as he bobbed his head up and down on Vic's shaft....

Vic's eyes met his. *You need to feel this too.*

In Saul's head, Crank stopped, shifting across to where Saul lay, and Saul knew what was coming. He shuddered as Crank's warm wet mouth surrounded his dick, unable to lie still, his hips in constant motion. Vic's lips fused with Saul's, and Saul moaned into the kiss as Crank took him deep.

Then it hit him. *If they can do this, so can I.*

The scene shifted, and Crank lay on his back, his hands on Vic's head, urging him deeper as Saul plunged into the ass he loved.

Aw fuck. That's hot. Vic groaned around Crank's cock as Saul drove his shaft home. Saul glanced up to meet Crank's smile, then reached out and pulled him into a kiss. Sounds filled the room as Crank moaned into Saul's mouth. Skin slapped against flesh as Saul drove into that tight channel around his cock with all the force he could muster, and Vic keened around the dick that stretched his lips.

Saul's heart sped up. This wasn't a fantasy. This was his future.

Crank coughed, and the images were gone. "Whoa. This is what I have to look forward to? 'Cause that's quite a leap, considering kissing a guy is as far as I've gone."

Saul gaped at Vic. "Oh my God. You weren't lying. He's straight."

Vic's eyes twinkled. "Yes." He glanced at Crank. "But we're going to change all that." Crank gave an exaggerated swallow and wiped his brow, and the sight was so comical, Vic burst out laughing. "I'm teasing you. We're not in the business of conversion therapy."

Saul laughed too, before a wave of fatigue rolled over him. "Just thinking about this wears me out."

Two hands met gently on his bandaged torso, and two pairs of eyes regarded him with obvious concern. "Then sleep," Vic urged. "We'll be here when you wake up."

"I'm not going anywhere," Crank assured him.

The door opened, and a guy Saul didn't recognize stepped into the room, carrying a cardboard tray with three polystyrene cups. His eyes widened when he saw Saul. "Hey, you're awake."

"Don't tell me." Saul managed a grin. "This is the fourth mate."

Vic laughed. "This is Scott. He's one of the Fridans, and he made sure the hospital knew what to expect when we landed."

Scott smiled. "I'm flattered, but I already have a mate. And finding *that* out was a big enough shock." His brow furrowed. "You look tired."

"He *is* tired," Vic confirmed. He leaned over and kissed Saul's forehead. "Now sleep."

Crank moved closer and kissed him in exactly the same spot. "What he said. There'll be time enough for talking when you've had more rest."

The wave of exhaustion was too much to fight, but he had to share what he'd learned. "Wait, no. I have to tell you—" But the men in his head were surrounding Saul with warmth and comfort, and he couldn't keep his eyes open. Whatever he wanted to say would wait, for a while.

VIC LED them out of Saul's room to the chairs in the hallway. "We can sit here." He took the proffered coffee. "I need this."

"He's going to be all right," Scott affirmed. "Have they worked out what's gotten into his bloodstream?" Vic told him about Dr. Martinez's diagnosis, and his face clouded. "How in hell did they do this? Bring half a dozen northern short-tailed shrew shifters—dear Lord, that's a tongue twister if ever I heard one—and have them shift and *nibble* on him? Because I didn't see bite marks." He shuddered. "Only those wounds on his chest and back."

"Look, can we change the subject?" Crank frowned. "Because something is bugging me. I thought mates were rare. Like, really, *really* rare. And that only shifters have mates. And yet here we are. Vic has two human mates, and you've got one too." He paused. "Are you a shifter?"

Scott nodded. "Yes, but nothing as majestic as Vic here."

Crank's frown was back. "Whatever you are, you're amazing, and don't let anyone tell you anything different." He bit his lip.

"You're dying to ask what I shift into, aren't you?"

"Well, yeah, but I figured it was kinda rude to ask."

Scott met Vic's gaze. "I like your mate."

"I'm getting pretty fond of him too," Vic murmured. He chuckled when Crank arched his eyebrows. Then he remembered he'd promised to address the issue of attraction. *Later. When Scott's not around.*

Scott returned his attention to Crank. "I'm a red panda."

Crank's jaw dropped. "Oh my God, how fucking adorable is that?"

Scott laughed. "Okay, I definitely like you."

"You said finding your mate was a shock," Vic commented. "Why was that?"

"Because like Crank, I believed in the rarity of mates. I've been working with the Fridans for a number of years, and recently I was assigned to work with Aelryn. So imagine my surprise when I walked into his office, and suddenly all my senses were on alert, telling me this man *meant* something to me. And then to find he had the same reaction." Scott gave a shy smile. "We don't have the telepathic connection that you three seem to share, or Horvan and his mates. But after meeting not one, but two sets of three mates, I'm optimistic."

"What about?" Vic inquired.

"That somewhere out there is our mate, and when we find him or her, we'll be complete. We'll have what *you* have."

"Her?" Crank stared at him. "You'd be okay with having a female mate?"

Scott nodded. "Both Aelryn and I are bi, so we'd be happy having a man or a woman. It wouldn't matter anyway. They would be part of us."

A phone buzzed, and all three of them checked. It was Scott's. His face glowed. "Hey. Yes, I'm still at the hospital. Hang on." He hugged his phone to his chest. "Guys, it's Aelryn."

As if Vic needed to hear. Scott had lit up like a Christmas tree at his voice. "Listen, if you want to go to him, that's fine. You were wonderful. Thank you for all your help."

Scott beamed. "You're welcome." He brought his phone back to his ear. "Yes, that's fine. ... Okay, I'll tell them. See you soon." He disconnected. "Horvan said to tell you he'll be on his way soon, with his group in the chopper. And I'm to go back to the school." He stood, his hand extended. "So I guess this is goodbye, for now at least."

Vic ignored the hand and lurched to his feet to seize Scott in a tight hug. "Thank you." When Vic released him, Crank gave him a brief hug too. Then Scott grabbed his jacket from the chair, picked up his cup of coffee, and walked off down the hallway.

"Wonder what H has discovered at the school," Crank murmured. "I hope to God it's something we can use to help us stop these bastards." He shook his head. "I gotta be honest. When we were back in Idaho, listening to that guy's chilling voice, I don't think any of us had a fucking clue how big this was gonna get."

"I don't think we had any idea how ruthless our enemy could be." Vic set his jaw. "I don't care that they're shifters too. Anyone who can have such a blatant disregard for life…." He locked gazes with Crank. "We can't underestimate them ever again."

Crank leaned forward, his hands wrapped around his cup. "So what now?"

"What do you mean?"

"What I said. What happens now? You and Saul have your life, I have my job. What are we supposed to do?"

Vic sighed. "You're asking *me*? I'm on the same page as you—just running to catch up." There were conversations to be had before any plans could be made.

And air to be cleared.

"HAVE YOU made arrangements to return to Chicago?" Aelryn asked Horvan as they waited while the pilot of the Kaman Seasprite did his preflight checks. It was getting late, and Horvan was bone tired and yearning for his bed.

The prospect of curling up around his mates might have made the yearning more acute.

"Not yet. I've got someone working on it." Horvan had called Duke to see if they could hitch a ride from somewhere. It might take them a while to get back to Homer Glen, but nowhere near the fourteen or so hours it would take to drive that distance.

First I need to pick up Crank. Horvan hoped Saul was in a more stable condition. The last thing he needed was a distracted Crank. Then he considered the situation. *Will he want to leave them?* Gods knew Horvan hated even the *idea* of being parted from Rael and Dellan.

And at some point we need to address the Brick situation too. That was Dellan.

Horvan nodded. *I know. Not looking forward to that part.* Brick appeared miserable as fuck standing next to Hashtag, and Horvan's heart went out to him. *How would I feel if we'd gotten here too late and Saul had been dead?* Horvan wouldn't have needed to deal with Brick—either Vic or Crank would have torn him apart, and Horvan wouldn't have blamed them.

You wouldn't let them do that. The firm edge to Rael's voice spoke of confidence.

Horvan sent up a silent prayer of thanks for his mates. They truly *got* him.

"And I meant what I said." Aelryn's eyes glinted. "We should combine forces and take the fight to them, once we have located any of the camps."

It made a lot of sense, and Horvan intended discussing the prospect with Duke when they got home.

Aelryn stared out at the darkness beyond the floodlit helipad. "I must confess, this situation with Vic and his mates… I do not understand it."

Horvan had been thinking the same thing. "How can a shifter suddenly have two *human* mates?" He peered at Aelryn. "And you really have no idea?" He'd hoped Aelryn had a line on it, because if anyone did, it would be someone like him, from a bloodline that stretched back to shifter antiquity.

"Fate is a wild and capricious thing. Who can say why or how something will happen? I can tell you, far better men than I are pondering this very question as we speak."

"Now that's what I call an enigmatic response." A not entirely satisfying one.

Aelryn sighed. "All it will ever be is theories. If it's the Fates or mysticism or biology, no one can ever *truly* know."

"H?" Roadkill pointed to where one of Aelryn's men was running toward them across the tarmac. One glance at the guy's expression was enough to tell Horvan this was *not* gonna be good.

He came to a halt in front of Aelryn, leaned in, and whispered in his ear. When all the color slid from Aelryn's tanned face, Horvan's suspicions were confirmed.

"What's happened?"

The man took a step back, his head bowed, and Aelryn drew in a breath. "My men have been conducting an in-depth search of the entire grounds," he said, his deep voice lowered. "They have found two bodies."

Aw fuck no. "Who are they? Any clue?"

Aelryn gave a brief nod. "They'd been concealed in one of the rooms off the tunnel that connects the main building with the rest of the school. Initial identification would point to them being…." He swallowed, and his gaze went to Brick.

Horvan's heart sank. *Those bastards.*

Brick jerked his head up. "What is it? What's wrong?"

Aelryn walked slowly over to him. "You need to be strong, my friend," he said softly.

Brick's face was the color of milk. "Tell me," he croaked.

"We require you to identify two bodies."

Brick took an involuntary step back, his eyes widening. "No," he whispered. "I did what they asked." His eyes met Horvan's. "Why did they do this if I was cooperating?"

"You don't understand." Aelryn's voice was so tender. "One of my medics has examined them. He believes they've been dead about three weeks or so."

Brick swayed on his feet, and Hashtag caught him, putting his arm around him. "I gotcha," he murmured. He caught Horvan's gaze. "Me and Roadkill will go with him. He's not doing this on his own."

We're all going with him. Dellan walked over to Brick, Rael joining him.

You got that right. Horvan squared his shoulders. "Let's go do this."

CHAPTER TWENTY-ONE

CRANK AND Vic sat on either side of Saul's hospital bed. When Crank's phone rang, Vic knew instantly from his expression who was calling. "Horvan's here, isn't he?"

"Almost. He says we need to talk."

Vic patted his hand. "Then go talk. We'll be here when you're done. Saul's not going anywhere, and neither am I."

"You sure?"

He sighed. "Will you just go? We're going to be fine, okay?" Besides, he needed Saul to himself for a while.

They had something to clear up.

Crank got up and walked to the door. "I won't be long."

Vic waved his hand. "Will you get out of here and go see your boss?"

Crank rolled his eyes. "He ain't my boss." Then he was gone.

Vic returned his attention to the bed. "I know you're awake," he murmured.

Saul opened his eyes. "Damn. I'm not gonna be able to hide a thing from you, am I? This telepathy business sucks."

"I'm sure there are ways around it." Vic made a mental note to talk to Horvan, Dellan, and Rael. They had to have figured *something* out, because none of them looked as pissed as Saul sounded.

Saul stiffened. "Er… can you see my dreams?" His face was flushed.

Vic arched his eyebrows. "No, but now you've got me curious. What was going on in your dream that you don't want me to see?"

"Oh, nothing," Saul replied quickly.

Too quickly.

Vic grinned. "Now you *have* to tell me."

Saul glared at him. "I was dreaming about Crank, okay? Well, you and Crank. And me. And we might have been… fucking."

"*Might* have been?" Vic was enjoying himself.

"Hey, you had dreams about Crank, he had dreams about you, I'm just catching up. And can I say—about freakin' time? I was feeling left out."

161

"Was it a hot dream?"

Saul bit his lip. "Hot enough that I'm annoyed I woke up. And as for *how* hot—" He grinned. "—here, lemme show you." Saul closed his eyes, and warmth stole through Vic's body. Crank's dick was buried in Vic's throat, slamming into his face, while Saul knelt at Vic's ass, matching Crank thrust for thrust.

Vic swallowed, then coughed. "Yeah, okay, that's… that's one hot dream."

Saul's eyes popped open. "So let me get back to it? I wanna be there for the finale."

"I'll let you go back to sleep in a bit." He cleared his throat. "We need to talk." He picked up the plastic cup and gave Saul another drink.

Saul pulled on the straw, his Adam's apple bobbing. Then he sagged back onto the pillow. "What about?"

"The way you left things when you went on the mission," he said simply.

"Oh. That."

"I get that your mindset might be a little different to what it was then."

Saul blinked. "Hmm. Let's see. I've got both of you in my head. I'd call that pretty momentous. Of course, that doesn't make the emotions any easier to deal with. I've never had to share you with anyone before. Not something I do well." When Vic frowned, Saul locked gazes with him. "Despite these dreams I'm suddenly having, until now I've never even *considered* sharing you, babe, so you have to know, this whole situation is confusing as fuck."

"Tell me about it. I've been in a state of constant self-loathing ever since I became aware of this attraction to Crank." An attraction Vic could no longer fight.

"So what happens now?"

Vic sighed. "Crank asked me the same question."

Saul narrowed his eyes. "Was Fielding's snow job just that, or was he right about something? Do we all have to bond? Because I don't think that's happened yet."

Vic shook his head. "It hasn't. *Nothing's* happened yet."

Saul's eyebrows shot up. "Like I said, I can hear you both in my head. I'd call that a pretty big *something*." He paused. "But do we have to… you know?"

"We don't have to do anything." Except Vic was sure he didn't want to walk away from whatever was developing between them. "But to be fair, we can't make any decisions without considering how they will affect Crank. Or without talking to him."

Saul flushed. "And now I feel like a shitheel for even discussing it while he's not around."

Vic held Saul's hand between his. "We will, all right?"

Saul's flush deepened. "I hope he'll be okay with me taking my time over this. I don't wanna rush into anything."

"*All* of us can work on it together," Vic assured him.

And hopefully we'll find a way to be together.

CRANK WAITED by the hospital's helipad, shivering a little in the cold night air. He caught the *whump, whump, whump* of the chopper blades and watched as it lowered to the ground. The door slid open, and Horvan got out. He strode across the tarmac toward Crank, but no one else followed.

Crank frowned as Horvan reached him. "What's going on?"

"There's a plane waiting for us at Hanscom Air Force Base, to take us back to Waukegan. It leaves within the hour."

Crank stilled. "We're going now?" What disconcerted him was the voice in his head, telling him he couldn't leave.

Horvan nodded. "Hashtag is gonna find that camp Vic thinks is in Montana. As soon as he does, we're organizing a joint raid with Aelryn's people. Duke okayed it." He locked gazes with Crank. "I need you to be one-hundred-percent focused on this, so I'm gonna ask you now—is that gonna be a problem?"

Crank swallowed. "No." The word even *tasted* like a lie. He'd give it his best shot, but he had no way of knowing how this whole business was going to affect him. "Have I got time to say goodbye?"

"Sure. Just don't be long about it. And Crank?" Horvan laid his hand on Crank's arm. "I know this can't be easy. God knows I found it a bitch to leave Dellan and Rael, and I've only done it once. So I do understand what you might be going through. But buddy, we've got a job to do."

Crank nodded. "I hear ya."

163

"And there's something you need to know before you get on that chopper." Horvan's face tightened. "The bastards killed Brick's parents, probably right after they took 'em."

"Aw fuck. How is he?" Crank shoved aside his feelings of animosity. *No one deserves this.*

"A fucking mess. I got one of Aelryn's medics to give him something so he could travel."

"What about Jamie? Did you find him?"

Horvan shook his head. "No sign of him, so we're assuming they've taken him to one of their camps. *Another* reason to get off our asses and find the fucking place." He inclined his head toward the main building. "I'll tell you the rest when we're on our way. Go say goodbye. The clock is ticking."

Crank didn't wait to be told twice. He hurried indoors and made his way through the maze of hallways until he was back at Saul's room. He paused outside, watching Vic and Saul through the glass. Saul was awake, and they appeared to be having a deep conversation, judging by Vic's somber expression.

Is this a private party, or can anyone join in?

Both men jerked their heads toward the window, and Crank pushed open the door. Then Vic widened his eyes. "Oh my God. Poor Brick."

Crank blinked. "Wow. I didn't even have to open my mouth."

"You didn't need to," Vic told him. "It's all there in your head. Along with…." He stiffened. "You're leaving."

Crank's heart sank to hear the sorrow in Vic's voice. "Yeah. Chopper's waiting for me. No rest for the wicked, right?" The quip felt wrong.

"You have to go. I get that." Saul looked him in the eye. "And it's okay. I've still got a lot of recovering to do, and Vic's going to take care of me."

"*Both* of us should be taking care of you."

Saul shook his head. "Looking after me is *not* a two-man job. Besides, you've got a few tasks to do. You've got to find the bastards who killed Brick's parents. *And* you've got to find Jamie. You're gonna be *way* too busy to be worrying about me." His features softened. "You need your head in the game, okay? We," he said, gesturing between him and Vic, "need you to come home safe and triumphant. Got it?"

That made the ache in Crank's chest lessen. "I got it."

Vic got up off the bed. "He's right. You need to go. Just remember one thing. The distance between us won't change anything, you hear me? You're still our mate. We'll stay in touch."

"I'm guessing we'll be too far apart for you to hear my thoughts." Not that Crank had a fucking *clue* how it worked over great distances.

"Probably." Saul took a deep breath. "Look, before you go there's something I have to tell you. Both of you."

The waves of misery rolling off Saul froze Crank to the spot. "What's wrong?"

Vic sat on the bed, taking Saul's hand. "Tell us. Whatever it is, it's causing you pain."

Saul's chest heaved. He gestured to his bandages. "You need to know how I came by these. And Dellan will need to know too." He met Crank's gaze. "I'll let *you* decide when's the best time to drop the bombshell. Because this is going to devastate him."

"I don't think I wanna hear this." Crank swallowed. "But I also don't think I have a choice."

Saul shook his head, his face solemn. "No, you don't." He took a deep breath. "Sit. Take my hand. I want to show you something."

His stomach churning, Crank sat on the opposite side of the bed to Vic and took Saul's proffered hand.

"Be warned. This is going to hurt."

Before Crank could get a word out, his head was filled with the image of a tall, dark man, his eyes glittering. His cruel smile gave Crank the shivers. *Who's he?*

That's Fielding. I'll go out on a limb and say he's big in whatever organization they've got going. Not gonna replay the whole memory, because it was just a lot of "we're better than you are" bullshit. This *is the bit you need to see.*

Crank watched as a young boy approached. *Is that one of the students?* The words dried in his throat as Fielding introduced Alec. His heart pounded when Alec raised his hands—except they *weren't* hands. Crank cried out as pain ripped through Saul's body and tore his hand from Saul's grasp. Vic did the same, gasping.

Saul was shaking. Vic's hands trembled as he passed Saul his water cup. "Jesus."

"Sorry." Saul took a drink. "It was easier to show you than tell you. And whatever toxin they found in my body, Alec had to have dipped his claws in it before… before he started carving me up like a turkey."

Crank shook his head. "No. That's not right." He forced himself to be calm as he replayed the memory. "There was nothing on his claws. I mean, they weren't dripping or anything."

"But that would mean"—Vic paled—"Alec's body somehow produced the toxin. They turned him into a weapon."

"What do you mean, 'turned'?" Saul's face was as pale as Vic's. "They fucking *engineered* him to be a weapon. And did you hear what Fielding said? About who Alec is?"

That was the part Crank wanted to obliterate from his mind. He was sick to his stomach, and his head was spinning. His first reaction was sheer incredulity, but he couldn't argue with the memory Saul had replayed for them.

They really did this. And if they could do that, what else might they be capable of?

Then he remembered. There was a chopper waiting.

"Guys, I have to go." He stood.

Vic's face was a picture of misery. "I know." He came around to Crank's side of the bed and hugged him. "We'll talk soon, okay? We're not going to forget about you."

"You'd better not," Crank whispered, holding Vic tight against him. When he let Vic go, he turned to Saul. "Get better soon, all right?"

Saul bit his lip. "I'll do my best." He held his arms wide, and Crank gingerly took a hug, aware of the tubes and wires. The heart monitor beeped faster, and Crank chuckled. "Is that for me?"

Saul laughed. "Maybe?" He cupped Crank's cheek. "Stay safe, you got that?"

"I got it." With a tremendous effort, Crank headed for the door. He paused, drinking in the sight of….

My mates.

Now *there* were two words he'd never expected to use.

That makes three of us. Vic smiled.

I am never *gonna get used to this.* Saul's smile faltered. *Please go. Before I get Vic to cuff you to the bed to stop you from leaving.*

"I'm going, I'm going." Crank was through the door and down the hallway before he had time to change his mind. Leaving them felt so wrong, but it wasn't as if he had a choice. Saul was right.

He had a job to do.

THEY WERE about an hour from landing in Chicago when Crank decided he couldn't stay silent a moment longer. They sat on opposite sides of the aircraft, the interior bare but for seating that ran in two lengths. No one spoke, and that in itself felt weird—even when they were returning from missions fraught with danger, there was always some banter, usually from Crank.

Horvan sat between Rael and Dellan, who leaned into him. Hashtag and Roadkill sat with their backs to the netting that covered the plane's interior skin, their eyes closed. Brick sat apart, his head in his hands, his shoulders shaking. That was what shocked Crank the most. As a shifter, Brick stood head and shoulders above most, and he was a *polar bear*, for Christ's sake.

No, that wasn't right. He was a man who'd had his world ripped apart. Even if he was still hurt by Brick's betrayal, his heart went out to the man.

Before Crank could utter a word, Brick jerked his head up. "H?"

"Yeah?"

Brick shuddered out a breath. "When we land, when we get back to the house, I'm gonna pack up my gear and go. I'm out. I-I can't deal with this shit. I need to be on my own for a while."

Horvan's eyes were kind. "Take as long as you need. Where will you go? Home?"

Brick shook his head. "Gonna get as far away from civilization as I can. Maybe Churchill in northern Manitoba?"

"What's in Manitoba?" Roadkill demanded.

"Polar bears." Brick's broad chest rose and fell. "I need to shift for a while."

Horvan nodded. "I hear ya. You know where to find us."

Crank was done. He got up from his seat next to Hashtag and crossed the space to where Dellan sat. He sat beside him. "Look, we need to talk. I know it's not exactly a good time to be sharing this, but you know what? There is *never* gonna be a good time for what I have to tell you."

Dellan frowned. "Now?"

"Can this wait?" Horvan asked.

Crank shook his head. "You need to know what we're up against before we go any further." He took a deep breath, then told them what he'd seen in Saul's head and the conclusions they'd arrived at.

Dellan became impossibly still for a moment, his amber-flecked green eyes huge. Finally, he shook his head violently. "No. No. It's not possible."

"Saul believed him."

"And why would he do that? What told him any of that... garbage could be even remotely true? Fielding lied."

Crank had been thinking the same thing, but something about Alec haunted him. "Back at the house, you got any family photo albums? Ones with pics of you as a little kid?"

"Yes, but—"

"Then when we get back, pull 'em out and show me."

Dellan gaped. "What will that prove?"

Crank sighed. "I can still see Alec." He tapped his temple. "In here. Believe me, I'm not likely to forget him. So if I see a photo of you and compare it to Alec, if there's no similarity whatsoever, then Fielding is truly a lying son of a bitch who deserves to rot for all eternity. But if there is—" He swallowed. "—then we need to realize what we're up against. Don't get me wrong. I'm praying it was all lies."

Because the alternative didn't bear thinking about.

"Can we not talk about this now?" Rael asked in a low voice. "We're all tired, and we're upset."

Crank nodded. "I had to tell you." He went back to his original seat, his stomach churning again.

This is such a fucking mess.

What made it worse? With every second, they closed the gap between their present position and Homer Glen—and increased the distance between Crank and his mates, to the point where he couldn't feel them in his thoughts anymore. It didn't matter that it made no sense. It didn't matter that Crank's head told him it couldn't be true.

His heart believed the opposite.

CHAPTER TWENTY-TWO

"CRANK. CRANK!"

He opened his eyes, his heart pounding, and sat bolt upright in bed. "'M ready. We gotta go someplace?"

Horvan sat on the bed beside him. "Whoa there. You were having a nightmare."

"How'd you know that?"

"Because you woke up the whole damn house," Hashtag grumbled from the doorway. "H, give him some warm milk or something, will ya? This makes three times this week." He gave Crank a sympathetic glance. "Get some sleep, buddy." Then he turned and walked away as Dellan appeared, carrying a steaming cup.

Dellan came closer and planted a tender kiss on Horvan's shoulder. "Go back to bed, sweetheart. I've got this. I'll be up in a minute."

Despite his frantic heartbeat, which was slowly returning to its normal rhythm, Crank bit back a smile. "Sweetheart. Aw." When Horvan jerked his head to glare at him, Crank held up his hands. "Hey, ain't nothing wrong with a little sentiment."

Horvan rolled his eyes. "At least you didn't say... you know." He shuffled out of the room.

Crank watched him, mouthing *Mama Bear*, and Dellan was clearly trying not to laugh. Horvan pulled the door shut behind him, and Dellan took Horvan's place on the bed. He held out the cup.

"Hot chocolate. Nothing like it for sending you to sleep."

Crank peered suspiciously at the dark-brown liquid. "Is that because you stirred something into it to knock me out?"

Dellan chuckled. "I wouldn't do that." He got onto the bed, his back against the footboard, his legs crossed at the ankles, his tan standing out against the white shorts. "Okay. Suppose you tell me what's been disturbing your sleep this past week. Hashtag's right. This isn't the first time." His eyes were warm. "Trust me, I know all about bad dreams."

Crank could believe that. One glance at Dellan's photo album had been enough to confirm Fielding's revelation. He'd tried to hide his reaction, but he should have known better. Dellan had been quiet for the rest of the day. "Does the hot chocolate help you?"

Dellan smiled. "Horvan has his own particular remedy for inducing sleep." There was a glint in his eyes.

Crank was glad he wasn't drinking at that moment. "Yeah, don't tell me. I've heard him *helping* you and Rael to sleep plenty of times."

"Until we find that camp, Horvan feels useless. He says all he can do is love me." Dellan flushed. "That's plenty in my book. And even when I wake up sweating and shivering at the same time, I know I'm damn lucky to have them in my life." He cocked his head to one side. "So. You haven't answered my question."

Crank swallowed a mouthful of hot chocolate. "You know how I dreamed about Saul? The night they were…." He couldn't bring himself to say the words.

Dellan nodded. "Yes."

"Well, ever since we got back a week ago, I've tried, but—" He gazed at Dellan, his stomach churning. "—I-I can't hear them."

"Oh, Crank." Dellan moved closer and took his hand. "I know how you feel. You remember when Horvan went to Duluth to meet with Saul?" Crank nodded, and Dellan's face tightened. "Horvan hadn't even been gone an hour when I realized he wasn't here anymore." He tapped his temple. "I couldn't hear him in my head, and God, that was the worst feeling. But I did have Rael. So I do know a little of how you're feeling, but it must be so much worse for you, with both of them out of range."

"You'll laugh." Crank didn't believe it himself.

"No, I won't." Dellan's earnest tone decided him.

Crank swallowed. "It feels lonely." Dellan's hand tightened on his. "It's like there's this emptiness inside of me that only they can fill. Which makes no fucking sense because we didn't get to spend all that much time together. We certainly didn't… connect like you guys did." He closed his eyes. "I've never needed anyone my whole goddamn life, and yet here I am, needing—wanting—them." He opened his eyes, his heart racing. "But what if I can't hear them because those fuckers have gone after Vic and Saul again?" Adrenaline shot through his system, and he knew it was panic-induced. His chest tingled, and nausea almost overwhelmed him.

"If you're worried, call them." Dellan's eyes widened. "Or maybe try something."

"Like what?" They'd shared calls, texts, emails, but it wasn't enough. And he hadn't told them about the turmoil inside his head. *They don't need to know that.*

"Close your eyes again." Crank did as instructed. "Now *feel* for them. Don't try to hear their thoughts, just seek them out. They're your mates, so you should be able to find them."

Crank shivered. "I've tried this. I can't."

"Then keep trying. Reach out for them."

It wasn't going to—

Two points of warmth registered, not much, but they were there. Crank stilled, homing in on them, taking deep, controlled breaths, letting his bedroom fall away as he concentrated on that soothing source of warmth. A feeling of well-being washed over him, settling in his chest.

"Aw shit, I feel them." Tears pricked the corners of his eyes as he dimly became aware of Dellan's hand stroking his.

"You'll never be alone, Crank. You've got us, but now you've got a growing family of your own."

Family? The word ricocheted through him as realization sank in. Vic and Saul were his family. His mates.

And Crank had... feelings for them.

He opened his eyes to find Dellan gazing at him with such compassion that his heart ached to see it. "Thank you."

Dellan patted his hand. "You're welcome. Now, drink that all up and then try to get some sleep. Dream of your mates—and stay focused on them." He got off the bed. "And now I'll go back to my room. I need a dose of Horvan and Rael."

Crank couldn't resist. "Taken internally, no doubt."

Dellan chuckled. "I'll see you at breakfast." He left the room.

Crank leaned back against his pillows, drinking his hot chocolate. Dellan's remark had set his mind on a particular track, one he needed to consider.

I'll talk to H in the morning.

Right then he wanted to hold on to that soothing warm feeling in his chest.

CRANK TRUDGED into the kitchen, following the delicious aroma of bacon. Mrs. Landon smiled when she saw him.

"I knew you'd be one of the first. The eggs are done, the bacon's in the oven, and there are two pots of coffee. I'll leave you all to it." She walked out of the kitchen.

From the breakfast bar, Horvan chuckled. "She knows us real well." He gestured to the stove. "Help yourself. Then we'll talk."

That stopped him short. "Am I in trouble?"

"No, but you've not been yourself this past week. I think it's time I asked the question."

Crank placed a couple of spoonfuls of eggs onto a warmed plate, then added strips of bacon. "I don't think I like the sound of this." He poured himself a coffee.

"Before we left Boston, I asked if you'd have a problem with your focus. Last night seems to prove you do."

Crank shook his head. "Actually? I'm okay." He couldn't miss Horvan's dubious expression. "No, really, I am. And I have Dellan to thank for that." That warmth had stayed with him for the rest of the night, and when he woke, it wasn't with the same pain in his chest that had been present ever since he'd left Boston.

Horvan blinked. "Oh. Okay."

"But there *was* something I wanted to ask you, before the others come down. And it's something I don't really wanna share." When Horvan arched his eyebrows, Crank groaned. "Look, it's about… sex, okay? I know Roadkill calls me the gayest straight man ever, but I've never… *you* know."

Horvan studied him for a moment. "Okay. You need to start thinking of attraction as a spectrum, a sliding scale. You are *not* one-hundred-percent straight, okay? I think such people are very rare, if they exist at all. You need to be more open to exploration, that's all. The logistics? That's pretty much what you can see on any gay porn site. You don't need me to advise you on that." His eyes sparkled. "Although I really *would* take Hashtag up on his offer to show you the trick with his tongue, or at least talk you through it. Because you *will* blow their minds, as well as their—"

Crank coughed loudly as Hashtag and Roadkill wandered into the kitchen, both making a beeline for the coffee. Horvan fell silent, but his eyes still held that evil glint Crank knew so well.

Exploration? The thought sent a shiver through him, but Crank knew it was something he wanted to pursue.

The only thing in his way? About five hundred miles between him and his mates.

When Dellan walked into the kitchen, Crank gave him a grateful smile. "Thanks for the late-night chat and chocolate. Worked like a charm."

Dellan beamed. "I'm glad. But right now I have a question for our resident techie." He went over to the coffeepot. "Hashtag, why has a very large antenna suddenly appeared in my backyard? Couldn't you get enough channels or something?"

Hashtag coughed. "Yeah, about that...."

"Is that what you went shopping for yesterday?" Crank asked.

Hashtag nodded. "Just an idea I got. If it pays off, I'll let you know." He glanced at Horvan. "It was something Crank said on the plane ride home, about knowing what we were up against. So far we've been playing by the rules, but these fuckers make up their own rules as they go along. So I thought if conventional means haven't helped me locate that camp, then maybe it was time for more unconventional ones."

Horvan narrowed his gaze. "Is that a euphemism for 'illegal'?"

Hashtag gazed back at him with an innocent expression that didn't fool Crank for a second. "I'm gonna pretend you didn't ask me that, okay?"

"H, let Hashtag work his magic. He's our best bet for finding them." Crank patted Hashtag on the back. "You've got this."

Hashtag blinked. "Thanks. Now, where is the real Crank? What have you done with him?"

Crank let out a gasp of mock horror, and the others laughed.

"Don't listen to him," Dellan said warmly. "I like this new Crank." His eyes sparkled. "Someone—or maybe a *couple* of someones—are obviously having a good influence on you."

That gave him pause for thought. Crank liked the Horvan who'd emerged since finding his mates. There was a depth and empathy to him that made him an even better leader.

Is that what love does? Change you?

Crank wasn't sure he was ready for change. Then he reconsidered.

I think I'm ready for them.

SAUL SAT in a chair by the window, a blanket over his knees. Outside, April was proving itself to be a contrary bitch. The temperature in the high fifties of two days before had plummeted to a chill thirty, and the winds had picked up.

Saul didn't want to be in that fucking chair, under that fucking blanket, in fucking *Duluth*. He wanted to be all healed up, no bandages, no pain.

He wanted to be in Illinois.

I can hear you, you know.

And that was another goddamn thing that busted his chops. "Can't a guy have any secrets?" he yelled toward the kitchen.

Vic strolled in with a tray, on which was a bowl of soup and a chunk of bread. "Nope. That ship has sailed. Lunch."

Saul narrowed his eyes. "Oh yeah? And what if I don't take your word for that?"

Vic placed the tray on Saul's knee, and Saul felt the hurt ripple through his mind. "You don't like hearing me inside your head?"

Aw fuck. "Yes, I do," he protested. "But I want to keep *some* secrets from you, babe. And I figure there has to be a way around that. So I want to call Dellan. Or Rael. See if they've found something that works for them. Something *we* can use."

"Okay. We'll call them—*after* you've eaten."

Saul arched his eyebrows. "You've turned into a real little mother hen, you know that? I'm feeling *so* much better, honest."

Vic stroked Saul's cheek. "I know. I just want you to feel one hundred percent, that's all. And for the record?" He leaned in and whispered, "I want to be in Illinois too."

Saul swallowed. "Yeah, I thought you might. I know we talk with him on the phone, but it's not the same. And I've got this feeling."

Vic sat on the end of the couch. "What kind of feeling?"

Saul hoped to God it wasn't some kind of premonition, and that by sharing it, he wasn't somehow talking it into existence. "They've got a huge mission coming up, right? Well, what if he goes to that camp... and he doesn't come back?" This was sheer craziness. A guy he'd met only a week ago had the ability to turn Saul inside out. "You remember at the hospital, when I told Crank to leave before I got you to cuff him to the bed? Maybe I had the right idea after all."

Vic nodded. "A very telling idea, if I might say so."

"What do you mean?"

"It was such a paradox. You weren't comfortable with Crank staying, but you sure weren't happy with him leaving."

Vic had nailed it. Every single thing he felt about Crank was a fucking paradox.

"How, Vic? How did he crawl into my heart, a place where I did *not* want him to go because it had this big sign on it, saying Reserved for Vic?"

"Maybe there's more room in your heart than you thought possible," Vic murmured. He pointed to the bowl. "Eat. And while *you* eat, *I'll* give Dellan a call. Deal?"

Knowing Vic felt as he did was all the balm Saul needed.

Vic picked up his phone and scrolled to Dellan's number. "Hey. You got a minute? … Can I put you on speaker?" He tapped the screen, and Dellan's voice burst from it.

"You must be a mind reader. I was going to call you later today. Saul, how are you?"

"On the mend, and thanks for asking." Then Vic gave him a mock glare. "Oops. My nursemaid wants me to eat, so you'd better talk to him."

Dellan laughed. "Sounds like Vic is taking care of you. So what can I do for you?"

"Saul wants to know if you guys have any way of shielding your thoughts from each other."

"Yes, we do."

Dellan's prompt reply had Saul straightening in his chair, almost sending his tray flying. "Really? Could we do that too?"

Dellan chuckled. "Well, I taught Horvan and Rael how to do it, so I think I can teach you two."

All the tension in Saul's back and shoulders seeped from his body, leaving him feeling unexpectedly light. "Thank you. But… you said you were going to call us. Why?"

"Well, I wanted to ask Vic for Doc Tranter's number."

Vic frowned. "But surely Horvan has his number?"

"Probably, but I-I wanted to talk to Doc about Alec."

"And you don't want Horvan to know it's been on your mind, is that it?" Saul surmised.

"That's it exactly."

"No problem. I'll send it to you," Vic told him.

"Hey, Dellan? About Alec…." Saul's throat seized. Even talking about him brought back the memories.

Dellan's sigh filled the air. "Crank took a look at photos of me as a kid. There seems little doubt Fielding was telling the truth. So I need to talk to Doc. Maybe he can shed some light on this."

"Was that the only reason for your call?" Vic asked.

"No. I wanted to know how you two were doing without Crank."

Saul met Vic's gaze. "Badly, if I'm honest." There was no reason to hide his feelings from Dellan.

"Yeah, I thought as much. So I've had an idea."

As Dellan spoke, Saul and Vic exchanged looks, and with each passing moment, Saul became aware of the emotion blossoming within him, the same emotion he could feel surging through Vic.

Excitement.

CHAPTER TWENTY-THREE

"H! H!"

Crank glanced up from his phone, his pulse quickening. "They're outside. I'll get him," he called out to Hashtag. He got up from the kitchen table, where he'd been drinking coffee and snacking on cookies, and went to the french doors, noting the three neat piles of clothes on the floor. Horvan, Rael, and Dellan were taking a break, except their version of a break involved a shifted chase, hidden behind the perimeter fences. Dellan seemed to be having the most fun. He ran up behind Horvan and gave his butt a playful nip, and suddenly it was Horvan doing the chasing, with Rael darting between both of them and running around them in circles.

"Guys! You'd better get in here." Crank opened both doors, and within seconds the air in the kitchen was a rich mixture of bear, lion, and tiger. The three shifted back. Crank never tired of the sight. One minute they were fur and sinew and teeth, the next, they were naked. Not that Crank was noticing their bodies. Horvan's muscles, Dellan's long, lithe torso, the way Rael's muscles flexed when he moved….

Nope. He definitely wasn't noticing them at all.

Then why are you thinking about seeing Vic and Saul naked? Why do you picture them writhing around on the bed with you? And that dream you had last night? The one where Saul was behind you and—

Fine! I get it. Goddamn internal thoughts, and *not* the ones he yearned to hear.

Horvan got into his jeans and headed toward Crank, rubbing his ass. "What's so urgent? Not that I'm complaining. Dellan gives quite a nip."

"And you love it," Rael said with a grin as he pulled on a pair of sweats and a tee. Dellan did the same.

Horvan aimed a mock glare at him. "Hey. No giving away my secrets."

Hashtag appeared in the doorway, his face alight. "I found it. I fucking *found* it. At least, I think I have. It can't be anything else."

Horvan grinned. "Awesome. I knew you would."

"Your idea paid off?" Crank said as he followed everyone into Dellan's office. Once inside, he couldn't miss the hardware cluttering up the desk. "Wow. You contacted any alien life-forms yet?"

"Only the one I saw in your bed this morning when I came to get your ass out of it," Hashtag teased. Crank gave him the finger. Hashtag sat at the desk. "Okay. Google Earth was getting me nowhere." He peered at them. "You know how Google Maps and Google Earth work, right? They buy their images from a small number of commercial satellite operators, but the technology is pretty basic. I mean, it's a decent enough resolution, but—"

"Hashtag." Horvan's voice was firm.

"Okay, okay, I'm getting to the important part. I think we can all agree our adversary has more power behind them than we first imagined." There were somber nods from everyone in the room. "So that got me thinking. Those images I've been searching through online… what if they're not showing what's actually there?"

Horvan frowned. "I don't get you."

"I *mean*, I've been scouring every inch of Montana for over a week and coming up with a big fat zero. Three times going over and over the same images." Hashtag drew in a deep breath. "So let's assume for a moment that the bad guys are everywhere." He shuddered. "Which gives *me* a screaming case of the heebie-jeebies, but let's not go there. What if the images we see online have been manipulated? So that certain installations don't show up?"

"Like the camp?" Dellan asked.

Hashtag nodded. "Yup. So I got to thinking. What if I used *another* source for the images? Such as US spy satellites that can pick out objects less than four inches across."

Crank gaped at him. "You can't hack a US spy satellite."

Hashtag bit his lip. "Oh. Okay. If you say so."

"Oh my fucking God, you did it. They're gonna turn up here and drag your ass to jail."

Hashtag grinned. "Either that or offer me a job. You have *no* idea what's involved in hacking a satellite. You have to know its orbital periods and positions, the frequencies it uses for command and control, the hardware to communicate via those frequencies…." Another grin. "A big enough antenna. Plus, you have to get through multiple layers of security. Because—"

"Hashtag, just tell us what you found." It sounded as if Horvan's patience was wearing a bit thin.

"Come and look."

They crowded around the back of Hashtag's chair, staring at the monitor. Crank leaned in. "All I see is green," he joked.

"Then let me show you what happens when I zoom in." Hashtag clicked on another tab, and an image opened. There were a lot of trees, but the outline of the camp was clearly visible. "I'm trying to gauge the size of it." He pointed to the perimeters, where there were square installations at regular intervals. "Remember the towers we saw in the photo of Dellan's dad? I think that's what these are—manned towers, to watch the inmates." His expression grew grim. "And these must be huts of some kind. The images were taken in very early morning, because I can't see anyone around. There seems to be a fence all around it, but there's only one access gate that I can see. What makes me positive this is the camp, however, is what happens when I go back to the online photos of the same area." He clicked on another tab.

"Holy fuck." Horvan leaned closer. "It's not there." He glanced at Hashtag. "Do you have the coordinates?"

"You bet." Hashtag sagged into his chair.

Horvan patted his shoulder. "You did it. You fucking *did* it." He straightened. "Okay. I'll send word to Aelryn and organize a Zoom meeting. Duke will need to be in on it too." He smiled. "We've got a raid to plan."

HASHTAG'S DISCOVERY had created a buzz of excitement throughout the house, which amplified after Horvan met up with Aelryn and Duke. Crank knew it wouldn't be long before they had a fixed date for the raid, once men, munitions, and transport had been arranged.

What rocked him to his core was the urgent need growing in him to settle his affairs before that date arrived. It made no sense. They'd barely acknowledged they were mates before Crank had had to leave. Why then did he miss them so freaking much?

We miss you too.

Crank froze. Hearing Vic's voice in his head sent a wave of pleasure through him. *How come I can hear you all the way from Duluth? Not that I'm complaining, you understand.*

Ah, well.... That was Saul. *That* might *be because we're not* in *Duluth.*

"Hey, Dellan?" Roadkill stuck his head around the door. "A taxi's pulled up outside. You expecting anyone?"

For a second Crank was rooted to the spot. *No way.* Then he lurched off the couch, pelted through the house, and skidded to a halt on the varnished floorboards in the hallway, stopping himself at the last moment from slamming into the front door. He yanked it open, and his heart soared to see Vic getting out of the taxi, then walking around to open the other rear door.

Oh God, they're really here.

He dashed outside, ignoring the gravel that dug into his bare soles, and came to a dead stop in front of Vic. "Come here." Crank hoisted him into his arms, his lips seeking Vic's, and to his delight Vic responded with a fierce kiss, his arms locked around Crank's neck, his legs caging Crank's waist.

"Now that's what I call a welcome," Vic whispered, his breath tickling Crank's ear.

Hey, do I get a kiss?

Crank gently lowered Vic to the ground, then peered inside the back of the taxi. Saul looked way better than the last time Crank had seen him, but there were dark circles under his eyes and a pallor Crank didn't like at all.

"Should you be traveling?"

Saul rolled his eyes. "For God's sake, did you and Vic study the same mother-hen handbook or something? You sound just like him."

Crank held out his hand, and Saul took it, allowing Crank to help him to his feet. There was maybe half a head's difference between them. Crank cupped Saul's chin, tilting his head up. "I am so fucking happy to see you," he murmured, before moving in to kiss Saul on the lips.

A cough from the driver broke the spell, and Crank took a step back. Saul frowned. "You'd better finish what you've started once we're indoors."

That was enough to create a fluttery sensation in Crank's belly.

Vic paid the driver and went around to the trunk to collect their bags. Heat radiated through Crank's chest at the sight of four bags. "Planning on staying a while?"

"Dellan said to figure on at least a couple of weeks," Vic told him.

Crank frowned. "Dellan did?"

Saul nodded. "He invited us to stay." He grinned. "He also said it would be a surprise."

"He got that right." Crank walked with them up to the door, where Dellan stood, smiling.

"Welcome, guys." He gave Vic and Saul a hug as they stepped into the hallway. "Nice timing. Dinner will be in about an hour, so you've got time to chill out a bit before then. You'll be sharing Crank's room—if that's okay with Crank, of course." Dellan gave him an inquiring glance. "Is it?"

The fluttery feeling in Crank's belly felt as though a million butterflies had gotten in there. *Oh hell.* He needed to get in the room before they did to make sure the lube and tissues were out of sight.

Horvan came into the hallway, his smile as broad as Dellan's. "Hey, I didn't know you were coming." More hugs were exchanged.

Dellan coughed. "And you have *no* idea how hard I worked at locking that thought out of sight." He gazed at Saul. "Maybe you should rest before dinner. I know you said you were strong enough to make the trip, but it has to have worn you out."

Saul nodded. "A lie down sounds good right now."

Crank picked up two of the bags. "I'll show you to your—our—room." His heart was hammering at the thought of sharing a bed with them.

Will they want to do more *than sleep?*

In his head Saul gave a chuckle. *Who said anything about sleeping?*

Stop that, Vic admonished. *Don't scare him. We've only just arrived, for God's sake.*

He led them up the stairs to the second floor, then along to his room. "It's a king bed, thank God," Crank said as he ushered them through the door, mentally heaving a sigh of relief that he had in fact cleaned up after himself that morning. "But if you two want to share it, I'll find someplace else to sleep." He had to give them the choice.

And what if we don't want that option? Saul inquired.

Crank shivered. "Fuck, this is weirding me out. You can hear every single goddamn thought in my head." Maybe it was time to talk to Horvan about that mental safety box thing he had going with Rael and Dellan.

"We can help with that," Vic said in a low voice. He glanced at Saul, who nodded. "Crank, sit down, please. We need to talk." And like that, the mood swung in a more serious direction.

Crank sat on the bed, and they joined him, flanking him. "What's up?"

"We've been doing a lot of thinking since the last time we were together at the hospital," Vic said.

181

"And a lot of talking too," Saul added.

Crank's heartbeat raced, sending shooting pains through his chest.

To his surprise, Vic placed his hand over Crank's heart. "Hey. Everything's okay. Honest. We wouldn't be here if it wasn't."

"Look, we know you've said you're straight, and we don't want to screw with your head." Saul took Crank's hand. "And I shouldn't have teased you like that. Dellan taught us how to lock away our thoughts, so Vic and I... we figure we can do that so we don't make you uncomfortable."

"Why would I be uncomfortable?" Crank looked from Saul to Vic in confusion.

"Well, if we're sharing a bed, and we want to *do* anything...," Saul proffered, "you won't see those thoughts."

Crank sighed. "Since those... images we shared in the hospital, all I can think about is being with you two. I keep meaning to ask one of the guys how to suck a dick to make it good for the... suckee. That would be *you*, by the way. And then there are the dreams."

Vic chuckled. "Ooh, I want to hear about those. Were they R-rated?"

Crank's face grew hot. "R? Sure, we'll go with that." He glanced at Saul's hand covering his. "Horvan told me that attraction is a spectrum. So maybe my bar is skewed and I'm not nearly as straight as I thought. I only know I want to explore this—with the two of you."

Saul's slow smile sent warmth spreading through him, kindling quickly into heat as Saul released his hand and stroked Crank's thigh. "Don't you think it's time we got better acquainted, then?"

Oh fuck.

CHAPTER TWENTY-FOUR

CRANK GAPED at him. "Are you for real? One, you just got here. Two, we're gonna be having dinner real soon. And three, you don't think everyone is gonna know *exactly* what we've been doing up here? Because there are three shifters downstairs who can probably smell cum from a thousand yards."

"He does have a point," Vic murmured. "Although a thousand yards might be pushing it a little." He chuckled. "Maybe nine hundred yards."

"You're not helping," Crank gritted out.

"So you're not saying no—you're saying not yet?" Saul pressed.

"Yes, that's what I'm saying." Except Crank was trying not to think about it.

"Guys?" There was a knock at the door. "Assuming you've had enough *rest*, you might wanna put some clothes on." Roadkill cackled. "There's coffee and cookies downstairs."

"You see?" Crank let out a growl. "For your information, we're all wearing clothes in here," he hollered, but Roadkill was already gone.

"Cookies? Before dinner?" Vic complained.

"Fine. We'll eat yours."

Saul stood. "We still need some time to ourselves. Everything happened so fucking fast in Boston, and we're all playing catch-up." He held out a hand to Crank, who took it, rising to his feet. "And what's really weird about that?" His face softened. "I missed you. I didn't expect to do that."

Crank swallowed. "Ditto. You've both been on my mind a lot." Then he was pulled into a three-way hug, Vic and Saul's hands on his back, the three of them connected, and *holy fuck*, it was as if something clicked into place.

"Trust me to end up with two mates who are both taller than me," Vic groused.

Crank lifted him into his arms, and Saul moved in behind Vic. "That's the awesome thing about being horizontal," Saul said, his voice husky. "Height doesn't matter." He kissed Vic's neck, and Vic shivered. Crank applied his lips to Vic's mouth, and all three let out a low moan of pleasure.

With extreme reluctance, Crank broke the kiss. "Guys, this will have to wait." He lowered Vic to the floor.

"Okay, but it *will* happen." Saul reached around and patted Crank's ass. "Don't worry. I'll be gentle." His eyes gleamed.

Crank erupted into a coughing fit. When he had himself under control, he leveled a hard stare at Saul. "You know what they say about assumptions, right?" Without waiting for a reply, he headed for the door, and they followed him. As they made their way down the stairs, Crank did his best to shove aside the question that plagued him.

Does Saul have a big dick?

Vic chuckled. "Oh yeah, he does."

That did it. Crank was going to talk to Horvan, Dellan, and Rael as a matter of urgency. Dellan and Rael were going to teach him how to block his thoughts, and Horvan? Well, he needed Horvan's advice on… other things.

VIC HAD to admit, it was good to be among his friends again. They sat around the dining table after dinner. Everyone was talking animatedly, while Saul leaned back, listening to the conversations, but Vic knew those green eyes missed nothing. Vic loved the way Horvan's team greeted Saul as if he were one of them.

Then it hit him. Saul was—just as he was. They were all united against a common enemy.

It wasn't until the coffee came out that he realized someone was missing. "Where's Brick?"

Horvan sighed. "He's gone. He's taking a little vacation. He'll be back after he gets his head together. Well, maybe."

Vic couldn't help but notice Horvan's usual confident tone was lacking from that last statement.

Hashtag put down his coffee cup and beamed. "You've heard about the camp, of course."

Vic stilled. "No, what?"

"We found it. Well, *I* found it."

"Way to go, Hashtag!" Then Vic stilled. "Wait. When was this?"

"A few days ago." Hashtag frowned. "I felt sure you'd have been told about it. I mean, what with the mission being planned and all…."

"Mission?" Vic jerked his head to glare at Crank. "You didn't say a word about it."

A flush crept across Crank's cheeks. "Didn't I?"

Vic stared at Horvan. "How soon are we talking for this mission?"

"Within the next week or so." Horvan's ears pinked.

Vic gave a slow nod, then returned his attention to Crank. "And we'll still be around. So have you thought about what you'd say when it came time to leave? 'Hey, guys, I'm going to the store'?" He gaped. "You never intended letting me go on it whether I was here or not." Then the full force of this new information hit him. "Does Aelryn know about this?"

Horvan nodded. "We discussed it."

"And neither of you said a fucking *word*?"

Horvan cleared his throat. "We made the decision not to invite you because we felt you'd want to stay with Saul in Duluth. Now that you've come, you two can stay here with Rael and Dellan."

Dellan's jaw dropped. "Excuse me? Are *all* of your guys in on this shit? So what are we in this equation? The womenfolk, to be left behind while all the menfolk go off and get their asses killed? Well, fuck all over that." He glared at Horvan. "You kept this shielded from us too."

"That was *not* how it went down," Horvan protested, his voice brittle. "We decided it was for the best not to take you with us because our attentions would be divided. We can't do our job if we're worried about you."

Saul snorted. "Do you know *how many* missions Vic has been on? He—"

"I'm sorry, what was your reason for being with Vic? Oh, I remember." Horvan locked gazes with Saul. "He needed a keeper."

That earned Horvan a death glare. "We *all* need a keeper, you asshole. Who do you think takes care of you? Oh, wait. Your mates. That's part and parcel of the whole package."

Horvan's shoulders slumped. "I-I can't risk losing them. After what happened to you—and to Brick's parents—I'm terrified of what they'd do if they got hold of Dellan or Rael."

Vic's anger slowed to a simmer. He couldn't argue with that. Not now.

"Can I be honest?" Crank's face clouded. "This past week or so has been torture. Not being able to hear either of you, I imagined the most

185

horrible things. That they'd come after you again, that they'd found you. I can't stand the thought of them getting to you or Vic," Crank admitted.

Before Saul could respond, Rael let out a growl. "Fine. We'll stay behind, like good, dutiful little wives. You big, strong men go ahead and go on your mission. Don't you worry about us."

"But I *am* worried," Horvan retorted. "I'm bringing in men to act as guards while we're gone, to keep you safe." He reached across the table for Rael's hand. "I'm sorry we had to do it this way."

Rael tugged his hand free. "The sad thing? I don't think you are."

"And you're forgetting a couple of very important details," Dellan added. "It's *my father* they have incarcerated in that place, my half brother too—at least, we hope to God that's where they've taken Jamie, because we don't have a whole lot to go on."

"You're thinking about Brick's parents, aren't you?" Hashtag's expression was glum.

Dellan shivered. "I don't even *want* to think about that." He regarded Crank with a sorrowful expression. "I can understand not wanting Saul to go—he'd probably agree with me that he's not in any condition to do that—but Vic? He's not a child, Crank. He can make up his own mind. And it's thanks to him that we even know about this camp. Not letting him in on the mission to shut it down seems kind of churlish. Selfish. Insert adjective here."

Vic regarded Dellan with affection. "Thank you for that." Then he turned to Crank. "I'm going on this mission. Dellan nailed it. I need to be in on this fight. I get what Horvan said, that your attention might be divided if I'm there, but if I'm not, I'll be going through much worse, imagining what's going on. Besides—" He stuck out his chin. "—you need all the men you can get."

Saul sighed. "You've lost, Crank. I know that look. Better live with it, because it's happening." He glanced at Dellan. "And for the record? I may not be one-hundred-percent fit, but that doesn't mean I don't want to go." When Dellan opened his mouth to reply, Saul held up his hand. "Relax. I know you're right. That doesn't mean I have to like it." He let out a yawn, then covered his mouth with his hand. "Sorry, guys, but can we continue this discussion in the morning? I'm beat. Think I'll call it a night."

Vic knew better. Saul was trying to end the conversation.

Dellan's smile was warm. "That sounds like a good idea. Crank, why don't you and Vic go up with Saul? I'm thinking of having an early night

186

too." When Rael blinked, his brow furrowed, Dellan gave him a steady look. "We all need to chill."

Rael's forehead smoothed out. "You're right."

Vic couldn't swear to it, but he had a feeling something private had been shared between them, something Horvan wasn't privy to.

Roadkill got up from the table. "In that case...." He walked toward the door. "Hashtag? Game of pool?"

"Sure. Why not?" His eyes twinkled. "Seeing as everyone else will be... busy." They left the room, both chuckling.

Vic said good night to Horvan, Rael, and Dellan and followed Crank from the dining room. As they climbed the stairs, Saul muttered. "Well, that was tense. Is it always like that?"

Crank shook his head. "Dellan and Rael are normally more laid-back, but I guess this situation has everyone riled." They reached the second floor, and he led them to his bedroom door. When he paused, Vic stroked his back.

"I can feel your panic. Let's get inside, and you can tell us what's bothering you." They went into the room, and Vic closed the door. "Now, you don't strike me as the kind of man who'd be nervous about getting into bed with two guys. You always seem so confident." And yet waves of heightened emotion were rolling off him, washing over Vic, swamping him.

Crank swallowed hard. "It's just that... well, the idea that I have mates is truly sinking in. Before, it was kinda ephemeral, I suppose, but with every minute you're here, I'm realizing that everything is about to change."

"Do you want things to go back to how they were?" Saul asked in a low voice.

Vic caught his breath, waiting.

CRANK SHOOK his head again. "Uh-uh. I don't want to go back. This is me now." He squared his shoulders. "It's just that there are new bits of me to discover, that's all." And he had to admit to a certain amount of curiosity.

Then Crank let out a strangled gasp, trying to pull air into his lungs as Saul kicked off his shoes, grasped his dark blue sweater by its hem, and leisurely pulled it up and over his head, revealing his bare torso.

Jesus.

The wounds were long, and there were a lot of them. Bruises too, but they had turned that orange color they always did when on their way out.

187

"It's okay," Saul said in a low voice. "It looks worse than it is. The stitches came out a day or two before we left Duluth. I have to be careful, that's all." He gestured to his back. "Got them here too. But that still leaves a lot of me you can touch."

Crank couldn't help himself. He took a breath, then moved in closer and pressed his lips to one of Saul's scars.

Saul's breathing caught. "Fuck."

Crank straightened and stroked Saul's muscular shoulders, the curve of his biceps, his well-defined abs, his firm torso.

"You like how I look? How I feel?" Saul murmured.

Crank nodded, unable to speak, his throat tight.

"Then let me see you." Saul leaned in and kissed Crank's neck. "Wanna see what you're hiding in those jeans," he whispered.

"I already know what *you're* packing," Crank quipped.

Saul aimed a hard stare at Vic, his lips twitching. "You giving away my secrets?"

"More a case of letting him know what he was in for," Vic said with a chuckle. Then he shifted closer, and Crank allowed himself to be undressed. His heart pounded as Vic's nimble fingers popped the button free on his waistband, then slid the zipper down.

Saul grabbed Crank's jeans and pulled them over his hips. His gaze drifted lower. Then he raised his chin, his smile of approval swelling Crank's chest. "Oh, honey, look at you." Crank's breathing hitched as Saul curled cool fingers around his already-stiffening shaft.

Vic peered at Crank's crotch. "Jesus. And I thought *you* were big."

Crank couldn't resist. "And now you know why they really call me Crank."

Saul grinned. "And now *you* know what a size queen our Vic is. Looks like it's your lucky day, Vic." He let go of Crank's dick and pushed his own jeans and underwear to the floor.

Oh my God. Saul's cock sprang up, smacking against his belly, hard and thick. It wasn't its length that caused Crank's heart to hammer, but its girth. *Vic takes that?*

And he loves it. Saul's eyes sparkled. *You will too, I promise.*

And there you go, making assumptions again. That earned Crank a throaty chuckle from Saul.

"You say assumptions—all *I* hear is ass." Saul stepped out of the denim and lay on the bed, patting the space beside him. "Come lie here, next to me."

As if in a dream, Crank did as he was instructed. Vic moved to the end of the bed and carefully placed his clothing over the footboard. Then he came around to climb onto the bed, and Saul spread for him.

"Come here, beautiful."

Vic moved in, as sinuously and stealthily as a predator, more like a big cat than a human. He crawled up Saul's body, lithe and graceful, until his elbow met Crank's face.

"Ow!" Crank rubbed his cheekbone.

Vic knelt up, his face flushed. "Oh God, I'm so sorry. I've never.... I haven't ever been in bed with two men. The logistics are challenging."

Saul laughed. "Hey. We're all trying way too hard to ensure this is good for everyone. What if we just relax and move slowly? There's no hurry, right? Let's get to know how each other feels, how we look." His eyes gleamed. "Because *fuck*, the visuals alone are amazing."

Crank was down with that.

Saul moved, and Crank found himself between them as Saul ran his hands over Crank's body, awakening every nerve and fiber. Vic leaned in to kiss him, and Crank closed his eyes, allowing the sensations to wash over him.

Does it feel good? Vic asked.

Better than I would've believed. Then Saul's lips were on his neck, and Crank pushed out a low moan. *Oh fuck, that feels awesome.* He opened his eyes to watch them kiss, aware of the heat flooding through Vic's body.

I've missed you. Vic cupped Saul's cheek.

"What do you mean, you've missed him?" Curiosity tore Crank from the moment.

"Well, we haven't... since he left for Boston."

Saul kissed Vic softly on the mouth. "I was in no state, and besides, we wanted to wait."

"For what?"

Saul's eyes met his. "You." He smiled. "And right now I want in Vic's beautiful ass."

Crank's face grew hot. *I've dreamed about that, watching you slide into him.*

Saul grinned. *Then let us make it a reality.* He gestured to his erect dick. *Suck it, babe, while Crank gets you ready for me.* He glanced at Crank. *You know what to do, right?*

Crank hoped his eye roll was answer enough.

Vic got on all fours between Saul's spread thighs and went down on his shaft, his head bobbing as he took Saul deep, his mouth full as he moaned. Crank reached into his nightstand drawer and grabbed the lube. He squeezed some onto his fingers, then knelt at Vic's ass, unable to tear his gaze away from that tight pucker.

"His hole sucks you right in," Saul said, reaching over Vic to pull his cheeks apart. "He loves being fingered."

Crank slowly pressed one finger into Vic's entrance, sighing as warm flesh tightened around it. Vic moaned, and Crank took that as a sign not to stop. He slid in and out of that hot little channel until Vic was pushing back, his body demanding more. By the time Crank had three fingers in Vic's ass, his own dick was like a rock.

Saul stroked Vic's bulging cheek. "You gonna ride me?"

Vic pulled free of Saul's cock and straddled him in a heartbeat. Crank knelt beside them, working his own shaft, his heart pounding.

Saul gave a nod toward the bottle of lube. "Now get my dick ready."

Crank applied lube to the thick cock, loving how Saul slid through his fingers. When Saul pressed his dick to Vic's opening, Crank winced. Even with him stretching Vic's hole, that had to fucking *hurt.*

Then he remembered and opened his mind to both of them. *I'll feel what you do.*

Saul nodded. *Oh yeah. There is no feeling on earth like sliding my cock into the man I love.* He gazed up at Vic. *Ready, baby?*

Vic guided Saul's dick into him, an inch at a time, and while there was an initial flash of discomfort, Vic soon relaxed. What stole through Crank's body could only be described as a sort of euphoria. Vic planted his hands on either side of Saul's broad chest and started to rock, an easy back-and-forth motion, his hips rolling as he rode Saul's cock.

Saul moaned. "Aw fuck, I'm home." He peered at Vic. "That feel good?"

Vic's face glowed. "*So* fucking good." The words almost sounded as if he was purring. He glanced over at Crank and smiled, then reached out and wrapped his hand around Crank's shaft, stroking it lazily while he undulated his body.

Saul stroked Vic's lean torso and thighs. "Much as I love it when you do all the work, I can't lie still. I have to fuck that ass."

"Then fucking *move*, Saul," Crank ground out. "I wanna see it."

Saul grinned. "That I can do." He bent his legs, placed his feet on the mattress, and tilted his hips, driving up into Vic's hole, his initial thrusts slow and measured but gaining in strength and tempo. Crank couldn't take his eyes off the sight of Vic's body, the skin so tight around Saul's meaty dick that slid in and out, glistening with lube.

Then Saul picked up speed, and Vic grabbed hold of the headboard, the bed rattling against the wall as Saul fucked him. "Oh yeah, like that," Vic said with a groan.

Oh my fucking God, this is amazing. The rush of pleasure that coursed through Vic now flowed through Crank, and he didn't want it to stop. It was all there, locked between the three of them: the emotions, the connection....

Sheer bliss.

Vic shot his load over Saul's chest, and Crank knelt up to claim Vic's mouth in a fierce kiss. Then he gasped as Saul turned his head and took Crank's dick between his lips. It only took three or four good hard sucks to have Crank coming, and Saul swallowed every drop as Crank trembled with the force of his orgasm.

Crank took it all in—their blissed-out expressions, the warm sated feeling that flowed through Vic, even the sweet ache where Saul's cock was still buried inside him.

"My turn," Saul whispered.

Vic nodded, lifting himself up and down on Saul's cock, his thumbs flicking Saul's nipples, teasing them. And when Saul came, Crank found himself drowning in sensation. He felt Saul's elation, Vic's climax... and *oh my God*, he could feel Saul's warmth inside Vic, as if it were *his* cock sheathed in Vic's body.

"Jesus."

"You say that a lot." Saul pushed out a wry chuckle. "I'm gonna take it as a compliment." He peered at Crank. "Well?"

Crank cleared his throat. "Wh-when did you say it was going to be my turn?"

CHAPTER TWENTY-FIVE

SAUL KNEW something was different the second he woke up—there were *two* bodies snuggled up to him. Vic's head was on his chest, and Crank's arm lay across his waist. Warmth surrounded him, and a slow wave of contentment washed over him.

I like this.

His face tingled when he recalled his initial resentment toward Crank. *How was I to know?* All he'd been able to think of was that he didn't share, and that went as far as a guy in Vic's dream. And Crank had turned out to be a hot AF guy.

You're thinking about my ass again, aren't you?

Saul laughed. "Good morning. And you got me." Then he gasped as Crank teased his nipple with his tongue. "Fuck, you learn fast."

"You mean I learn to speak Saul fast, right?" Crank tugged gently on his nipple, and electricity shot all the way down to Saul's dick.

"God, I felt that." Vic opened his eyes. "Is this a private party, or can I join in?"

Saul put his arms around both of them and pulled them in close. "Morning," he murmured. "I know exactly how I want my day to start." He wanted to watch Crank fuck Vic.

"What a coincidence. Me too." Vic's expression grew wistful, and Saul knew whatever was on his mind had nothing to do with sex.

"Tell me."

"I think I know." Crank sat up in bed, throwing back the sheets. "Come on. I'll show Saul where the wetsuits are."

Saul blinked. "Wetsuits? You both got a thing for neoprene that I don't know about?" Then he stilled and smacked his hand against his forehead. "I am so *stupid*. There's a lake out back, isn't there?"

Vic grinned as he got up from the bed. "No one will be up yet. It's still early. Come and swim with me."

192

Saul didn't move. "Both of us?" A brief flash of bitterness lanced through him at seeing Crank's obvious enthusiasm for the prospect. "Have you swum together before?"

"Just the once," Crank said as he stepped into his jeans.

Vic reached out to caress Saul's cheek. "But now I want *both* my mates with me."

Saul's pangs of jealousy melted away at the warmth in Vic's voice. "Then let's get out there."

They crept through the quiet house, Crank leading the way to the kitchen and into the utility room that also housed a couple of bikes, a set of skis, and several wetsuits in varying sizes.

"Why does Dellan have all these different suits?" Saul asked.

"He bought them once he'd met Horvan," Crank informed him. He grinned. "Actually, once he met all of us. He said he'd buy a bunch of suits, just in case. He even got one that would fit Brick, but he prefers to shift and jump into the water." Crank grabbed two of them and handed one to Saul. "This might fit you." He shucked off his jeans and tee, and Saul was momentarily distracted by Crank's freed shaft. Crank's eyes twinkled. "Later. Our mate needs a swim first." Then he frowned. "Hey, should you be doing this?"

He had a point, but no way was Saul about to sit and watch them swim without him.

"He'll be fine," Vic assured Crank. "Besides, neither of you will be swimming—you'll both be holding onto me while I drag you around the lake." He was vibrating with need. "Now can we get out there?"

Saul gave him a quick peck on the lips. "Go shift. We'll join you when we've squirmed into these."

Vic bit his lip. "As long as you don't take too much time helping Crank's *dick* into his wetsuit." Then he was out the door and running toward the lake.

Saul stared after him. "He really does know me."

"But that's a good thing, right?" Crank surprised him with a kiss. "Now hurry up and take your clothes off. He's waiting for us."

They helped each other into the suits. Crank groaned and glanced over his shoulder. "Excuse me? If you keep touching my ass like that, I'm never gonna get this zipped up."

Saul leaned in and whispered, "But it *calls* to me."

"Oh yeah? You speak ass now? And what is it saying?"

Saul grinned. "Eat me."

Crank whirled around. "Out there. Right this second."

"Did I hit a nerve?"

"No, but I'll hit something in a minute." He narrowed his gaze. "Look, are you sure you should be swimming? I mean, the stitches might be out, but—"

Saul put his hands on his hips. "If you think I'm going to forgo one of my greatest pleasures because I had a few pieces of string in my skin, you're crazy."

Crank arched his eyebrows. "A few? How many? And don't lie, because I'll know."

Saul rolled his eyes. "Seventy-eight, all right?" He smiled. "See? I'm strung together tight as a drum. I'll be fine."

Crank huffed. "You know best, I guess." He grabbed some towels from a shelf above the dryer, and then they walked across the patio toward the lake. There was no sign of Vic, except for a heap of clothing at the water's edge. Crank waded in, shielding his eyes from the morning sun as he gazed out over the still water.

"Can you see him?" Saul asked as he strode through the water toward Crank.

"I think we need to go out a little deeper."

They swam toward the middle of the lake, and suddenly a wave lifted both of them.

Grab on.

Saul grasped the slim fin that rose up, slicing through the water, and on the opposite side Crank did the same, their hands touching. Then Vic swam in a wide circle, and they laughed as they tried to hold on. Vic's mood was clearly playful as he swam in a broad figure eight.

Saul's heartbeat raced as warmth radiated throughout his body. *This feels amazing.* What heightened the experience was to realize Vic and Crank's elation matched his own. The sheer joy of sharing the moment and sensing every emotion that tumbled through them was overwhelming.

What struck him most vividly was their *connection.*

Had enough?

Saul laughed out loud, enjoying the exhilaration. *We're still holding tight, aren't we?*

Crank snorted. *This is way better than a roller coaster.*

They swam like that until the sun had climbed higher in the sky. Then a voice from the bank broke the spell.

"If you three want breakfast, you'd better hustle, or it'll be gone." Hashtag grinned. "And I'm sure you've all worked up an appetite." He strolled back toward the house, whistling.

Then Saul suddenly had his arms full of a naked Vic, who slid like a slippery eel from his grasp and swam away from him.

"Last one out gets to bottom!" Saul hollered, then struck out for the bank before either of them had the chance to tell him to take it easy. Crank matched him, stroke for stroke. When they reached land, Vic stood there in a towel, laughing. "Wow. I'm not sure who won—it was that close. Maybe you need to flip. I get to watch."

Crank heaved himself out of the water. "You forgot to tell me he can be a mischievous little fucker."

Saul chuckled. "You have *no* idea. He's just warming up." It delighted him to see Vic so relaxed. Then Saul realized he'd never felt so content. *Maybe whoever decides on who mates with whom knows their stuff. Maybe all we needed was each other.*

The thought was oddly comforting.

"That was great," Crank proclaimed as he rubbed his head dry. "Thanks for letting me come along."

"Both of you seemed to enjoy it." Vic gazed out at the lake. "This is heaven. I have to shift fairly regularly, but things have been so hectic, there hasn't been time. Whenever I go out, you're both welcome to come with me. I liked having the company. Swimming is fun, but when you're alone, it gets old fast."

Saul kissed Vic's shoulder. "Okay, confession time. I've always thought of swimming with you as our special thing, but having Crank there with us?" He glanced at Crank. "I don't know that anything ever felt so right."

Vic's breathing caught. "I was thinking that exact phrase. It was right."

The full import of Vic's words hit home. "But... I didn't hear your voice in my head," Saul told him.

Vic grinned. "Score one for Dellan's mental safety boxes."

Saul winced, and Crank noticed, damn him. "You overdid it, didn't you? I knew you—"

Saul stopped Crank's words with a kiss. Then he drew back and looked Crank in the eye. "Okay, yeah, the skin is pulling a little. But I'll live. And I wouldn't have missed this for anything." He smiled. "Now, if I promise to be a good boy and not exert myself for the rest of today, will you quit mothering me?"

Crank regarded him in silence for a moment. "How did you do this? How did you crawl into my heart and make it ache for you?"

Saul responded the only way he could. With another kiss.

Vic walked over to them and put his hands to their faces. "I'm missing out here. Kiss me, and then we'll go see what they've left us for breakfast."

Three mouths met in a tender kiss. Saul had to admit, he could become a fan of three-way kisses. Then he gave an internal chuckle.

Three-ways sounded like a whole lot of fun.

Crank broke the kiss. "One thing does seem a little odd about your shark, now I think about it."

"And what's that?"

"Well, you shift into this enormous creature, but your fin is tiny. Okay, so I'm no expert, and the only shark I've got to go on is *Jaws*, but—"

Saul chuckled. "Ooh, you just strayed into dangerous territory."

"Greenland sharks have tiny fins, all right?" Vic protested.

Saul glanced over him and said in a stage whisper, "Fin envy. Told you he was a size queen." Then he let out a loud *ouch* when Vic whacked his arm.

"I have to tell you guys something," Crank murmured. "It was when we were out there and Vic said *grab on*. Jesus, that was my dream, the one I had over and over again, where I was about to drown and Vic saved me."

"When was this?" Saul asked.

"Late March." Crank flushed. "Of course, that wasn't all he did. Only that was the part that weirded me out."

Vic grinned. "Do tell. What was I doing?"

"Sucking me off. I got so goddamn tired of waking up covered in cum."

Vic's eyes gleamed. "I think I need to experience this for myself."

Saul smacked his ass. "Down, boy. Breakfast, remember? You can try Crank's protein shake later." In fact, he had a list of all the things he wanted to try with Crank.

Number one was finding out what that gorgeous ass felt like on Saul's dick.

"ARE YOU still sore at me?"

Crank aimed a glare at Roadkill. "Damn straight." He'd walked into the kitchen to find an inflatable cushion on his chair and Roadkill making sympathetic noises, asking how his ass was. "Is this what I have to look forward to every morning of their stay?" Then he realized what he'd said, and suddenly there was a heaviness in his chest and limbs.

"What's wrong?" Dellan asked.

Vic covered Crank's hand with his. "He's thinking that at some point this stay will be over. He's right. His life is all over the place. So is mine a lot of the time. Not exactly a good starting point for a stable relationship."

Before Crank could comment, Dellan flashed Horvan and Rael a glance, then got up from the table. "Could you three come with me for a little walk? It won't take long."

Crank's scalp prickled. *Something is up.*

They went through the french doors out onto the patio, and Dellan led them toward the lake. They stopped at the bank, all of them gazing at the still waters.

"It's so beautiful here," Vic murmured.

"I'm glad you think so." Dellan flung out his arm to encompass the lake. "I think this would be a great view. Imagine looking out from your front porch and seeing all this."

"Quit teasing," Crank grumbled.

To his surprise, Dellan arched his eyebrows. "Who's teasing? I'm being very serious. You could build a place of your own here. Okay, nothing like the size of mine, but how big would it have to be to house the three of you? And I do have five acres. I'd be willing to give up some of it for a house for you three if it means you have a place of your own."

What the fuck? Crank was lost. "But… how could they just move here? Didn't Vic say they have their own lives?"

"That leads me to the second part of this idea. Come on back to the house."

They strode across the lawn, Crank's head in a whirl. *Does this make any sense to you guys?*

Nope. That was Saul. *But color me intrigued.*

When they got back to the kitchen, Dellan looked at Horvan and smiled. "Over to you, then."

Horvan gestured to the table. "Sit down. We need to talk. *All* of us."

The prickling sensation spread out from Crank's scalp to his arms. "What's going on, H?"

Horvan cocked his head to one side. "Where's home to you, Crank?"

197

He snorted. "What's that? Certainly not that crappy apartment where I store my stuff and where I flop between missions. I wouldn't call it a home." He gestured to the room. "Now *this* is a home, and I'm real happy for you guys, honest. But for the rest of us? We live out of our duffels because we never know when we'll be sent on assignment."

Vic pointed to Saul. "Up till now? Home was where Saul was. And although I love Dellan's idea for a house, I don't see how we could make it work."

Horvan cleared his throat. "Well, I have a—" Rael coughed and gave him a pointed stare. "Okay, *we* have a plan. We talked with Duke about the present situation. It's always a clusterfuck trying to set up missions because no one is ever in one spot. Take this year when I called you guys to come help us save Dellan. You flew in from all over. So what if we had a base? Someplace from which we go to wherever we're needed."

"Keep talking." Crank folded his arms.

"Nothing is set in stone yet, and there are logistics to work out, but what if we change that? What if we make Chicago our base of operations?"

"Yeah, but we can't *all* live here," Hashtag reminded him with a grin. "Bad enough now. Some of you guys are getting pretty ripe."

Horvan gave him the finger.

"No, Hashtag is right." Dellan gazed at the group of men around the table. "We can't all live here. Our place isn't big enough to house everybody. But I spoke with some people in my company, and I've discovered we have holdings in Chicago, including some that we're looking into renovating. There's one building that sits on six acres. It has several outbuildings and one large warehouse." His eyes shone. "That could be made into dormitory-style housing. The buildings around it could become gyms, sparring rooms, arsenals—"

Roadkill cackled. "Yeah, I can see it now. Like they're going to let us have a bazooka in downtown Chicago."

Dellan laughed. "It's not downtown, but it's close enough that you could get there in thirty minutes. And Duke said he could make it happen, so I think we're good to go." He beamed. "Think about it. You three would live on the grounds with us. Hashtag and Roadkill, you'd get to choose whether to stay with us or live in Chicago in the new dormitory housing. The rest of the men could stay in dormitories, and they could finally have a place they could call home. There'd be space for Aelryn's people too, if they needed it, plus room for when there's a big op planned and we bring in more men."

"But I don't work for Duke," Vic said quietly. "And neither does Saul."

Horvan chuckled. "Not now, you don't. But you *could*, both of you." He held up his hands. "Hey, you'd still do your job as shifter archivist, but someone else would pay you. And Saul's already proved he's a good man to have around."

"And we have a lot more work to do if we're going to stop the Gerans." Rael's expression grew solemn. "This isn't going to be an easy fix, guys. This could take a while. But they have to be stopped. You know that, right?"

Hashtag nudged Saul. "You got some deep emotional attachment to Duluth or something?"

Saul laughed out loud. "We chose Duluth because of its proximity to Lake Superior. And then Dellan goes and offers us land for a house right on a lake." His gaze focused on Crank. "Better yet, a house where all three of us could live. What's not to love about that?"

Vic squeezed Crank's hand. "What do you say, Crank? Do you want to build a home with us?"

The time had come for total honesty.

Crank stared at his fingers, laced with Vic's. "Since I left the military, my whole life has been about the team. Getting laid occasionally."

Hashtag almost choked on his coffee. "Occasionally?"

Crank glared at him. "Hey, if H can have a past where he knows all about your so-called talented tongue, then *I* can have a past too. Because it *is* the past. Beyond those hookups? Nothing. No emotional attachments, because I never knew whether I'd be back to that town again."

"And now?" Saul asked.

Crank met his gaze. "Now? It's starting to look like I could have a home. We're talking putting down actual roots. It always scared me before, but now… it doesn't."

And ain't that the fucking miracle of the century?

Dellan got up from his chair and went to stand between Horvan and Rael. "I think our family just got bigger."

Hashtag chuckled. "You don't fool me, Dellan. That house idea for Crank? You weren't thinking about giving them space—you're more concerned about how many beds you're gonna go through while they're under this roof."

"Damn. You saw straight through me." Dellan rolled his eyes.

"Hashtag, don't you have a satellite to hack?" Crank retorted.

Hashtag got up from the table. "Come on," he said, tugging on Roadkill's arm. "You can keep me company while I check for up-to-date images. We have to be ready for when the word is given." They left the kitchen.

"There's one good thing about Crank giving up his room—eventually," Vic remarked. When Dellan gave him an inquiring glance, he said softly, "That way you'll have a room for your dad when we find him, plus another for Jamie, if he wants to stay."

Dellan's eyes glistened. "I love that idea." He wiped his cheeks. "Excuse me. I have to see to… something." He walked quickly out of the room, and Horvan and Rael hurried after him.

"We're gonna find them." Crank had never been more determined.

"I've been thinking about that house plan," Saul murmured. "Five acres isn't all that big, you know. A little smaller than five football fields. I hope this house is far enough away from here that everyone won't hear Vic when he screams."

"Hey!" Vic's eyes flashed.

Saul gave him a sweet smile. "Did I lie?"

"That is *so* not the point," Vic said with a growl.

"Oh, I think it is. You scream when there's one guy fucking you. What do you think you'll be like with two of us?"

"At the same time," Crank added with a grin.

"Are we talking spit roasting?" Vic's eyes were wide.

Crank bit his lip. "Sure. We'll go with that if it makes you happy. For now." Right then, Crank was the happy one. In the course of two conversations, his life had been turned around again. So what if his job was fraught with danger?

He had someone to go home to. Someone to live for.

Actually? Two someones.

CHAPTER TWENTY-SIX

DELLAN WAITED until Horvan was in the office with Crank, Hashtag, Roadkill, and Vic, then pulled his phone from his pocket and went out onto the patio. Rael had gone into town with Mrs. Landon. Saul was taking a nap after both Crank and Vic had insisted. He was looking better with each new day, but there was no way he'd be going on the mission.

Looks like he'll be with us. Except Dellan had no intention of waiting it out in Illinois, and he was pretty sure once he outlined his plan, Saul would be on board with it.

Dellan reached the water's edge and squatted on the grass. He scrolled through his contacts until he found Doc's number, then clicked Call, his heart racing.

Please, Doc, be available. Dellan had wanted to call before, but every time he'd gotten as far as bringing up the number, he'd chickened out. *Maybe I'm better off not knowing.*

Except that was bullshit. He *had* to know.

By the time the call had reached five rings, Dellan was ready to try again later, but then Doc's voice filled his ear. "Hello?"

"Doc, this is Dellan Carson."

"Dellan. How are you?" The delight in Doc's voice warmed him.

"I'm fine. Well, maybe not fine. A lot has happened since we last saw you. But Doc, I need your help."

"What can I do for you?"

"Have you got a moment? I don't want to be dragging you away from something important."

"I'm packing for a trip, but it can wait. What's up?"

Dellan took a deep breath. "Okay, this is going to sound really farfetched, and more like science-fiction than reality, but…." He paused, his heart pounding.

"Dellan." Doc spoke calmly. "Tell me."

Dellan related what had happened to Saul, including everything Fielding had told him about Alec, not forgetting to add the part about the toxin. Doc listened in silence. "So I guess what I'm asking is… is such a thing possible?"

Yet more silence.

"Doc?"

"You think you've heard everything, and then…." Doc sighed. "Is it possible? For any *reputable* doctor or scientist, I'd say no. But this group?" He snorted. "They don't seem to have any morals or ethics. If you're asking if such a thing can happen, I'd *like* to say no, but I can't, because one day science *will* find a way. They'll do it through legitimate methods, and it will take many years. If they skirted the rules, it might come faster, but it comes with much greater risks."

"I was coming to that." Dellan's heart quaked. "If they've really done this, I mean, accelerated his growth rate—and whatever modifications they've made to allow him to produce this toxin—what's his life expectancy? What if this whole process makes him unstable?"

"I don't have answers for you. Well, maybe one theory, but I don't think you'll like it."

"I still want to hear it."

"Did you ever read about Dolly, the cloned sheep?"

For a second, Dellan was lost. "The what?"

"In the late nineties, someone thought it would be a good idea to clone a sheep, whom they called Dolly. In February 2003, she was euthanized because she had a progressive lung disease and severe arthritis. Her breed has a life expectancy of around eleven to twelve years, but Dolly lived for six and a half. Now, I know cloning is not what we're discussing here, but the principles are the same. They're tinkering with nature. I have to ask myself, have they already done this successfully, or is Alec a prototype? Do they have any idea how long he'll live?"

Dellan shivered. "We have to get Alec away from them. I don't know how long he's got left, but I *do* know they'll abandon him without hesitation once he's outlived his usefulness." The thought of him being used as a weapon made Dellan's blood curdle.

"Maybe he's at the camp."

Dellan froze. "And how do *you* know about that?"

After a moment's pause, Doc cleared his throat. "Because I'm part of the mission. Horvan contacted me a few days ago. He said they might need a medic, and he wanted me along because I knew your father. Yes, he told me that part too. I think he knew I'd agree in a heartbeat." Another pause. "That's why I'm packing. I'm getting ready. I expect the call any day now."

"But a call to go where?" All Dellan had was Bozeman, where the conversation between the two shifters had been overheard.

"I don't understand."

"Where are you going? No one is telling us anything."

"Who precisely is *us*?" Doc's voice was gentle.

"Me, Rael, Saul—that's Vic and Crank's mate—are being left here in Illinois."

Before he could get any further, Doc interrupted. "Wait. Did you say Vic and Crank have a *mate*? How is that even possible?"

Dellan snorted. "If a direct descendant of Ansfrid doesn't know the answer to that, there's little hope any of us will come up with one."

"A direct—oh my, you're keeping some exalted company these days. But back to what you were saying. You're staying there?"

"It's my father they're going to rescue, possibly my half brother, and maybe my son, but *nooo*, I can't be involved." Dellan knew he sounded bitter, but he couldn't help it.

"And what would you do if you *were* there?"

"We'd be a damn sight closer to our mates if they needed us, for one thing. There wouldn't be almost *one and a half thousand miles* between us, too far a distance to know what they're going through, what they're feeling…."

Another silence fell.

"Doc?"

Doc's sigh sounded heavy. "I think you're right to be unhappy with the situation. And I'm probably going to regret this, but…. Right now I have no information to give you, but when I know more, I'll contact you. Please don't tell Horvan how you found out, okay?"

"Seriously?" Dellan's pulse quickened. "You mean it?"

"I'll send you the location as soon as I know it. Hopefully that will give you enough time to make travel arrangements. I'm assuming you'll leave once Horvan and the team have gone."

"Doc, I'll be waiting for your text. And thank you."

"Anything for Jake's son. I-I loved your parents, Dellan, and I want you to find him. Dear God, you *have* to find him."

The barely concealed emotion in Doc's voice brought tears to Dellan's eyes. "We will." It was more than words.

It was a vow.

Dellan thanked him again and then disconnected. He sat quietly for a moment, locking away his elation. *Can't let Horvan see any of this.*

He intended sharing it with Rael and Saul the first chance he got.

VIC TYPED Gallatin County in Google Maps and pulled up the image on his tablet. "So what are we looking for?"

"Gooch Hill Road," Hashtag told him. The others were also on phones or tablets. "You'll see what looks like a farm with several outbuildings. It's the only property for miles. What interests *us* is that large structure at the bottom right of the boundary. It's a barn, and the farmer doesn't use it anymore. It's perfect for our purposes. We can bring our guys there in batches and stay hidden until we're ready to make our move."

"And the farmer is gonna sit there and let us take over his barn?" Crank inquired.

Horvan chuckled. "Hardly. We're paying him a lot for the privilege. What matters most about this place is that it's only half a mile from the gates to the camp. According to Hashtag's recent photos, there's a long dirt road that leads from those gates to the heart of the camp, and usually there's one, maybe two guards patrolling it."

"What do the locals think the camp is?" Roadkill asked.

"Some kind of research station, studying encephalitis and meningitis in cattle," Hashtag replied.

"We'll be hitting the place from two different sides," Horvan announced. "Team one will go in at 1:50, creating a diversion so that team two can infiltrate ten minutes later. Team one's objective will be to engage and neutralize the targets if they can, while team two gets inside and tries to get the people out. I'm leading team two, and I want all of you in it with me." He glanced at Vic and Crank. "I'm keeping you two together. I figured that was for the best."

Vic heaved a sigh of relief. *Thank God.* He wanted to keep Crank close.

I'm as relieved as you are. Crank's gaze locked on to his. *We can keep each other safe.*

Horvan coughed. "I do know what you're doing. Can you save the internal conversation for another time?" His voice was gruff, but that twinkle in his eye belied his tone. "We'll need to be as stealthy as possible, but once we've got all those extra bodies with us, that will be unlikely, so everyone will need to move like hell."

"Do we have any intelligence as to how many people are in there?" Vic wanted to know.

"So far, not much. Hashtag has been checking images whenever the satellite comes within range, but he hasn't seen a lot of activity on the ground. That's why we're taking as many men with us as we can. Aelryn is sending men too. He's organizing team one. And Doc Tranter will be there," Horvan announced with a smile.

Roadkill grinned. "Did you ask him, or did he already know about it and invite himself along?"

"I asked. I figured he'd want to be involved. We can always use a medic, and he was best friends with Dellan's parents."

"We don't need our guys with guns," Hashtag said with a grin. "Just have Doc shift into an elephant and trample all the bad guys." The others laughed.

"That's all for now." Horvan closed the folder on his lap. "Once we know we have a place to set up a base, Duke will organize flights to Bozeman Yellowstone airport and ground transportation to the site."

Vic shut down his tablet, then caught his breath as an image appeared in his head. It was a heavy, full cock—Saul's cock—and Saul was pulling it down, then allowing it to spring back up with a *smack* against his belly, only to repeat the motion.

Dear Gods. Talking about playing dirty.

Crank coughed, his face turning a shade of dark red, and Vic knew he wasn't the only one on the receiving end of that image.

"You okay there, Crank?" Horvan regarded him with concern.

When Crank had stopped spluttering, he wiped his mouth. "I'm fine. I think I swallowed wrong." Then another image appeared in Vic's head, of Crank sucking Saul's cock, his mouth stretched wide around it. Crank snuck a glance at Vic. *I'm gonna fucking kill him.*

Will that be before or after he puts that in your ass?

Crank's coughing fit returned with a vengeance.

Vic got up from his chair. "Are we done here? Because I need to check on Saul."

Hashtag grinned. "Gonna take his temperature? Three guesses what you're gonna use for a thermometer—and where you're gonna stick it."

"See you at lunch," Horvan said with an evil glint in his eye. "Unless you want to take yours in your room?"

Crank glared at him. "Did any of us make comments about how much time you spent in Dellan's room when we first got here? Hmm? No, we did not."

Vic's chest swelled with pride. *Good for you.* Horvan flushed, and Vic knew Crank's observation had hit home.

"Go spend time with your mates. We'll see you all… when we see you."

Crank smiled. "Thanks for that." He got up and followed Vic from the room. As soon as the door closed, Saul's voice filled Vic's head.

This dick isn't going to suck itself.

Vic laughed as he sprinted toward the stairs, happier than he'd been in a long time. Crank was hot on his heels as they raced to the bedroom, and Vic realized Crank's eagerness for what was to come was as great as his own.

Whoever put us together knew what they were doing.

CRANK PUSHED open the bedroom door and barged in, feigning anger. "We were in a meeting." It was difficult to keep up the pretense, however, when faced with a naked Saul kneeling on the bed, giving his solid shaft leisurely tugs.

Saul arched his eyebrows. "I waited until the meeting had finished before sending that image. I think that was very considerate of me." He gave a smug grin. "And which would you rather be doing—talking with Horvan and the others or sucking on this?" He smacked his dick on his palm.

Vic rolled his eyes. "Talk about a stupid question." He was out of his clothes in a heartbeat, then launched himself onto the bed, getting on all fours in front of Saul. He peered up at Saul before swallowing his cock to the root.

Saul groaned and grabbed Vic's head, pumping into his mouth. "Fuck. You're good at that." He nodded toward Vic's ass. "You need to taste our boy."

Boy? Vic pulled off and stared at him, before Saul grabbed his head and ground his dick into Vic's face.

"We're not talking shark years, we're talking human years. And you're our boy, so get used to it."

Not going to argue with that. Vic's head bobbed as he took Saul deep once more, and Saul's groans multiplied.

Crank undressed, getting his arms caught up in his tee as he pulled it over his head. He shucked off his jeans and got onto the bed behind Vic, spreading Vic's asscheeks to reveal his tight little hole. He gave it a tentative lick, and the shiver that coursed through Vic emboldened him to continue.

Oh gods, yeah, like that.

Crank smiled to himself as he licked and sucked Vic's pucker. *I know how to do this part.*

Vic shivered as Crank stabbed at his hole with his tongue. *Not going to argue with that.*

The combination of Vic's hole loosening for him and the constant moans in his head from both Vic and Saul stoked the heat building inside him until his need was white hot. Then he stilled, straightening. "Do we need condoms?"

Saul came to a halt, his hands on Vic's head, stroking his hair. "Vic's a shifter, and I get regular physicals. I'm assuming you have them too as part of your job." Crank nodded. "So there's nothing wrong with you that we need to know about?"

"Not a goddamn thing. And I haven't gotten laid since February."

"Seriously? Then you've got some making up to do." Saul's eyes glittered. "And no, no need for condoms. We're good to go."

Vic growled and knelt upright. "Guys. I'm a shifter, you're both healthy—now can we stop talking?" Then he flopped onto his back between them, grabbed both their dicks, and tugged them toward him.

"Is he usually this bossy?" Crank asked.

Saul laughed. "Only when he's hungry for cock." Then he groaned as Vic slid his lips along Saul's shaft. "Fuck, you're ravenous, aren't you?"

Vic pulled free and turned his head to take Crank's cock deep, and Crank cupped Vic's cheek, thrusting into his mouth.

Vic broke off to wrap his fingers around his own shaft. "You know how to rim, but how are you at sucking dick?"

Crank grinned. "Let's find out." He leaned over, his face within inches of Vic's hard-as-steel shaft. "Such a pretty cock." He rubbed it against his face before licking a line from root to head.

You've been taking lessons. Saul grabbed Vic's dick and guided it between Crank's lips, encouraging him to go deeper. *That's it. Make our boy's heart sing.*

Crank held still while Vic thrust, his hips rolling up off the bed as he pumped into Crank's mouth. Then he smacked Crank's hip. "Give me your cock again."

They got into a rhythm: Vic sucked them off alternately, pausing now and then while they took it in turn to worship Vic's shaft. Crank's heart pounded when his lips met Saul's as they mouthed Vic's shaft, and when those lips claimed his in a fervent, heated kiss, Vic's moan of pleasure rang in his head.

The sights and sounds sent heat surging through Crank—add to that the emotional tumult raging inside both his mates and he was fighting not to bust too soon. And when Vic lay on his belly, Saul's dick buried in his throat, and Crank finally slid his lubed cock into Vic's tight body, the sensation was so overwhelming that he had to stop for a moment to regain his control.

Vic shuddered and pulled free of Saul's shaft. "Fuck, you're hard."

Crank shivered. "Don't think I've ever been this hard. Part of it is being inside you." His dick was sheathed in tight muscle.

Vic twisted to look at him. "What's the other part?"

"When Saul is inside you and I feel your emotions?" Crank swallowed. "I want to feel that too." He'd been thinking about it every time they shared a bed. Saul hadn't pushed, and Crank was grateful for that, but that hadn't stopped the images from invading his mind.

Saul regarded him with wide eyes. "Are you sure? I mean, I know I tease you about taking your ass, but I'd never do it unless you wanted it."

"Six months ago, if anyone had told me I would consider taking a cock, especially one the size of Saul's, up my ass, I'd have punched them in the mouth. But you two have shown me it's not weird or strange. So yeah, I want to experience that."

"Does this strike either of you as a very odd conversation to be having while Crank's dick is in my ass?" Vic's eyes sparkled. "Not that I'm complaining, you understand. Because it feels amazing."

Saul smiled. "Before we met you, I imagined I could feel how much Vic enjoyed it when we had sex. Now? I realize that's exactly what I was feeling. Well, kinda. When you came along, it all became sharper. And *now* I know what I was feeling was his pleasure as well as mine. Maybe… maybe it's time I experience it too."

Crank blinked. "You want to bottom?" Then he pushed aside his incredulity. "Not that there's anything wrong with that."

Saul chuckled. "Vic has never wanted to top, and—"

"Still don't," Vic responded promptly. Both Crank and Saul chuckled at that.

Saul stroked Vic's head. "But maybe, if you're willing, we could all explore a little more. I'm not saying *right now*, but one day…."

"Can we go back to the part where Crank was about to fuck me?" Vic exclaimed.

Crank covered Vic with his body and slowly withdrew his cock, before driving it back in. "Like that?"

Vic trembled. "Exactly like that."

Crank rocked into him, keeping the pace gentle. "Fuck. Sliding into you is… exquisite." There was no other word that did justice to the sensation. Crank's arms took his weight as he rolled his hips, aware of Vic's warm back against his chest, the way he tilted his ass to meet Crank's thrusts.

Then Saul moved around the bed, and Crank gasped as strong fingers pried his asscheeks apart and a warm, wet tongue licked over his hole. "H-holy fuck." Then Saul rubbed his beard through Crank's crease. "Jesus fucking *Christ*."

"What the hell did you just do?" Vic demanded. "Because you really need to do that again."

"What he said." He moaned as Saul pressed his tongue to Crank's pucker. "Aw fuck. Don't stop."

"Hey, *you* stopped!" Vic remonstrated.

"Well, having Saul's face in my ass is kinda distracting, okay?"

"Get back to fucking our boy," Saul whispered in his ear. "I've got something else I wanna try." The *click* that followed had Crank's heart pistoning, and he froze as Saul pressed a cool, slick finger into his body.

"Oh God. Oh God." Crank was torn to say which felt better: Saul's finger or Vic's hole.

"Want me to stop?" Saul inquired, stilling inside him.

"Don't even think about it," Crank ground out. Then he rocked out of Vic, forcing Saul deeper into his body. *Oh fuck, Saul....*

It wasn't long before Crank was fucking himself on Saul's fingers, shuttling between his mates, crying out as each new delicious sensation washed over and through him. And when Saul smacked Crank's asscheek with his hefty cock and asked if he was ready for it, Crank spread his legs wide at the knees, tilted his ass high, and waited, his heart pounding.

The bliss that accompanied Saul's unhurried penetration left him in no doubt that this was meant to be—the three of them connected, in mind as well as body, moving together in sinuous harmony toward their goal.

It was almost perfect.

"I want to see your faces," he cried out.

Saul withdrew instantly, and Crank flopped onto his back, only to have Saul tug him toward the edge of the bed. Vic pushed Crank's knees to his chest, folding him in half, then straddled his ass, crouching over Crank's still rigid dick as he guided it back into him. Saul stood beside the bed, his hands on Crank's asscheeks. The head of Saul's cock kissed Crank's hole, he pushed, and they were joined once more.

Crank looked into their eyes. *Now make me come.*

Vic nodded. *You're close. I can feel it.* He moaned as Saul moved in and out of Crank, each thrust sending Crank deeper into Vic's body, until all three were rocking, their breathing harsh.

Crank didn't know what brought him to the edge so goddamn fast. Maybe it was being in a guy's ass for the first time, or having a dick in his, or the fact that his mind went into overload trying to assimilate the sensations. All he knew was that moment when his whole body was on fire. He was the first to let go, and he groaned as he shot his load, his cock pulsing inside Vic. *Oh Jesus, I feel that.* Every wave of pleasure that broke over Vic caught Crank in its wake, and a moment later warmth coated Crank's chest as Vic came.

I wanted this to last, but I can't hold back any longer. Saul's hips jerked as he picked up speed, slamming into Crank's ass, his breathing staccato as he drove his shaft all the way home. Then he pushed Vic onto Crank and covered them both, and Crank caught his breath as Saul's dick throbbed inside him.

Oh dear God, this is heaven.

They lay together, a fusion of arms, legs, lips, and tongues. Crank's shaft was still buried in Vic's ass, and Saul was balls-deep in Crank. Little by little, their breathing returned to its usual cadence, but Crank didn't want to move. He wanted to hold on to this moment for as long as he could.

"We don't have anywhere to be, do we?"

Vic kissed him, a slow, tender kiss that was as comforting as a blanket on a winter's night. "Nowhere at all." Then he turned his head, Saul leaned in, and three mouths met.

"Now I have two men to take care of," Saul whispered as they parted.

Crank stiffened. *I can take care of myself. I've been doing it for a long time.*

And just like that, the afterglow vanished as if it had never been.

CHAPTER TWENTY-SEVEN

VIC FLINCHED as if Crank had slapped him across the face. Behind him, Saul eased out of Crank and stood there, his face tight. "What's wrong with me wanting to take care of you?" The words came out strangled.

Vic disengaged himself from Crank and knelt beside him, his stomach churning. Saul's hurt was palpable, echoing the sharp pain that lanced through Vic.

Crank's breathing hitched. "Oh Christ. Now I've ruined everything." He sat up on the bed, leaning against the pillows. "It's just that… I've kinda gotten used to being self-sufficient. I've been that way since I was in my teens. Not gonna talk about what led up to it, but I left home when I was fifteen. I bummed around for a while, worked all over the place, and when I turned eighteen, I joined the army." He bit his lip. "That changed me, a little. I learned what it meant to be part of a team, but also how to take care of others." He shrugged. "I'm still doing that."

"Maybe that needs to stop." Saul's voice was steadier. "Maybe it's time you let someone take care of *you* too." He ran a hand over Vic's back, and Vic arched into his touch. "They sent me to Vic because he needed a handler. I can be that for you too, you know. *We* can be that for you."

Crank's face clouded. "That sounds an awful lot like pity. I don't need that."

Saul's eyes widened. "It has nothing to do with pity. We want to take care of you because you're our mate. And it goes both ways. I'd hope you'd want to take care of us too." He climbed onto the bed and knelt on the comforter. "Come here."

Crank crawled over to him, and Saul pulled him upright, enfolding him in his arms. "I don't care that I've known you for about five minutes." He grasped Crank's wrist and brought his hand to Saul's chest, where his wounds were etched over his heart. "You're already in here. So taking care of you? It's kinda automatic." He let go of Crank's hand and cupped his chin. "Now kiss me, because I need it."

Crank's mouth was on his in an instant, his tongue seeking access, both of them letting out soft sounds that spoke of pleasure and arousal. And then Vic pulled both of them down to the mattress, lying between them as they kissed and touched and stroked, no goal beyond that of learning each other's bodies. Vic rolled onto his side to face Saul, and Crank snuggled up behind him, caressing both his mates, enjoying the feel of Vic's warm skin against his.

"I'm sorry I spoiled the mood," he murmured.

Saul stroked his arm, then lifted Crank's hand to his lips and kissed the tips of his fingers. "It's okay, as long as we understand one another better because of it."

Vic craned his neck to look at Crank. "Why is your cock poking me in the ass again? Didn't you get enough? Your cum is still in there, for God's sake."

Crank kissed Vic's neck, loving the shiver that trickled through him. "Truthfully? I don't think I'll ever get enough of the two of you."

Vic's smile reached his eyes, and his face glowed. He reached back and gave Crank's dick a slow pull. Saul grabbed the lube, and then he tugged Vic's leg, hooking it over his hip, spreading him. He wiped slick fingers over Vic's hole, and seconds later Crank was inside him again. He sighed as he bottomed out.

This is where I'm meant to be.

Saul kissed Vic, then Crank. *This is where all three of us are meant to be.* In each other's arms.

SAUL LAY on the bed, his eyes closed. He seemed to be sleeping more than he usually did, but the doctor at the hospital had warned him his recovery might be slow. It didn't help that Vic and Crank were busy with preparations for the mission. The word had come down from Aelryn the previous day: forty-eight hours until both forces met in Montana. Neither Vic nor Crank had disclosed exactly *where* in Montana, and Saul guessed he could understand the reasoning behind that decision: after the Brick episode, information was not to be bandied about. The importance of the mission made it high priority, and Saul had been around the military long enough to understand the demand for secrecy.

The soft knock at his door roused him from his doze. "Come in." When Dellan and Rael entered, Saul sat up immediately. "Is anything wrong?"

"This can't get back to Crank or Vic, all right?" Dellan sat on the bed, and Rael went around it to sit on the opposite side.

"Gotcha." Saul gazed at him, intrigued. "What's this about?"

"I only need to know one thing." Dellan tilted his head to the side. "Do you *really* want to stay here while they go off on their mission?"

Saul snorted. "What do you think?"

Dellan gave a satisfied nod. "Okay, then. We're going to Montana."

He frowned. "What?"

"You heard me. I know where they're going, where their base of operations will be, what time the mission kicks off…." Dellan smiled. "I know everything. So am I booking three seats on the flight to Bozeman?"

"How? Did Horvan suddenly forget to lock everything away or something?"

"Never mind about how I know." Dellan speared him with a look. "You took weapons to Boston, right?" Saul nodded. "Where are they now?"

Saul inclined his head toward the closet. "My Glock is in there. They took my Sig Sauer."

"And you can take that on the plane, can't you?"

"Sure, as long as I let them know about it and it goes as cargo." He stilled. "We're really going?"

Dellan nodded. "I don't know about you, but I don't want to be so far away from Horvan."

"Then why do I need my gun?"

"Don't get me wrong—I have no intention of putting either myself or Rael in harm's way, but we might need protection."

Saul drew in a deep breath. "Count me in." He gazed at both of them. "And I'll keep you safe."

Rael took his hand and squeezed it. "Thank you. Now, lock this conversation away. We don't want them to have even the slightest notion that we're doing this."

"Will that work? Crank said he could sort of 'feel' me and Vic when we were in Duluth. Won't they know we're nearby?"

Dellan sighed. "I'm counting on them being so focused on their mission that we can sneak up on them."

Saul blinked. "That's it? You're basically hoping they don't get wind of us?"

Dellan gave him a hard stare. "Well, do you have any better ideas?"

"Okay, okay. We'll go with hope. Now, what's the plan?"

"They're leaving at dawn tomorrow. I don't have all the details, but I'm assuming they're heading for Waukegan. I've got three tickets on the 10:55 out of O'Hare. It gets into Bozeman Yellowstone airport at threeish. That should be hours after Horvan and the others arrive there. We'll hire a car at the airport and drive to Bozeman. Then we keep out of sight until they leave the base, which is around 2:00 a.m."

Saul arched his eyebrows. "For someone who doesn't have all the details, you sure know a lot."

Dellan chuckled. "I have my sources."

His words sank in. "Wait—you've already bought three tickets? What if I'd said no?"

Dellan bit his lip. "I had a hunch." He got up from the bed. "Now get some rest. We've got a big day tomorrow." Rael relinquished Saul's hand, and the two men left the bedroom.

Saul lay back on the pillows. *I might not be able to fight, but I can take care of Horvan's mates.* Except in his heart, he hoped for the chance to deliver a little retribution for what he'd suffered at the hands of Fielding and his men.

Just a little.

THE MOOD around the dining table was more solemn than usual. Rael could understand that. Their minds had to be focused on the mission. Horvan kept firing glances at him and Dellan, but Rael was confident they'd hidden their plans deep out of sight. What made Rael's heart pound was the thought that he now had a better idea of what the guys were up against.

Is there even a small chance some of them might not come back?

He couldn't afford to think like that.

You okay?

Rael jerked his head up to meet Horvan's warm gaze. *I'm fine. A little worried, that's all. I'm sure I don't have to explain why.*

Horvan wiped his lips with his napkin and leaned back with a sigh. "I know this is tough for you, Dellan, and Saul, and normally I'd tell you everything, but…. Well, after Brick—who only did what he did because he wanted to keep his parents safe—we're keeping things on a strictly need-to-know basis." He glanced around the table. "In the military, you get to

215

appreciate the need for secrecy." Horvan returned his attention to Dellan and Rael. "It isn't that we don't trust you. I hope you realize that."

"Yes, we do," Rael assured him. "You're looking out for everyone who is going with you. You have to do what you can to keep them safe, and if that means restricting access to information, then that's what you do." He waggled his eyebrows. "Doesn't mean we have to like it, or that Dellan and I won't make you pay for it at some point." Hoots and chuckles erupted from Hashtag and Roadkill at that.

Horvan grinned. "Is that a threat or a promise?"

Dellan chuckled. "A bit of both. But seriously, don't worry about us. You have far more important things to concern you."

Rael's chest tightened at Horvan's pained expression. "Just so we're clear? *No one* and *nothing* is more important to me than you two."

His declaration sent a pang of guilt lancing through Rael, and he could feel Dellan's similar reaction. *We are right to do this, aren't we?*

Yes, we are. Dellan's response was prompt and emphatic.

Then Horvan cleared his throat. "Guys? Bedtime. We all need to get some sleep." His gaze met Rael's. *But not right away. Something I need to do first.*

Rael had a good idea what that meant—Horvan making love to both of them.

He smiled. *Who needs sleep anyway?*

CRANK UNDRESSED in silence, as did Vic and Saul. Horvan's words at dinner had resonated within him. He hated keeping Saul in the dark, but Saul had been through enough. What shocked him were the twitchy feelings he couldn't shake whenever he was alone with Vic and Saul, the way his heartbeat quickened when they drew near, and the sense of calm and contentment that pervaded him in their presence.

Crank had never succumbed to being sappy in his entire life, and he wasn't sure he was ready to start now.

"You two have turned me inside out, upside down, back to front...," he muttered as he climbed into bed. Saul got in beside him, and Crank ached to touch him.

"Are you complaining?" Saul leaned over and kissed him, a slow, intimate kiss that made Crank's heart beat even faster.

Crank chuckled. "The crazy thing is? Horvan said weeks ago that one day someone would crawl into my heart and turn it to mush. Of course, he thought that would be a woman, so he was almost right."

Vic slid beneath the sheets, and Crank caught his breath as warm fingers encircled his dick. "Are you always hard?" Vic murmured.

Crank chuckled. "Around you two? Duh." A momentary flare of panic speared through him, and he couldn't hide it fast enough.

Saul curved his body around Crank's, his arm across Crank's chest. "What's wrong?"

Crank swallowed. "I always told myself this was why I didn't get involved with anyone, why I didn't do relationships. Because there was always the possibility that something wouldn't go to plan and I wouldn't come home. I hated the idea of leaving someone to grieve for me."

"But you *are* going to come home," Saul said fervently. "And then it'll be the three of us. We'll build a house by the lake, go swimming every day with Vic—"

"And make love every night," Vic said softly. He gave Crank's shaft a leisurely tug. "Two or three times."

Saul chuckled. "You haven't discovered it yet, but Vic is pretty insatiable. Probably why he's good with two mates. You can fuck him while I rest up, and vice versa."

"Then what about me?" Crank asked. Teasing hid his nerves.

"Oh, I'll be able to fuck you too, don't you worry. We might have to work out a schedule, though."

Vic trailed his finger along the length of Crank's dick. "Don't think we're not aware you're prevaricating, Crank."

Crank's heartbeat stuttered, and tears pricked the corners of his eyes. They really *did* know him. "Until you two came along, the people I was closest to in the whole world were Horvan, Roadkill, and Hashtag. We looked out for each other. We had each other's backs. They were my family."

Vic cupped Crank's cheek. "Can't you tell us what happened? I mean, why you ended up on your own at so young an age?"

"Too many kids at home, so I left to make it easier on my mom?" The lie came easily, except he'd forgotten for a moment who he was lying to.

Saul's breath tickled his ear. "Wanna try that again?"

Crank sighed. "You've heard the story a million times. A dad who sometimes forgot that a belt is made for wearing. A dad whose address should've been the local bar, because they sure as shit saw more of him than his family ever did. A dad who was careful not to leave bruises or marks where anyone might see 'em. That all adds up to a kid who had enough and got out of there before things got worse."

Vic paled. "Did he ever hit your mom?"

Crank snorted. "That's the most fucked-up part. He said no decent man should ever resort to hitting a woman. So did that make him decent because he took out his rage on me instead? Because there was just me and two sisters, so that obviously meant I was his personal punching bag, right?"

"Couldn't you tell anyone what was going on? Did your mom know?" Saul asked.

"She knew all right. The fact that she did nothing about it was what convinced me I had to get out of there. So I stole what money I could find in the house, raided my piggy bank, and left. I got on a bus and kept going until I had no more money to buy tickets. I figured that meant I had to stay put for a while. I looked older than I was, thank God, and I found a job working in a warehouse. I slept there too. I moved from job to job till I was eighteen. You know the rest."

"You do know how awesome you are, don't you?" Vic looked him in the eye. "You became someone who fights to help others."

"And if you hadn't gone into the military, we might never have found you," Saul added.

Crank shook his head. "I think our paths would've crossed at some point. Not sure in what circumstances, but yeah, we were always going to meet."

"You really believe that, don't you?" Vic's voice held awe. He placed his hand on Crank's chest. "I can feel it here." Then he leaned in, and Crank surrendered to the sweetest kiss he'd ever experienced.

"What do you want?" Saul whispered, tracing the line of Crank's cheek with a finger.

"The three of us, connected, like we were the first time we fucked."

Saul nodded. "We can do that." Then two pairs of lips met Crank's, and Crank moaned into the three-way kiss. "Let us make love to you."

Crank tried to push the thought from his mind, but it wouldn't budge. *In case it's the last time.*

CHAPTER TWENTY-EIGHT

HORVAN TAPPED his earpiece. "Troy, we're in place." There were ten in his team, all dressed in black, crouched low in the trees. The gates were about twenty feet away, and no light could be seen in the camp beyond. Night vision goggles had revealed only one guard on duty. "One bad guy to take out."

"Copy that. We're registering about seven guards around the perimeter. Can't tell how many people are in the huts." A pause. "Seven's not a lot, Horvan. I'd expected more."

So had Horvan, and it made him nervous. "Remember, nonlethal force unless absolutely necessary. We wanna talk to these guys."

"Copy that." A pause. "Okay, we're going in."

"Copy that." Horvan signaled to the others who'd been listening. Crank patted the long slim barrel of his rifle, and Horvan nodded. Crank wouldn't miss.

An eruption of gunfire shattered the quiet, and Horvan tensed. Then light flooded the camp. "Fuck." So much for infrared. "Change of plan. We're going in now. Doc, Scott, you too." More gunfire rang out.

"Taking out the gate guard now." Crank aimed, fired, and the man crumpled to the ground, yelling and clutching his calf. Horvan and the others scurried across to the gate, and Roadkill secured the guard's wrists.

Horvan tapped his earpiece. "Kelly? One for collection, main gate. Wound to lower leg."

"Copy that."

Then they ducked under the barrier and sprinted along the dirt road that led to the camp.

A loud boom filled the air. "Christ." Horvan had heard enough landmines to recognize the sound. He tapped the earpiece again. "Everything okay, Troy?"

"Yes. Detonated a mine. The dogs had pretty much identified where they're located when they did a circuit of the fence. They seem to have only mined the outer part of the camp."

Horvan smiled. Shifter noses detected mines better than any devices designed for that purpose.

"Horvan, something's wrong here."

"What do you mean?"

"These guards we're taking down. Some of them are good shots, but others? If I was standing in front of them, they couldn't hit me."

"We're on our way." He signaled to Doc, Scott, and five others to head for the huts they'd seen during reconnaissance, and he, Crank, and Vic ran toward the center of the camp, where all the noise was coming from.

Troy stood in the center of the compound along with six members of his team, their guns pointed at the seven guards who knelt on the ground, their hands behind their heads. "I think this is all of them," he called out to Horvan as he approached. Then gunfire broke out from one of the huts.

"Horvan, we got us a sniper. They must have guards in there too." That was Hashtag.

Troy aimed his gun at the nearest guard. "How many more of you are there?"

The guard stared at him, his lips twisted into a sneer. "As if I'd tell a human."

Troy rolled his eyes. "Please, someone shift and wipe the smile off this fucker's face."

"My pleasure." Horvan removed his boots, ripped the clothing from his body, and shifted, lumbering toward the kneeling guards. He waited until he was only inches from the sneering guy's face before letting loose with a growl, baring his teeth. The guard paled, and Horvan shifted back. "Crank, you got my spare kit on you?"

Crank reached into his backpack and tossed Horvan a pair of jeans and a black tee. "You love getting your clothes off, don'tcha? And don't think I didn't get you digging the whole ripping clothes routine." He grinned. "Come on, fess up. You always wanted to be a stripper, didn't ya?" That got a chuckle from Troy.

Horvan ignored him, scanning the guards. "Now talk," he demanded, pulling on the jeans and tee. "How many more guards are there?" No one spoke. Then an explosion made everyone jump. "What was that? Roadkill, talk to me."

"They rigged the doors to the huts. We didn't see it. Mike's been injured."

"I'm on it, Horvan." That was Doc. "But you need to see this."

"Copy that." He glanced at Troy. "Looks like you've got this covered."

Troy nodded. "We'll secure them."

Horvan hurried toward the first hut, Crank and Vic keeping pace with him. Hashtag met them at the gaping hole where the door had been. "This is fucking unbelievable." His face appeared haggard. When Horvan went to step inside, Hashtag stopped him with a hand to his chest. "There are four more huts, but they're empty. We've checked them all. The sniper was in this one, but we took him out. He was a guard. But then we met gunfire from some of the inmates."

Horvan gaped. "Wait—the people we're supposed to be liberating were shooting at us?"

Hashtag nodded. "We've taken all the weapons. But H"—his expression was grave—"they're in an awful state. We've got people who are wounded, emaciated, sick...." His face tightened. "We shot at them before we saw who we were firing at. All we knew was we had to stop the gunfire. We injured a few. I'm more concerned about some of the others. I really don't think they'll make it."

The truth dawned. "They were abandoned. Expendable. How many people?"

"At a rough head count, maybe fifty? Looks like they were all crammed into a hut that sleeps half that number. And here's another thing. If they rigged the doors, they didn't care how many of the inmates would die as a result. But H"—Hashtag's gaze locked onto his—"Dellan's dad isn't one of them. Nor is Jamie. And no one like the kid Saul described."

"Aw fuck." This would break Dellan.

"Doc says he can't cope with this many people in need of care. There are wounds that need attending to, for one thing, and we only have Doc and Scott."

Horvan had to see for himself.

He stepped across the broken wooden door frame and into the large hut. Its inhabitants were herded together, and the air was thick with the smell of blood and infection. They were mostly women in their late forties or fifties, men with wounds that appeared badly tended to, a young man in his early twenties, and three or four children.

"Jesus," he muttered. The silence in the hut was oppressive. Doc and Scott moved among the inmates, silently assessing their patients. Doc glanced at Horvan, and his anger was obvious.

Horvan approached the nearest man and crouched beside him. "We're here to help you," he said in a low voice. The guy was way too thin, and Horvan couldn't miss the waves of fear rolling off him.

The man sniffed. "You... you're a shifter." When Horvan nodded, he stared at him in obvious puzzlement. "But I don't understand."

"Why were you armed?"

He swallowed. "They... they gave us guns and told us to protect this place. They said... they said if we refused, they'd kill us all, and that it would be a mercy compared to what *you'd* subject us to."

"Us?" Horvan frowned.

The man nodded. "Yeah, humans. Only, you're not human." He inclined his head to where Hashtag, Roadkill and a few of the others stood. "They are, though."

"Let me see if I've got this right. They told you humans would be here to kill you?"

"Yes."

"We've got company," Crank yelled from outside. "And you're not gonna believe this."

"Don't bet on it," Horvan muttered. After what he'd just seen.... He strode out of the hut and came to a dead halt when he saw who stood next to Crank. "Brick? What the fuck are you doing here?"

Brick was in camo, a rifle slung over his shoulder. "I had to come. They were calling me."

What the fuck?

"Someone from team one came across him, crawling under the wire," Crank told him. "Luckily for Brick. He was about to encounter a landmine."

Horvan holstered his gun. "Okay, from the beginning. When did you get here?"

"A couple days ago. I've been searching everywhere, but I couldn't hear them. I thought I was going nuts."

"Couldn't hear who, Brick?"

He blinked. "The voices in my head. Two of them. Young."

"Oh shit," Crank murmured.

"I've been hearing them for about a week now. I thought it was just grief, that maybe I was cracking up. At first they were only whispers, but they kept getting louder." He locked eyes with Horvan. "I was gonna call you to let you know I might need a doctor, but then yesterday... suddenly...." He swallowed. "It wasn't voices anymore. I got flashes of faces, conversations. And then the screams started." He took another hard swallow. "All they kept saying was 'They're coming, they're coming.' I tried to work out where the voices started from, but it was useless until I quit trying so hard and *felt* for them instead."

"Why didn't you call me?" Horvan demanded. "If you'd done that, we could've told you about the mission, and you could have come in with us."

"I wasn't thinking straight, all right?" Brick's face was ashen. "The voices thought they were going to die. They were *begging* me to save them. The only explanation I can come up with is they could be my mates. I can't hear them now, though, and it's scaring me. Either I've gone off the deep end, or—"

"You came!" The young man Horvan had seen in the hut burst through the gaping doorway and raced for Brick, barging past Horvan's men. When he got to where Brick stood, he threw himself into Brick's arms. "Seth said you would," he wailed, snuggling against Brick's chest.

Brick enfolded the guy in his arms. "I gotcha, I gotcha," he murmured in a soothing voice. "What's your name?"

"Aric." He was short, with dark-brown hair and large eyes. So small, he was lost in Brick's arms. Horvan noted the wounds on his hands and arms. Defensive wounds.

Doc emerged from the hut. "Hey, I haven't finished with you." He hurried over to them and stretched out his hand toward Aric.

All hell broke loose.

Brick screamed, "Don't you touch him!"

Horvan held out his hands. "Brick, stand down, let Doc—"

Brick snarled, pushing Aric behind him. "If you try to take him from me, I'll kill you!"

"Hey, dude." Crank's voice was soft. "No one's gonna take him from you, okay? But he's been hurt. Doc just wants to treat him." With each sentence he got a little closer, until at last his hand was on Brick's arm. "Brick, he's been hurt. You don't want him in pain, do you?"

Horvan stood still, letting Crank do his stuff.

223

Brick shuddered out a breath. "Okay, Doc. Take care of him. But I'm coming too."

"No problem. Is it okay if Scott takes a look while I talk to Horvan? You've met Scott, haven't you?" He gestured to Scott, who was watching the proceedings.

Brick nodded. "Yeah, I remember him." Scott took Aric by the arm and led him away from the hut, Brick following.

Doc waited until they were at a safe distance, then spoke to Horvan. "I need more help. There are wounds to be cleaned up, bandaged. We don't have the manpower."

"Then what do you suggest I do?" Horvan threw his hands up.

"Well, Dellan and Rael would help. Saul too. Call them." Doc flushed.

Both Horvan and Vic froze. Horvan narrowed his gaze. "Why do I have the feeling you don't mean call them in Illinois?" He concentrated, searching for them. *The jig is up. Where are you?*

At the base. Even in Horvan's head, Dellan sounded sheepish.

Then get your asses over here. Saul there too?

Yeah. That was Rael.

Bring him. And we are *gonna talk about this. You know that, right?* When no response came, Horvan chuckled. *Yeah, you know it.* He was torn between joy that they were so close and the urge to spank the pair of them.

Then he reconsidered. They might enjoy the spanking.

Vic OPENED his mind. *Saul Alexander Emory, what the fuck are you doing here?*

Hi, babe.

Don't you hi babe me. You might be my keeper, but motherfuck am I gonna kill you.

And when he gets through with you, it's my turn, Crank added.

That brought Vic a smile.

Doc cleared his throat. "I take it my help is on its way?"

Horvan snorted. "Well, that depends. I still need to figure out how they knew where we were, 'cause I don't believe in fairies. Of course, there's always the possibility that some well-meaning person might have tipped them off."

Doc coughed, and his flush deepened. "Hey, we need them." He glanced toward the hut. "A lot of these people are going to need psychiatric help when this is all over. I've been talking to some of them, and they've been living in a climate of fear. We need to make sure they're taken care of."

Horvan nodded. "And we'll do that." He tapped his earpiece. "Troy? Can you get a message to Aelryn? We're gonna need those medics."

"Copy that."

Then Doc's face crumpled, and Vic's chest grew tight. "Hey, what is it?"

"Jake isn't here." Tears trickled down his cheeks, and he gave them a savage wipe. "Look at me. I'm such an old fool."

"Doc? You and Jake were close?"

"All three of us. Then I went off to medical school, and although we stayed in touch for a while, communication dried up eventually. They told me about Dellan, even sent me pictures." Doc smiled. "Beautiful kid." His Adam's apple bobbed. "And if they've really done this... horrible thing to Dellan's son, we have to stop them. We have to find Jake. And Jamie." Then his eyes grew flinty. "It's obvious from talking to those poor people that their captors knew we were coming. They told me a load of buses turned up here, and most of the inmates were herded onto them. Then they gave orders to defend the camp, even convinced a few of their prisoners to help the remaining guards."

Horvan let out a growl. "You know what? We've been dancing to their fucking tune from the beginning. At every step, they've found ways to beat us to the punch." He set his jaw. "That has to stop. We need to think outside the box."

"And how do you propose to do that?" Vic asked.

"The team needs a change of leadership."

Vic's stomach churned. "You're not leaving, are you?"

Horvan shook his head. "No, but I think Saul should lead us now."

Vic frowned. "Saul? But he's not part of your group."

"And that's why we need him. He has ideas we might never have thought of." Horvan's eyes twinkled. "I can take orders from Saul without risking my fragile masculine ego. Besides, these bastards hurt our mates, they have Dellan's father, and they might have his half brother *and* his son. We need to help find them. So I will do whatever I have to in order to take these bastards down." He peered at Vic. "And will *you* work for us?"

Vic snorted. "Dellan's giving us land so we can build a house for the three of us. You really think I'm going to say no to that?"

"Horvan? You got a sec?" Brick stood with Aric, a damn sight calmer than he had been. "Aric here has been telling me some things, and I think you need to hear him out."

Horvan tapped his earpiece. "Everything contained, Troy? … Great. Give me a few minutes and we'll start to ship the bad guys outta here, then do the same with the wounded, as soon as the choppers arrive with the medics." Then Horvan faced Brick. "Okay. Talk to me."

Brick gave Aric a nudge. "Tell him. He's a good guy." Aric bit his lip, and Brick nodded encouragingly.

"I met Seth here at the camp. I knew right away he was something special. We… we clicked, y'know?"

Horvan glanced at Vic before responding. "Yeah, we know."

"Well, the guys who run this place, they were really interested in him."

"Why?" Vic demanded. "Do they want to breed him too?"

When Aric nodded, Horvan frowned. "What is it about Seth that they want to replicate?"

Aric shivered. "He has a talent. Not for speed or agility or anything like that. But he can do things with his mind."

"We talking psychic talent?" Horvan asked.

Aric nodded again. "When… when Seth and I tried to reach out to find someone to help us, we found we could send our thoughts farther when we were together. Alone? Nowhere near as far. But it's Seth's talent that makes it possible, not mine. So when they said they were going to take him away to a new camp, we knew we had to find help, and fast."

"A new camp?" a familiar voice asked.

Horvan whirled around to find Dellan, Rael, and Saul standing behind him. Saul headed straight for Vic and Crank, and Horvan's heart soared to see the joy in their faces as the three connected in a fierce hug.

Do we get one of those, or are you still mad at us? Dellan inquired.

Horvan didn't hesitate. He took two steps and grabbed hold of his mates, then pulled them against his chest.

You are both gonna get your asses kicked for this when I get you home.

Dellan smiled. *Will the ass-kicking be before or after you fuck us through the mattress?*

Rael kissed him. *Love you. And we had to come.*

Dellan broke away from him and approached Aric. "Tell us what you know about this new camp."

"That's where they took Seth. And they took his dad too. Usually they don't keep kids with their parents, but they wouldn't split Seth and his dad up. Never did find out why."

Dellan stared at Horvan. "They have a new camp."

"And we'll find it, okay?" Horvan glanced at Brick. "Because now we've got to rescue Brick and Aric's mate."

Rael stepped forward to join Dellan. "Hey. I'm Rael, and this is Dellan. What kind of shifter are you?"

"I'm a… cat."

Horvan gave him a warm smile. "What kind of cat? Jaguar? Leopard? Cheetah?"

Aric blushed. "No, just a regular old housecat." He snuck a peek at Brick. "You know, the kind that likes to curl up in your lap and purrs when he's happy and content. Only there wasn't much of that until I met Seth." Then he gazed openly at Brick. "And you."

Brick stroked Aric's hair. "I always was a cat person," he murmured. Then he cleared his throat. "And apparently I'm now a guy person too."

That stopped Horvan in his tracks. "Oh wow. You've never…?"

"Nope. Not ever." Brick gazed into Aric's eyes. "I guess there's a first time for everything."

"And what about Seth?" Dellan asked. "What kind of shifter is he?"

"He's a tiger." Aric's tone held so much pride. "His dad is too."

Horvan felt the tension in Dellan before the words left his lips.

"What's his dad's name?"

"Jake."

CHAPTER TWENTY-NINE

DELLAN RECOILED in shock. *It can't be.* Except that was a stupid reaction. They knew about Alec, about Jamie, and given how long the Gerans had his dad captive, God knew how many kids he'd sired. *Why not? He probably knows Mom is dead.*

Don't go jumping to conclusions. Horvan's voice was firm but kind. *There have to be a lot of guys called Jake.*

Who are also tiger shifters? There was one way to prove it once and for all.

Dellan reached into his jacket pocket and removed his phone. He scrolled through his pics until he found what he was looking for. "Aric, does Seth's dad look like this?" He held it up for Aric to see.

One look at Aric's wide eyes and open mouth and Dellan had his answer.

"Horvan."

Roadkill's low, urgent voice broke through Dellan's thoughts, and he went to pat Aric's arm, then thought better of it. He liked his hands where they were. "We'll talk more about this later, okay?" Aric gave a single nod, then pressed his slim body against Brick, who wrapped his arms around him. Dellan followed Horvan and the rest of the team away from the hut.

Roadkill came to a halt close to one of the watchtowers. "We've been talking to the inmates, trying to find out why they were brought here in the first place. The easiest answer appears to be they were used as breeding stock. They talked about genetic testing. The Gerans wanted certain shifters for their DNA. And another thing. There was a lab set up in one of the huts. Nothing there to help us—it was trashed before they left. But if Fielding was telling the truth, any manipulation they tried out would have been made that much more powerful if they were using their strongest shifters."

"But why leave them here? And why leave them alive? It doesn't fit their MO," Horvan mused.

"I can tell you why." Troy joined them. "I finally got one of the guards to talk. She said the Gerans wanted us to storm in here and kill everyone.

228

That was why they gave the inmates weapons. They wanted us to think we were facing a far greater force than they actually were. So we'd be slaughtering innocents." He grimaced. "The way she said it made my blood run cold. They liked the idea of us killing the very people we'd come in here to rescue. But there was a backup plan. If we hadn't shown up within three days of them leaving, the guards were to kill everyone, then flee. That was when the food would run out anyway."

"What food?" Crank growled. "These people look as if they've been starved."

"What will you do with them all?" Dellan asked Horvan.

Horvan got out his phone and hit speed dial. "Aelryn? Are you sending enough transportation for all these people? … Great. … Yeah, keep me in the loop, please. … Yeah, about that too." He gave a tired chuckle. "That sounds like a wonderful idea. Let's talk tomorrow." He disconnected. "Okay. Aelryn said his people will keep us informed about all the inmates, and the students too, but that we're done here. Oh, and he said to go home."

Dellan had a sudden yearning for his own bed. "I like the sound of that." He gazed at the floodlit camp. "Did we accomplish what we set out to do here?"

Horvan pulled him close, and Rael moved in too. "I know we didn't find them, but we did save all these people."

"If they all make it," Rael murmured. "Some are in a really bad way, Hashtag said."

"Some of them haven't." Doc sounded weary as he approached them. "We've lost three so far." He met Horvan's gaze. "When you get your next lead on Jake, call me, okay? I'm in."

Horvan nodded. "You got it. You wanna come back to Illinois with us?"

"Thanks, but no. I'll go with Aelryn's team. Some things I need to discuss with them before I go home."

Horvan released Dellan and gave Doc a tight hug. "Take care, and stay in touch."

"I will. And you take care of all these mates." Doc smiled. "What I wouldn't give for a mate of my own right now." And with that he walked back toward the hut.

Is Doc all right? Dellan was struck by the sadness that emanated from the doctor.

I'm not sure. Not finding Jake was obviously a huge blow.

"Horvan?"

He turned to face Brick and Aric. "What's up?"

Brick's brow furrowed. "Can we…?" Then he turned away. "Never mind."

Dellan's heart went out to Brick. *Horvan, can we help him?*

"You wanna bring your mate and come back with us?" Horvan put a hand on Brick's shoulder. "We never wanted you to leave in the first place. We're stronger when we're together."

"But Crank—"

"Was wrong," Crank blurted out. "I let my emotions get away from me. Not really very military. I'm sorry."

Brick's eyes widened. "No, *I'm* the one that's sorry. I put everyone in danger and—"

Crank held up his hand. "It's over, Brick. We've all been through enough, and I'll be damned if I lose any friends over what these sons of bitches have done." He held his arms open. "Bring it in, big guy."

Brick threw his arms around Crank and hefted him off the ground. "Thank you."

"No, thank *you*. When the chips were down, you came through. It was because of you we saved all those kids and my mate."

Brick frowned. "How do you figure that?"

Crank smiled. "Because you decided what side you were on." Then he whooshed out a breath. "Lord, but I'm tired. Call the pilot, H. I wanna go home."

"I second that." Dellan put his arms around Rael and Horvan. "Let's go home."

SAUL WAS sandwiched between Crank and Vic, and he had to admit, it was a pleasant situation to be in, even if the plane was lacking in the comfort department. Over on their left, Horvan, Dellan, and Rael were huddled together, their arms entwined, and facing him, Brick sat with Aric's head on his lap, gently stroking his hair.

Hashtag and Roadkill sat together, staring at the men around them. Roadkill's eyes twinkled. "I don't know about you, Hashtag," he said in a loud voice, "but I'm starting to feel as if I'm in a minority here."

"I know what you mean." Hashtag grinned. "Maybe we should hook up."

Roadkill's eyes lit up. "Hey, that's not a bad idea. You can show me that thing you do with your tongue." He puckered up. "Lay a kiss on me?"

Hashtag cackled. "I'll pass. Too tired right now. Maybe later when we have time to... you know." Tired chuckles came from all sides.

"I've been thinking," Dellan announced suddenly. "This psychic talent of Seth's—what if he inherited it from my dad? What if I have it too? That might explain why I could connect with Rael in dreams."

"Where are you going with this?" Horvan asked.

"Well, if Seth is with my dad, what's to stop them trying to reach out to Aric? They might be able to tell him where they've been taken."

Saul couldn't miss the note of hope in Dellan's voice.

"It's a possibility, I guess." Horvan didn't sound optimistic.

"I didn't find what I was looking for," Saul murmured.

"What did you expect to find?" Vic asked quietly.

"An opportunity to hit those bastards where it hurt, maybe? A little revenge would've been sweet. But to see that camp, to see the lengths the Gerans were prepared to go to so we didn't win...."

"Maybe I can help with that," Horvan said suddenly. "I think you should lead this team. You've got the experience. Hell, you've got more of that than I have with *your* background."

Saul blinked. "I can't lead these guys. They're your team, always will be."

"Then let's lead them together." Horvan's eyes met his. "What do you say?"

Saul took a moment to gaze at the men around him. Hashtag and Roadkill straightened, staring at him with obvious expectation. Brick wore the same expression, and Vic's and Crank's hands were at Saul's back. Horvan's earnest air hadn't changed.

He means it. That was Crank.

And we'll have your back. Vic cupped his cheek. *Always.*

Saul took a deep breath. "They've taken our mates and our children, killed our parents, tortured us. They've been one step ahead this entire time." He squared his shoulders. "That ends now. We will get our people back, and we will drive this darkness back into the hole it crawled out of." He shifted his gaze to encompass the group. "This is my vow, both to you and to myself."

And this is mine. I love you. Vic kissed him, a soft, fleeting brush of lips.

I'd die for you. Crank gazed at both of them. *So I guess… if that ain't love, what is?*

Saul kissed Crank, then Vic. Planning could wait until the following day. Right then, all Saul wanted was to get into bed with his mates so they could find their center again. Each other.

FIELDING SAT in his master's presence, not daring to move. "They did not win."

Dark eyes flashed. "No? That might be the case, but they've been a thorn in our sides long enough. They've brought production of our drugs to a screeching halt, cost us millions, and created more work for us, what with setting up new camps and new schools. We lost so many precious soldiers. Well, no more. I will not accept any defeat, and especially not at the hands of so weak an enemy." When Fielding frowned, he glared. "Any species that mates for love rather than strength is weak. And they think they can win this battle. They actually believe they have a chance against us." Cold eyes met Fielding's. "It's time they learned the truth. It's time to wipe the Fridans off the face of the earth."

Fielding smiled. It was all going to plan.

K.C. WELLS lives on an island off the south coast of the UK, surrounded by natural beauty. She writes about men who love men, and can't even contemplate a life that doesn't include writing.

The rainbow rose tattoo on her back with the words 'Love is Love' and 'Love Wins' is her way of hoisting a flag. She plans to be writing about men in love – be it sweet and slow, hot or kinky - for a long while to come.

If you want to follow her exploits, you can sign up for her monthly newsletter: http://eepurl.com/cNKHlT

You can stalk – er, find – her in the following places:

Email: k.c.wells@btinternet.com
Facebook: www.facebook.com/KCWellsWorld
KC's men In Love (my readers group): http://bit.ly/2hXL6wJ
Amazon: https://www.amazon.com/K-C-Wells/e/B00AECQ1LQ
Twitter: @K_C_Wells
Website: www.kcwellswrites.com
Instagram: www.instagram.com/k.c.wells
BookBub: https://www.bookbub.com/authors/k-c-wells

A GROWL, A ROAR, AND A PURR

K.C. WELLS

Lions & Tigers & Bears: Book One

In the human world, shifters are a myth.

In the shifter world, mates are a myth too. So how can tiger shifter Dellan Carson have two of them?

Dellan has been trapped in his shifted form for so long, he's almost forgotten how it feels to walk on two legs. Then photojournalist Rael Parton comes to interview the big-pharma CEO who holds Dellan captive in a glass-fronted cage in his office, and Dellan's world is rocked to its core.

When lion shifter Rael finds his newfound mate locked in shifted form, he's shocked but determined to free him from his prison… and that means he needs help.

Enter ex-military consultant and bear shifter Horvan Kojik. Horvan is the perfect guy to rescue Dellan. But mates? He's never imagined settling down with one guy, let alone two.

Rescuing Dellan and helping him to regain his humanity is only the start. The three lovers have dark secrets to uncover and even darker forces to overcome….

www.dreamspinnerpress.com

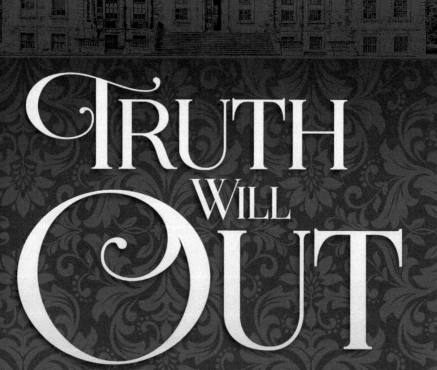

K.C. WELLS

TRUTH WILL OUT

A Merrychurch Mysteries Case

Jonathon de Mountford's visit to Merrychurch village to stay with his uncle Dominic gets off to a bad start when Dominic fails to appear at the railway station. But when Jonathon finds him dead in his study, apparently as the result of a fall, everything changes. For one thing, Jonathon is the next in line to inherit the manor house. For another, he's not so sure it was an accident, and with the help of Mike Tattersall, the owner of the village pub, Jonathon sets out to prove his theory—if he can concentrate long enough without getting distracted by the handsome Mike.

They discover an increasingly long list of people who had reason to want Dominic dead. And when events take an unexpected turn, the amateur sleuths are left bewildered. It doesn't help that the police inspector brought in to solve the case is the last person Mike wants to see, especially when they are told to keep their noses out of police business.

In Jonathon's case, that's like a red rag to a bull....

www.dreamspinnerpress.com

UNDER
THE COVERS

K.C. Wells

Will they find their HEA in Romancelandia?

Can they find their HEA in Romancelandia?

Chris Tyler loves his job. He photographs some of the hottest guys on the planet, but none stir him like Jase Mitchell. He'll never let Jase know – he values their friendship too much to spoil it.

Jase is looking forward to the Under The Covers Romance convention. It's a great opportunity to connect with readers who want to meet their favorite cover model, but more importantly, with agents who could advance his career. Too bad the only person he yearns to connect with is Chris.

What Chris wants is Jase in his life, but he's afraid that's sheer fantasy. What Jase desires is a Hollywood dream, but that will mean leaving Chris behind. What both crave is a real-life romance and their own Happily Ever After.

www.dreamspinnerpress.com